in the Society of Women

The Ladies Occult Society

in the Society of Women

The Ladies Occult Society

KRISTA D. BALL

Cover Art © 2024 by Niken Anindita
Interior Layout by Indigo Chick Designs
Edited by Skyla Dawn Cameron

Paperback 978-1-7380746-6-2
Hardcover 978-1-7380746-7-9

The Characters of the Ladies Occult Society Series

The Knight Household at Bryden Rectory

Mr. Knight: The patriarch of the Knight household and undeserving of a Christian name thus far in the series. The local rector.

Isabella: Also known as Mrs. Knight, not to be confused with the previous Mrs. Knights. Isabella is Mr. Knight's third wife.

Elizabeth: Called Elizabeth or Eliza by those related or close friends. Also known as Miss Knight, as she is the eldest.

Mary: Known as Mrs. James Fitzharding or Mrs. Fitzharding. Rich, and lives at Ashbrook House.

Charles: Sometimes just called Knight by other men; currently finishing schooling to join the Church.

Cassandra: Always called Cassie, unless in serious trouble with her eldest sister; known as Miss Cassie in polite society.

Theodosia: Always called Thea, unless in serious trouble with her eldest two sisters; also known as Miss Thea or Miss Theodosia in polite society.

Georgiana: Usually called G, unless in serious trouble with…well, you get the family dynamic by this point. Also known as Miss G in polite society.

Mr. Knight's Previous Wives

Lucy Knight: Deceased. The mother of Elizabeth and Mary.

Augusta Knight: Deceased. The mother of Charles, Cassie, Thea, and G.

Ladies Occult Society

Miss Alice Thorne: Miss Thorne, or amongst excellent female friends, Alice. Rich. Unwed, and likely to remain so since she has a strong enjoyment of female company.

Miss Susan Markson: Miss Susan, generally, as she had been a schoolteacher for the Royal Occult Society and it was a form of address that stuck.

Mrs. Egerton: A ghost, very opinionated. Specializes in custom spellworking.

Miss Gibbs: A ghost, aggressively cheery. Specializes in healing magic.

Elizabeth's Circle of Friends, Family, and Acquaintances

Cassandra Spencer: Aunt Cass or Mrs. George Spencer.

Mr. Osborne: A local bookseller and publisher, who has his eye on Miss Susan.

Mr. Grant: Aunt Cass' attorney who also assists Elizabeth with various legal and business affairs, as she is a woman.

Maria Thorne: Mrs. Thorne, Mrs. Henry Thorne. Elizabeth's oldest friend. Rich in her own right, married a rich man. Likes to complain about her husband, but clearly adores him. Loves to be helpful.

Henry Thorne: Mr. Thorne. Maria Thorne's husband. Occasionally gambles, but not so much as to anger his wife on a regular basis. Likes to pretend to be a wastrel, but is always supportive of Elizabeth and her family.

Mr. Sidney Sinclair: The local curate, which makes no sense to anyone since he is wealthy enough not to need employment. Every unmarried woman under thirty is in love with him, except Elizabeth, who complains he wears his collars too high for her liking.

Servants, Staff, and Local Trades

Julia: Bryden Rectory's 17-year-old kitchenmaid, the daughter of the rectory's old cook.

Miss Sims: The local seamstress, who has a lot of nieces living with her and who work as day maids for various people in the village.

Mrs. Green: The local midwife.

Mr. Collins: The current, younger, apothecary.

Mrs. Cook: Aunt Cass' cook.

Sally: Aunt Cass' housemaid.

James the Butler: Aunt Cass' butler.

Historian's Note

DETAILING SERVANT WAGES in this era is complicated, since we need to consider rank, wealth, position, location, and the individual temperaments of the employers. Also, one's position in the world dictated how many servants one hired. Even the poorest families hired help, even if just temporarily or for a few hours a week, for the various household tasks. A family with several small children, for example, might hire the neighbour's daughter to babysit while the mother and the older children worked.

The Victorian cookbook and lifestyle author Isabella Beeton recommended the number of servants the working and middle classes needed to live comfortably. To quote from my own book, *Hustlers, Harlots, and Heroes*, "those making £150-£200 per annum should keep a maid-of-all-work and bring in a girl for occasional or casual jobs as needed. The £300 bracket could afford a maid-of-all-work and a nurserymaid. The £500 a year family could afford a cook, a housemaid, and a nursemaid. The £750 households could not get by without a cook, a housemaid, nursemaid, and a footboy. Finally, the £1000 year per annum households required a cook, upper and under housemaids, nursemaid, and a man servant."

Housemaids were paid £5 in the late 1700s (this book is set in 1811). A maid-of-all-work made about £6 in the early 1800s, and general domestic servants made about £16. A manservant could make upwards of £42.

By 1856, author John Henry Walsh recommended housemaids make £10-£16, cooks be paid £10-£24, and maids-of-all-work incomes should be around £4-£10. If these salaries did not include rations of tea and sugar, or did not include laundry, they should be paid extra to cover those expenses.

Employers, such as Aunt Cass, could afford to pay more and some did. Some did not, and often wrote letters complaining about how good help was impossible to find. Rural areas might run into problems finding workers, simply due to the population size. Urban areas would heavily use word-of-mouth, recommendations, or even various types of employment services (including advertising), especially if one was looking to move to a different part of the country (or the world).

Chapter 1

February 8, 1811
Friday

IT IS A truth universally acknowledged that a young lady will want to be the prettiest girl at a ball. And when there are several young ladies living under the same roof, the eldest will be called upon to prevent sisterly resentment.

The winter had not been easy on Elizabeth's youngest sister. Poor Georgiana's coming out ball had been delayed so long that the local seamstress had to let out the bodices of G's new gowns, lest the seams burst during the first two dances.

Even more frustrating for poor G was that there was no one person to blame. She could not point and declared, "*They* caused the delay." Instead, illness had struck Bryden, and soon the neighbouring villages. The sickness even took away the rectory's own cook along with two servants at Vane Park. They also lost their second kitchenmaid, Alice, who had to return home to assist with the sick and dying in her own family.

And to make the winter more worrisome, their own father had contracted the illness as he did his duty visiting the poor and sick. As winter lingered, their father's health still had not returned to its full vigor, if he had even been in such high health back in November. For which Elizabeth was not certain.

"Eliza! G stole my good gloves!" Thea cried out.

"G, you must ask before taking things," Elizabeth called out rather automatically from the upper drawing room.

She opened the newly-arrived letter from Charles. The *weekly* letter from her brother, in fact. He had become Elizabeth's regular correspondent over the course of the winter, as he finished his studies, gained his ordination, and prepared for his transition to becoming an independent man. And Charles' letters were growing more affectionate, more jovial, and indeed more of a steady man accepting his situation in life and braving up to the task ahead, as opposed to a resentful one, wishing he had been born someone he was not. Elizabeth hoped it would continue, for she rather enjoyed this new brother of hers, who reminded her so much of the little boy he'd once been.

"I need them!" G shouted, though Elizabeth was not certain if it was directed at her or Thea, so she ignored the declaration of despair.

Charles' letter was filled with the usual details, though he confirmed that their brother-in-law, Mr. James Fitzharding, had officially invited Charles to stay at his and Mary's estate when his new curacy would be available.

> *Mary says I must stay at Ashbrook, for the curate's house (according to her) is in a shocking state and that she would not allow a pigeon to live there. I have yet to see the place, but she has ordered several improvements to the house, since it is unoccupied. What am I to do? I can afford to have the chimneys cleaned, I assure you, but Mary will not listen. Is there any possible way I can persuade you to write to her? I do not wish to sound ungrateful! But gracious be, if I leave her to it, she will tear the place down and rebuild it stone by stone to her satisfaction.*

Elizabeth chuckled, even as G shouted that Thea had stolen her best hair ribbon. She would write to Mary, for Charles' sake. Firstly, no one should be subjected to Mary's improvements without consultation, but secondly, Charles had been one third of the reason tonight's ball was happening.

Charles arrived home just after Christmas, and formed a coalition with Mr. Thorne and Mr. Sinclair. All three men marched upon her father's study, to announce that Maria Thorne must be allowed to set a date for the ball. While Elizabeth had not been in the room, Thea and Cassie had listened at the door, as indelicate as it was. They'd reported that the three men convinced their father that there would be no peace in England until G got to dance at least one night until the first break of dawn.

And, upon that truth, Charles struck with a line that fairness was a Christian virtue, and that G must have her ball, just as all of her other sisters had enjoyed.

Charles was now, of course, G's favourite person in the world, with Mr. Sinclair and Mr. Thorne being very excellent men, too. Though Elizabeth's own opinion of Charles remained guarded, she promised herself she was permitted to change her mind if she witnessed *repeated* growth on the part of her wayward brother. And his frequent kindnesses as of late did help soften past actions. Actions, she began to consider in a new light. Perhaps it had all still been his old illness, lingering, and festering, alongside a lack of maturity too common in those who had spent formative months in bed.

So in that light, Elizabeth wrote to her brother with the assurances of Mary's good intentions intermixed with the promises to drop hints to their sister that their brother was indeed a grown man, and should be allowed to live in his own house, shabby though it might be (in Mary's eye, if no one else's).

She did not finish off the letter, as there would be a need to recount the ball's details tomorrow. Instead, she moved on to the next unopened letter. Aunt Cass' letter had been far longer than Charles', and Elizabeth attempted to read it as the household once more erupted in howls and protests about ribbons, bobbles, and gloves.

"Ladies!" Elizabeth called out, having only managed to read the first paragraph. "God help you if your shrieking brings our father's attention upon you."

> *My dear niece, I have expressed this to the others, but I shall say it to you. It continues to amaze me that the occult has opened an entire world of possibilities for you ladies to explore —except it cannot offer the ability to make this hateful rain cease! It has not stopped for three days now! My lungs have not appreciated this damp, and now to make me even more miserable, my headaches have returned!*
>
> *My physician has threatened—actually threatened!—to call upon David, of all the people on this Earth, to convince him to make me go to Cornwall for the improvement of my health. As if anyone's health as been improved by a visit to Cornwall! And I would be forced to see your father's terrible brother if I went there, and I would rather be sent to France to join the laundresses and servants that follow the army.*
>
> *Oh, I do wish you would come visit us again soon! We were cheated out of our Christmas visit this year with the unhappy events.*

For it had not only been poor G who'd been affected by the terrible winter, but the entire household of Aunt Cass had been plagued with unhappiness. Poor Miss Susan, one of their lady occultists, lost her own aunt, Mrs. Taylor. She had been in service to the family for years, and died in her sleep. In the same week, Aunt Cass lost her housekeeper, Mrs. Dover. Not to death, but duty to her dead sister.

> *I have persuaded Miss Susan to leave her mourning weeds behind; her aunt would not have wished the girl to be in black for the rest of eternity. And Mrs. Dover has written to state she is settled in Liverpool, and is growing*

used to the children, and they to her. I have arranged for a generous annuity to support them, and have dispatched a trustworthy courier with gifts for the children, as well as coin to help set up their new abode. Through the courier, I have also sent instructions to her landlord, to have the rents paid via Mr. Grant's office. Many would say I am too generous with my servants, but I know you will support me.

Of course Elizabeth would support her aunt, and she was certain her aunt's lawyer, Mr. Grant, would do as instructed. Or, even if he did not agree, the man was far too sensible to utter a word beyond that of common-sense support. Elizabeth trusted him with her own inheritance; for a poor lady like herself, what greater compliment in a man's worth could exist?

"Eliza!" That was Cassie this time, though she had the good sense to stick her head into the drawing room as opposed to shout across the house like a common labourer. "Have you seen my yellow petticoat? The pale one?"

"It's in my closet, second drawer from the bottom, on the left," Elizabeth said, picturing the hidden garment in her mind. Then, considering, "You will require a new hiding place once the other two see you did not lose it."

"I shall see if Isabella has room in her trunk," Cassie said before ducking out.

At least little Miss Puss Puss remains, for the beast had grown so fond of us that Mrs. Dover feared removing her would just cause the cat to run away back to London. I am not fond of cats, as you have heard me complain (because of the kittens that always show up), but we refuse to let the cat outside when she is in heat. So while we have to endure the howling wails at all hours, we do not need to deal with kittens. So there is that blessing.

And, I must also confess though it pains me, Miss Puss Puss has quite destroyed the mouse population in our house and Sir William's. Mrs. Arthur Gateway across the street is so impressed that she approached us about hiring Miss Puss Puss for a weekend, to see if our little huntress can clear out her pantry. However, James—yes, my very stoic butler—does not feel this is wise, as we do not want Miss Puss Puss to feel abandoned. Yes, those were his words. I swear, that cat has possessed us all.

Your brother, Charles, visited the other day. He was only in town for two days he said, and stayed with a friend's mother, that is what he told me. I did not recognize the name—a Mrs. Talbot, I believe he said—

"Elizabeth?" That was Isabella, her pregnant stepmother. Again. Not that Elizabeth was annoyed at her father for it. For that was a woman's plight in life. No, why would she be annoyed by the natural consequence of marriage

She put on a smile and asked, in the calmest voice she could muster, even though she just wanted to read her letter in peace. "Can I assist?"

"Have you seen your father's pocket watch? Not the good one, but his everyday one?"

"Papa left it on the dining table this morning," Elizabeth said.

"Thank you, I shall go look," Isabella said. "Sorry to interrupt."

"Oh, there is no need to apologize," Elizabeth said with the usual graces hammered into her at a very young age.

"Miss Knight? Oh, do excuse me Mrs. Knight." That was Julia, the maid. "Miss Knight? Your father wishes to know where he put his bible. Not his everyday one, but the family bible."

"Pray tell him it is in the small trunk that is under the table with Augusta's vase."

"Ah, I did not think to look there," Julia said. She curtsied and rushed off.

Elizabeth waited to see if anyone else needed her; they apparently did not. Therefore, she turned back to Aunt Cass' letter while there was blessed silence. For all of Aunt Cass' frequent protests about the girls writing long letters, this was four pages, front and back! On and on went Aunt Cass' letter, detailing the weather, what they'd eaten for dinner, the company they kept, any evenings out, and long laments about Miss Susan and Mr. Osborne having not sealed any marriage contract between them.

The letter had been a part of an entire parcel and delivered via John, their bailiff who had been in London on business. With the letter came several swatches of fabrics and ribbons, and three drawings of very fashionable gowns cut from a lady's magazine. Elizabeth instantly felt her dear friend, Maria Thorne, would like one of the gowns from the drawings made using the yellow silk swatch. Her sister Cassie would probably prefer the blue muslin turned into one of the other gowns, though altered to be less flamboyant.

The swatch of red net, a nearly see-thru windowpane of cloth, would have sent their father to his deathbed, despite the fact that Maria Thorne's ballgowns were that thin and, yet, the world did not see anything beyond her coloured silk slip underneath, whose sole purpose was to cast a delightful hue through the gown. And, there was still her petticoat and her shift underneath, but if her father made the connection between that tiny swatch of netting and the gowns Maria Thorne wore, he would be preaching from the pulpit about naked ladies in the streets.

She considered her father's current disposition and believed, yes, he truly would do that. She would have to be very cagey to keep the samples away from her father.

"Eliza! Isabella will not let me borrow her pearl hairpins!" Thea bellowed.

Without looking up from the fabric swatches, she called out, "Those hairpins were inherited from her grandmother and not for your use. Shall I remind you that you lost the three hairpins I purchased for you in London?"

"I will not lose them!"

"I am quite firm," Elizabeth said, even as footsteps approached the drawing room. She did not bother to look up. "Isabella is right not to lend them, and if she has relented, I will insist upon you returning them to her."

Thea sighed in a manner that would make the great actresses of the age take note. "May I borrow Mama's amber hair pins then?"

Elizabeth ignored how the request sounded closer to a demand than anything else. "I lent those out to Mary at Christmas, as you well remember."

The hairpins had been Augusta's originally, and Elizabeth held the safekeeping of them. Augusta Knight, the second of three Knight wives, had left enough jewelry and bobbles to share amongst all of the Knight girls. So when Mary politely inquired about them, Elizabeth was rather comforted to let Mary participate in the sharing. Especially after all the fighting previously over jewelry, there had been an understanding. A new day, as it were.

A moment later, a door slammed shut, though Thea could be heard wailing about the meanness of elder sisters. Perhaps accurate—Elizabeth had no elder sister to compare, after all—but this might mean she had another few moments of peace and therefore opened Mary's letter.

Mary's was more open than their previous exchanges. She wrote this one from London, where her husband was still suffering the recovery of having two teeth pulled. Mary's letter reported the teeth were in the back, and therefore did not affect her husband's smile, thankfully. The two teeth were so tightly wedged that both became infected. And one tooth was at such a terrible angle that Mr. Fitzharding completely fainted during the surgery, the poor man.

My dear husband is still only allowed beef tea (without eating the beef, of course), finely mashed potatoes or carrots, and the thinnest gruel you can ever imagine, for fear of the food dislodging the scabs and causing infection. He is not yet up for company, and can barely tolerate even my presence. He requested the children not be left to linger with him; he does not wish to take anything for the pain beyond brandy, so his suffering is great. However, I have insisted his request be honored, and so the servants are on the strictest instructions not to slip anything into his drink or food.

Onwards went the letter, detailing her husband's grisly situation. Then, Elizabeth arrived at the underlined section, where Mary meant the news for her only, and not for the letter to be shared.

Now, here is where I must turn this letter to private information. In a fit of confusion, our father has accused Charles of having gambling debts and has ordered us not to assist him. I visited with Charles yesterday, in fact—he is here in London on an errand from the university and is staying with the mother of a friend of his. I do not recall the name, but my housekeeper here in town assures me the family is of excellent, if reduced, circumstances.

I have investigated the situation fully, and I wish to assure you that Charles has no gambling debts. He has run up about thirty pounds in town at the shops, but that was under my instruction for the fitting up of the house. There is no impropriety nor anything else of the former nature.

The misunderstanding is solely due to poor Charles. He wrote to our father detailing his purchases, just in the usual manner that we would do such a thing. However, our father misconstrued the letter somehow. You can well imagine the rest. Therefore, I ask that any and all requests of a financial nature concerning Charles not be told to our father for the foreseeable future.

At least his curacy has been finalized and I have arranged for the workmen to begin making the house livable. I realize that it has not had an occupant in five years, but surely that is no excuse for the state of it. The chimneys! The sorry lack of any furniture! I am appalled, I tell you this now.

And do not write imploring me not to spend my own money fixing this place up for my brother, Elizabeth. I know you and your ways, and I will not be swayed from my current course.

Elizabeth chuckled to herself. Oh, siblings know each other far too well for their own good sometimes.

"Eliza! I need you!" G called from the other room.

An ethereal voice whispered in Elizabeth's ear. "Miss Knight, may I offer a suggestion?"

"Are you about to suggest that I run away to Scotland with the first man who looks at me tonight?" Elizabeth sighed. "For that is what I am thinking."

"I would never dream of encouraging you to be so rash. No, I wished to hint that you will find no peace today, and that you should attend your sisters lest they set the house ablaze in a fit of pique."

"Eliza!" G shouted again. This time, with approaching footsteps accompanying the shout.

"There will be no peace until after this ball," came the ghostly guidance of Mrs. Egerton. "Go. For no other reason than to keep your father well disposed."

The ghost was right, as ever, and Elizabeth whispered her thanks. She folded up her letters and placed them into her writing desk, and then locked the entire thing before slipping the key into her apron's pocket.

In the hallway, she was confronted with three girls all in high temper about who was outshining whom, with their poor, pregnant stepmother seated on a chair giving orders about who should do what with their hair. All this hours before they were to leave for a ball!

"Finally!" G declared. She was wearing a muslin dress with the softest hint of pink. In one hand was a white muslin gown. And in the other hand, she held up a very pretty yellow silk dress. "I cannot decide."

"Girls! The ball is not for another eight hours," Elizabeth said. "I worry if you dress now, you shall spill food upon your gowns and then what?"

G made a disgusted sound. Elizabeth and Isabella both chided her, in the exact same tone. The two women looked at each other and smiled. Some habits are ingrained so deeply that the chiding came naturally, it seemed.

"Do not give us that look, Miss Georgiana Knight," Elizabeth said sternly, though she let the hint of a smile show. Her father had been strict enough lately, that the girls did not need further scolding. "Pick the blue dress if you must have my opinion."

"I shall wear the white," G announced, as Elizabeth knew she would. That was why she picked the blue; the white was the best gown for her debut event.

"Does that mean I cannot wear white, Eliza?" Cassie asked.

Elizabeth looked at Cassie's white muslin with the delicate eyelet embroidery that Cassie had done herself. "It would be a disappointment not to see you in the gown tonight, especially since you have finished the embroidery. However, looking at it, I wonder if we should add a ribbon to match your work. Nothing extravagantly coloured, but perhaps a pale yellow?"

Isabella's expression perked up. "I believe my yellow gloves would also do the trick."

"Oh!" Thea exclaimed. "Those are so delicate and pale, too! With the embroidery and a new ribbon, I wager everyone will think it is a new gown!"

That seemed to both please Cassie, and mollify a defiant G who did not want all of her sisters in white alongside her.

Thea announced she was wearing the pale pink gown, as it still fit.

"I should hope so!" Elizabeth said with a little chuckle. "It is not even a year old!"

"But it's still in fashion, I think, yes?" Thea asked.

"My dear girl," Isabella said, "it is a fine gown in a timeless style, and you have taken such excellent care of it."

"And, even when fashion changes a little, as it always does," Elizabeth said, "a new pair of gloves, a shawl, or a ribbon, and it would immediately appear new."

Thea frowned down at the gown in her hand. "I do not wish to be mocked, that is all."

"Who would dare laugh at you?" Elizabeth demanded in a tone of an offended eldest sister.

"I would send Mary after anyone who dared," Isabella said.

"You must wear the pink!" G insisted. "I am wearing a pink ribbon in my hair and we must match!"

Thea rolled her eyes. "Then I shall wear a white ribbon to match both you and Cassie."

With the tension of decision-making released, the sisters fell into the typical, excited tones of girls mere hours away from a ball. Elizabeth cautioned them to lower their voices, but it was too late, and the heavy footsteps approached from below.

She gave them a stern look, bidding them to behave. Their father approached the stairs, and Elizabeth could hear him wheezing even before he appeared. Elizabeth had noticed at breakfast how swollen his fingers were, and Isabella had confided that his feet looked the same, and sometimes up as far as his calves.

Yet, whenever someone suggested they call for Mr. Collins, to offer his expert advice as an apothecary, Mr. Knight became angry. Some days, he became enraged at the notion in such a way that frightened Elizabeth. For her father never behaved in such a manner. He was thoughtless, for sure, but never frightening.

Worse, Mr. Knight occasionally forgot that Mr. Collins was their local apothecary now, and would still talk about Mr. Clarke, who'd moved away months before. And his anger would be stoked at the reminder his memory had lapsed.

Isabella spoke to Mr. Collins on the sly, and he began to make a weekly visit, under the guise of administering his advice to Isabella, and then would offer his assistance to Mr. Knight. It was underhanded, and possibly even a lie, but Elizabeth was certain God would understand the need for such deception in matters of health.

"What is all of this noise?" her father demanded as he neared the top of the stairs. "What is this? New gowns again? Are we made of money?"

"No, indeed, Papa," Elizabeth said in her calmest tone. Out of them all, she seemed to be the one who could pacify her father's moods the fastest. "The Thornes' ball is tonight and we are emptying the closets."

Her father looked genuinely confused. "What ball? Why are the Thornes having a ball? In this weather?"

Elizabeth did not let her expression change at her father's forgetfulness. "The Thornes are throwing a coming out ball for G. We're all going."

"No one informed me of this!" her father declared, clearly forgetting the breakfast conversation on the topic. He turned to Isabella. "You cannot go. Not in your state!"

"But Papa!" Elizabeth interjected. "I apologize, as I thought you heard Mr. Collins and Mrs. Green when they said the exercise would do her good. Yesterday, at tea. I was there when they said it."

Her father's expression grew confused. "I don't remember that. But she cannot dance! Not in her condition!"

"My dear sir, I have no intention of dancing!" Isabella said with a nervous laugh. "My only plan for the evening is to move between an open window and a roaring fire, to achieve the perfect balance of comfort at all moments."

The girls made nervous chuckles.

"Open windows? You plan to be near open windows? In February?" He made a disgusted sound. "I have never heard of such foolishness. A woman in your condition near open windows! No midwife worth a ha'penny would ever dare suggest it!"

"Medicine changes, dear Papa." Elizabeth tried to smile. No one moved. "Even Mary has said how they treat her headaches now is not how they did when she was little. Now, tell me before I forget, Papa, because it has quite escaped my mind. Did you still wish to stay home tonight? Mr. Sinclair has offered to forego the ball and sit in front of your fire with you, if you prefer. But I do not recollect if you agreed to that plan or not."

Thea made a disappointed sound, and Elizabeth could see Cassie give her an elbow of correction. "Why would I need company? I don't need company! All of you get out and go to your ball. I'm sick of the very sight of you. And tell that Mr. Sinclair to keep his smiles away from here. I am in no mood for company. Company! Can not a man have some peace and quiet in his own study without company always coming by wanting tea and conversation? The nerve of that man! Will there be anything decent to eat today or will you all leave me to starve to death while you dance the night away?"

"The maids are baking rolls as we speak, for you to have with your ragout tonight," Isabella said.

"Why would I want to eat that?" Mr. Knight snarled. "I'd rather starve."

Elizabeth interjected before Mr. Knight could start complaining about his favourite meal. "Oh, Papa! Before I forget, did you see that Mary wrote yesterday? She was asking if we needed any strawberry cuttings once the ground thaws. I was thinking, since our own strawberry bed is still establishing itself, wouldn't it be a good excuse to ask her for some and then she could come visit us?"

Mr. Knight had been turning to walk away partway through Elizabeth's speech. Then he asked, "Why would I want company?"

"Because seeing Mary always cheers you up," she said.

"I don't need cheering! What's for supper?"

"Ragout," Isabella said.

"I like it with mushrooms," Mr. Knight said. "They never put in enough for my taste."

"I will remind Julia to add extra," Isabella said.

Once their father waved off their questions and he announced he was sick of gowns and balls, Elizabeth motioned for silence until they heard his study door close. Then, and only then, did the girls all exhale.

It was Cassie who spoke first. "He is getting worse, isn't he?"

Elizabeth nodded. "Yes."

"What is wrong with him?" G demanded as much as one could in a whisper.

"I do not know precisely, except that it is not improving." Elizabeth forced cheer into her voice as she said, "Now, let us put aside gloomy thoughts, as we have a ball to prepare for, and I will not accept a single drawn or sad face for the rest of this day. No indeed! We must find ribbons for your hair. Come girls!"

Chapter 2

THE PRIVATE BALL at Vane Park was perfect, or so G announced upon their arrival at the estate. After the usual exchange of boots for dancing shoes, the three younger Knight girls stormed the dance floor, arm-in-arm, ready to conquer the hearts of every young man within fifty miles.

Cassie's white gown was the talk of the ball, with her own embroidery painstakingly designed along the hem. Thankfully, G was still the centre of attention, in her own white gown with a bodice that was a touch too low for Elizabeth's tastes. However, she reminded herself that fashions changed, and that a young woman was allowed to express herself. She reminded herself of that fact three times in quick succession, as G seemed to frequently need to pick things up off the floor whenever a young man was nearby.

Despite the flirtations of her sisters, Elizabeth found herself in high spirits as the evening progressed. Her sisters were never without dancing partners. In fact, Cassie had danced two of three dances with a young gentleman Elizabeth did not recognize. G was busy flirting, and Thea was constantly grinning too widely at the young men. All in all, an excellent ball for her sisters, it seemed.

As for Elizabeth? There were too few young men to rescue her from her third glass of wine, but her spirits were high (and not solely due to the excellent wine), but she vowed she would take this glass slowly. It would be some time before supper, and she did not wish to become *giddy*.

Speaking of giddy, Mr. Sinclair came into view. He offered her a wide grin when he met her gaze and he walked toward her with his outrageous collar. Once at her side, he asked, "My dear, Miss Knight, why are you not dancing every dance?"

She took a sip of her wine. "I find there are not enough willing partners this evening. I believe my father is on to something about this new crop of young men. I remember being G's age and the young men were throwing themselves in the way of us young ladies. Nowadays, I find them huddled amongst themselves in dark corners gossiping like old women."

Mr. Sinclair glanced over at such a congregation of young men and sighed. "Have some pity. It is not easy being eighteen."

"Pish," Elizabeth said. "I was eighteen once, and I survived well enough."

"Did the young men of the village?" Mr. Sinclair asked.

Elizabeth laughed, a short, abrupt sound, and she covered her mouth with her fan to hide her toothy smile lest one of the old gossips see and inform her father. "Pray, tell me. Do you know that young man that is dancing with Cassie?"

Mr. Sinclair looked about until his face brightened with recognition. "Oh! That is Mr. John Baldwin."

"Any relation to Miss Phoebe Baldwin?" She asked, inquiring after her sister's rather wealthy friend from London.

"I cannot recall the exact connection, but he is related to Miss Baldwin. He has only just arrived today, for the ball, and is staying with the Parsons'."

"Well, at least there is one young man not afraid to flirt with the young ladies," Elizabeth said with a laugh.

Mr. Sinclair chuckled at that. He glanced at her glass and said, "Might I be so bold as to suggest a slice of cake with that glass of wine?"

"Alas, the young men have consumed all of the cake." She sighed dramatically. "I must contend myself with only wine, Mr. Sinclair."

"Oh, do not speak to me of wine. My mother sent me twenty bottles of the stuff. It arrived this morning."

"Why on Earth did your mother send you wine?" Elizabeth tried not to laugh as she asked the question, but she couldn't help it.

Mr. Sinclair raised his chin and put on a haughty tone, and raised his voice to be higher in pitch. "My dear boy, you live in such backwards retirement. You must be starving to death, and deprived of anything remotely decent to drink, adding further indignity to your reduced circumstances. The only reason I tolerate you holding such a degrading title as curate is because of my devotion to the Almighty who sees into our hearts."

"Then, I shall speak to Isabella to invite you to dinner as soon as possible, so that you will have an excuse to share some of this excellent Bath wine. It would be rather tasteless for a young man to drink that much wine alone."

"Well, I agree with that part, but I have to warn you that the wine is the same quality as you normally serve at your table, only it cost my mother two shillings more per bottle."

"Your poor mother has been robbed!" Elizabeth declared.

They chatted on like that, as the music played happily. Mr. Sinclair's attention was caught by Isabella walking near, and he said, "I am surprised to see her tonight. I understood she was on bedrest."

"To be charitable, no one medically inclined decreed that. The apothecary finally convinced my father that a little fresh air would not kill Isabella, and besides, imprisoning a woman against her will is frowned upon in today's enlightened society."

"She looked well," Mr. Sinclair said.

"Yes, I believe this one will last," she said.

"You seem disappointed?" Mr. Sinclair asked.

"That was not my intention. But, surely you understand, coming from such a large family. Tell me, what did your eldest siblings say when the younger showed up?"

"From what I gather, they all complained loudly and advocated for separate houses for my parents, as separate bedrooms were clearly not enough distance."

"Mr. Sinclair!" Elizabeth exclaimed. She swatted his arm with her fan. "Now, let us find you a young lady who has been sitting alone for far too long."

Mr. Sinclair sighed, and in an exaggerated tone, said, "Miss Knight, why are you constantly trying to marry me off to all of the saddest women in the county?"

"Because sad young ladies deserve to be happy as much as the gay ones."

"I...I suppose I cannot argue with that logic," he said with a laugh. "Well, then I shall be at your service. Always madam." He bowed. "I shall *always* be at your service."

"If that were true, my good sir, you would not wear such flashy clothes in the country."

He leaned toward her ear to whisper, "And that, my dear Miss Knight, is why I do it."

"I shall pretend I am shocked by such scandalous intentions," she said. She rolled her eyes so fully that even Mrs. Egerton would've admonished her for unladylike behaviour.

But she led Mr. Sinclair over to introduce him to a cousin of Mr. Thorne's, one of the many Thorne female cousins, and secured for her the next two dances with Mr. Sinclair. And his ridiculously starched collar. If she were not to dance every dance, that was God's will. But she would step in and give the other young ladies the opportunity to flirt and smile.

IT WAS PAST eleven and Elizabeth's stomach began to protest the wine and lack of cake. The servants arrived with more, after the young men ravished the platters, but sadly there was not even one slice of a cake she preferred. Still, she suffered in silence, with the fortification of Portuguese wine.

Isabella was in good spirits, and Elizabeth said so when her stepmother approached her.

"I have been taking breaks all evening. My poor feet," Isabella said. "But it is good to get the exercise, even if it is occasionally too hot tonight for my tastes. But the servants have been letting me escape into one of the closed rooms, and that has been most agreeable."

"That is where you keep disappearing," Elizabeth said. "I had wondered."

"Elizabeth, who is that young man who Cassie keeps dancing with, and thinks we do not notice," Isabella inquired.

"Apparently, his name is Mr. John Baldwin, some relation of both Mr. Parsons and Miss Phoebe Baldwin," Elizabeth said. "She has been very sly, and after their first two dances together, they have been very good with only dancing every other dance together. I would wager, however, that he is currently with Thea so that he can have the next dance with Cassie, and then be the gentleman who escorts her to supper."

Isabella watched the dancing couples before asking for her source. When Elizabeth said Mr. Sinclair. "Ah, of course. When a lady needs well-investigated gossip, we can always trust Mr. Sinclair to supply."

Elizabeth chuckled. "Indeed, the man had a gift for ferreting out the truth in any situation. I credit his mother for having so many children. There must not be any secrets in that household."

The two ladies chatted. About the gowns. The ribbons. About how Mr. Parsons finally abandoned wearing his wig and was growing out an excellent beard. The outrageous number of wax candles that must've cost upwards of twenty pounds.

"G was beside herself when she saw the eight-hour candles," Elizabeth said. "I worried she had already gotten into the wine by her heightened giddiness!"

Isabella glanced down pointedly at Elizabeth's glass. She laughed. "Technically, this is my fourth, but that is only because I had to put down my glass when Mr. Thorne asked me to dance, so it should not be held against me. Oh, there is Mr. Sinclair again."

He had his back to them, with two flute glasses in hand, and was looking about. He finally spun around, continuing his examination of the crowd, and then spotted them. His face brightened and he approached. "Miss Knight, I have secured us both a glass of Punch à la Romaine. Alas, Mrs. Knight, I did not see you with our esteemed Miss Knight when I was gathering the desserts."

Isabella laughed and said, "In my condition, I fear even the tiniest bit of champagne would have me snoring in a corner in a most uncouth manner."

"I, however, have no such fears!" Elizabeth said with a laugh and accepted her dessert. It was cold and tart, and perfect to help cool her from the heat of the ballroom. "Ah, thank you ever so much, Mr. Sinclair! What a surprise."

Isabella's attention was caught by someone in the distance and she said, "Alas, it appears I am needed. Can I trust the two of you not to cause mischief?"

"My dear lady, I am offended" Mr. Sinclair said, feigning shock.

"Well, I have never trusted a man in such a bright yellow coat before, but I shall attempt to be open minded," Isabella said before leaving them to their desserts and conversation.

Mr. Sinclair, glass in hand, looked down at his very fashionable attire. "Would we call this bright?"

Elizabeth stopped spooning semi-frozen goodness into her mouth to make a show of inspecting the local curate. She made a contemplative sound. "I hate to disagree with anyone of my fair sex, but if pressed, I would personally call this mustard, as opposed to bright."

"This is very fashionable in London, I assure you," Mr. Sinclair said.

Elizabeth looked about. "Alas, sir, we do not find ourselves in London this evening."

That seemed to amuse him. Elizabeth expressed her enjoyment of the dessert, of which Mr. Sinclair said, "Yes, I remember you mentioning it last week when we were discussing our hopes and dreams for tonight's menu."

Elizabeth chuckled and said, "I had no idea you were listening so attentively. Now I know to always be on my guard, for it seems you never forget anything."

"Oh, I forget a great many things, according to my mother," he said. "Do you have a partner for the next dance?"

"Alas, no, but just as well. Let the young ladies find a willing partner to sit next to them during supper!" she said with a smile.

"Then, will you do me the pleasure of the next dance? And, your company during supper?"

Elizabeth readily agreed, for there were no other prospects and she always enjoyed Mr. Sinclair's company. They finished their desserts in time to join the next call for dancers, and it wasn't until a full five minutes into the dance with Mr. Sinclair smiling and staring and smiling some more that Elizabeth began to wonder if four glasses of wine and a champagne-based dessert were playing tricks on her fragile old maid's mind.

"What was that look?" Mr. Sinclair said with a laugh as they linked arms to spin about.

They pulled apart and she linked arms with Mr. John Baldwin who said, "You are Miss Cassandra Knight's sister, yes?"

"Indeed I am, sir!"

"Pleasure to meet your…Hello Mrs. Thorne!" As they parted company.

She returned to Mr. Sinclair who said, "The look, madam!"

"I cannot even remember now!" She laughed as she was spun about once more.

And on they went, up and down, spinning about, all interspersed with moments of standing across from one another, smiling and staring with no privacy to speak, back to spinning about with others in a circle. Until, finally, the dance ended and she was flushed from exercise, and *perhaps* the alcohol.

With the announcement for supper, Mr. Sinclair escorted her to the dining area. Due to the number of guests, two dining tables were set up, and Elizabeth took her place next to Mr. Sinclair, and near enough to her sisters to flash an instructive elder sister glare if necessary.

The table was covered with a magnificent display of all of the best dishes of the season, with a handful of footmen about ready to offer assistance if needed, but mostly they were expected to dig into the dishes before them, which is what happened at Elizabeth's end of the table.

Elizabeth skipped the soup all together, and instead helped herself to a little of the duck, some boiled potatoes, and the ragout of beef and mushrooms. She was enjoying the friendly conversations about her when she noticed Mr. John Baldwin popping a mushroom into Cassie's mouth, making her blush and giggle.

"Ah, I see the eldest sister has caught the villain in the act of flirting," Mr. Sinclair said as she continued to watch her sister and this young man from across the table. "Shall we intervene and make a scene?"

"Oh, I believe we shall allow it, sir," Elizabeth said, matching his lowered volume, as much as one could whisper in a noisy dining room.

"Flirting at a ball! My mother would faint at the scandal," Mr. Sinclair said.

"Your mother had fifteen children, if I recall. I believe she has seen her fair share of flirting in her time, and yet you all have lived to tell the tale." Elizabeth was interrupted by G's very loud laughter. "I suppose it is too late to repeat my sisterly advice to take care with one's wine consumption at a ball."

He chuckled and said, "I believe, Miss Knight, it would very unsisterly of you, given your own wine situation."

"You disagreeable man!" Elizabeth said with a laugh. A little too loudly, catching the eye of all three of her sisters, and some of the matrons from the next table over. She felt her cheeks heat up and said loudly across the table, "And how is the ball thus far, girls?"

A downpour of three Knight girls all talking over each other was proof enough that the ball was going well with enough young men to cause no true jealousy.

Elizabeth ate, but not too much in case she was needed to occupy a gentleman's arm. She certainly did not wish to be bouncing and skipping with a stuffed stomach. G had no such worries, though she noticed Thea and Cassie paced themselves; both having made themselves a little ill at their own coming out balls. Maria Thorne, ever the gracious host, ensured there were dishes to Thea's particular needs delivered directly to her by the footmen before placed upon the table within reach of the others.

But too soon the musicians began striking their first notes, and the eager dancers abandoned the food. After all, it was only midnight, and the young people had several more hours before the candles burned down.

Thea approached them with big, sad eyes and announced she did not have a single offer for the next dance while she stared at Mr. Sinclair. Elizabeth managed to hide her laughter as Thea extracted an invitation to join him on the dance floor. Elizabeth's hand was requested by Mr. Parsons, and she happily danced with the gentleman, who (for all of his wigs and age) was still an excellent dancer.

Afterward, Cassie brought by her Mr. Baldwin for introductions—apparently, he was a cousin of Miss Phoebe Baldwin and had a small income, but nothing flashy. A third son. A good match, therefore, for Cassie, for a rich wife would be preferred for the eldest and…

Elizabeth managed to stop herself before she turned into Mary. She even let out a little laugh, which caught the attention of her new acquaintance, but she quickly asked if they had witnessed Thea's blatant display to get Mr. Sinclair.

"Speaking of dancing, I promised Miss Georgiana Knight my arm for this dance, and I believe I'm expected immediately!" Mr. Baldwin said, bowing to them before rushing off.

"I believe I shall like him," Elizabeth declared.

"Indeed?" Cassie said with hope in her voice. Then, a sigh. "He is an excellent man."

"Has Mary met him?"

"Not yet," Cassie said. Another sigh. "I do not wish her to find him … wanting."

"Oh, do not despair. Mary can be very reasonable," Elizabeth said.

Cassie made a sound that said she was not as confident, and she accepted a glass of wine from a passing footman. Then, in a rather innocent, airy tone that Elizabeth immediately found suspicious, Cassie said, "Mr. Sinclair has been very chatty this evening."

"Yes, I believe he is in excellent spirits." She let out a little snort. "Or, perhaps he has gotten into Mr. Thorne's excellent spirits."

In that moment, he caught her eye and smiled at her. She smiled back, self-conscious that her sister was watching, though she had no idea why she would feel thus. When she glanced at

Cassie, she saw the look of a sister wishing to say more. "Say what is on your mind or those wrinkles will remain forever."

"Mr. Sinclair smiles a lot when you are around," Cassie said.

Elizabeth laughed. "That is because he smiles a lot no matter the circumstance."

Then, a little quieter, Cassie said, "Elizabeth, he smiles more when *you* are around."

Elizabeth was unable to reply, to ask what Cassie was insinuating, for Mr. Thorne arrived at their side.

"Forgive me, Miss Knight, but your sister has escaped my arm all evening, and I see there is a space for us to slip into the dance unnoticed! If she will have me, of course. And do not worry about convention! If you wish to save yourself for the unmarried men, I will not take offence, I assure you."

"I would be honoured, sir!" Cassie said, and happily took Mr. Thorne's arm to go join the dance.

Mr. Sinclair met her eyes and Elizabeth smiled. Then, her expression froze in place, when she saw the sad eyes of Thea dancing opposite of him, who was so very obviously in love with Mr. Sinclair. And how Mr. Sinclair, for all his smiling, was not in love with his dance partner.

A voice, a tiny, tiny voice whispered perhaps he was in love with her. But, she was not a girl barely seventeen in a new gown thinking she would have an offer of marriage by the end of the month. What she and Mr. Sinclair had was friendship, the rare kind that could exist between a young man of a good income, and a young woman who, for all of her charms, would slowly sink with age.

So when he looked at her again, she smiled openly and did not trick herself into believing he saw her as anything other than a friend, a proxy even, until his family found him a woman of means.

And so she drank half her glass of wine, and made the promise no more after this one.

She finished the glass.

Well. Perhaps one more.

Chapter 3

February 9, 1811
Saturday

Elizabeth arose only slightly blurry eyed at her usual time, and made her way down to the breakfast table for ten sharp, despite the five (or was it six?) glasses of wine the night before, and despite having arrived home just as the dawn's light cracked the sky.

The rectory was so silent that Elizabeth was surprised to see her father at the dining table, reading a newspaper. He flipped down the top and said, "Ah! Someone moderated themselves last night, at least."

"Am I the first to arrive?" Elizabeth asked, sitting down to the table.

"Isabella stirred earlier to announce she was too old to be at balls at all hours of the night and returned to her bed to sleep off her revelry," he said. Then, he made a joke about how Isabella's knees did not even crack in the morning yet, so she was not so old.

Elizabeth was surprised to see her father in such good spirits, but she went along with them. He asked plenty of questions about the ball, more than he'd ever asked her before, and she happily answered his inquiries as she helped herself to a hearty breakfast.

There was a knock at the door, and then Mr. Sinclair was ushered in by a maid at the same time that Cassie stumbled into the dining room yawning and barely dressed.

"Cassandra! We have a guest," Elizabeth said.

Cassie yawned before pulling her dressing gown tighter. "I apologize, Elizabeth. Papa. Mr. Sinclair." Another yawn, then Cassie shook her head. "I have been sent by G and Thea to ask if they can have permission to sleep further. And, also, for myself, please."

"Oh, go on with you, girl," her father said. He yawned. "See what you did? Go! Back to bed with you."

Cassie curtsied to Mr. Sinclair, and yawned so hard that all of them ended up doing the same, which caused a great deal of laughter.

"Ah, Sidney, come my boy. Now, I do not see any black marks underneath your eyes. It appears you and my eldest are the only sensible people of my acquaintance, for even my own wife is unable to string together three words of sense," Mr. Knight said. "Of course, I did not hear Elizabeth giggling in her room at six this morning, unlike some other ladies in my household."

"I have more experience with balls, sir, so I will not abuse my sisters for making the same mistakes I did at their age."

"Did I hear our Miss Knight admit she has made a mistake, sir? Surely not!" Mr. Sinclair said, warranting a great deal of laughter from her father.

"I assure you, sir, I have made a number of mistakes in my life, and I still do, too, and every day."

"As do we all, daughter! As do we all," Mr. Knight said as he folded his newspaper. "Now, Mr. Sinclair, pull up a chair and join our little party. It is no Vane Park, but our Julia makes an excellent breakfast."

Mr. Knight's spirits remained high all through breakfast. Apparently, the ragout the night before had been excellent, and he was in mostly good memory. He had confused two engagements, and had accidentally done the one Mr. Sinclair was to do earlier that morning, but Mr. Sinclair smoothly dealt with the situation, stating he'd misunderstood and thought he was to do both, and so was happy to hear his day's work had immediately lightened. Then, before her father could say anything, Mr. Sinclair asked who in the village required a visit.

They went on like that for three-quarters of an hour, until Mr. Knight declared himself, "sick of company, my good Mr. Sinclair," for which the young curate laughed. Then, Mr. Knight offered up Elizabeth to walk with Mr. Sinclair to Vane Park, as that was the man's next stop, since "no one will be awake in this house for hours yet," and Elizabeth found herself gathering up her outdoor clothing before she'd had the opportunity to finish the food on her plate.

And so, the two young people walked along the lane. They discussed the ball, then weather, the state of the roads, the health of this or that person in the village, before finally, they fell into silence. One of them would have to bring up her father eventually, and she determined that it would not be her.

"At least it is not too muddy," Elizabeth declared. "Provided one avoids the puddles, of course."

"I know I shall complain of the heat in a few months, but I confess I grow weary of complaining about the cold."

"I believe I have known you long enough, sir, to boldly state that there are only about four days out of the year where you are not complaining about the weather."

Mr. Sinclair considered that for a moment before a wicked smile came across his face. "I get it from my mother."

Elizabeth laughed. "I think I should like to meet your mother one day. I believe we will be fast friends."

"That is my greatest fear," he said.

However, that topic soon exhausted itself and they fell into silence once more. It did not feel oppressive, not to Elizabeth's senses. Rather, it felt as if they were friends, where quiet could overtake them without awkwardness.

Except, Mr. Sinclair grew more awkward as the walk progressed. Something was on the man's mind, of that Elizabeth was certain. Finally, he spoke in a heavy, almost pained voice. "Miss Knight, I feel I must apologize to you."

"Apologize?" she asked. "Whatever for?"

"I have not been the active curate your family requires in this trying time." He frowned and fussed before saying, "Miss Knight?

May we, just this once, dispense with the niceties of society and speak as if we were lifelong friends so that I can be open and honest with you?"

"Sidney," she said with feeling. "It is my hope we shall always be friends, so you may always speak to me as such. But, sir, you are frightening me. Whatever is pressing upon you? I can see it in your face. What has happened?"

His mouth quirked curiously, an expression she'd never seen before. Was it…embarrassment? He let out a little chuckle, and surely the red upon his cheeks was from the February air and not anything else. "My dear Miss Knight, or shall I also be bold and call you my dear Elizabeth?"

That made her laugh, a short, harsh bark that would have drawn Augusta's sharp rebuke when she was still alive. Even now, she could hear her former stepmother's voice, telling her only women of loose morals laughed in the company of men.

"What was that look?" Mr. Sinclair—Sidney—asked her.

"Have you ever heard your mother's, or in my case my former stepmother's, voice in your head at the most interesting moments?"

"Endlessly," he said, dragging the word out until he rolled his eyes at the end for emphasis. "And what does this voice tell you?"

"That perhaps you may call me Elizabeth when we are alone, but perhaps not around others, for the gossips of the village will certainly have us married by special licence before Easter."

"Ah, yes, that would be terrible indeed," he said without humor. Or, at least he attempted so, for she spied one corner of his mouth twitching.

"Terrible indeed!" Elizabeth said with a laugh, ignoring Augusta's voice. Then, growing somber once more, she said, "Now, there is no one about, so tell me what is pressing upon your heart."

"One hundred thousand pounds," he said. "And a few shillings. And a gold clock."

Elizabeth stopped walking. She stared at him, right there on the side of the lane. Stunned into silence. "My dear Sidney, tell me, please, that you are not indebted to that degree."

"Oh, Miss Knight, no you misunderstand me." He was not laughing, nor even smiling. His face was one of sorrow and oppression. "I find myself in rather an opposite position. And, I thought we were now using our Christian names, being lifelong friends."

She rolled her eyes. "Sidney Sinclair, do not vex me, or I shall use your Christian name but not in the manner of which you request. Now, tell me about this absurd wealth. Who has inherited it, and are they single?"

Mr. Sinclar began walking again, and said, "I am very single, indeed."

Elizabeth's smile faded as the meaning of his words settled in her mind, with the full weight of that reality. She turned to him and said, "Surely you are not implying..."

"Alas, it appears I am the luckiest man in England, for a distant relation has died and left me his entire fortune. All one hundred thousand pounds, and a few shillings. And, curiously, a gold clock that is currently trying to make its way from Italy."

Elizabeth's mouth moved, but no words came from it. Finally, she managed to blurt out, "Why are you still working as a curate?"

He did not smile when he said, "I believe those will be my mother's exact words and tone when I can no longer fight off the attorneys from letting the news slip. In fact, upon your good opinion of the man, I hired Mr. Grant of London to assist in the transfer of assets, and all of the work that has come with inheriting such a large fortune. I had hoped hiring outside of my family's usual circle of connections would grant me a few extra weeks of peace before my life is ruined."

"Ruined? Good God! You just inherited a fortune!" Heat was rising within Elizabeth's chest and she found it difficult to breathe. Then, a thought stabbed her in the heart. "Oh. Then you will leave us. Bryden, I mean. You will leave Bryden." And in a quieter, sadder voice, she whispered, "And all of us."

"Oh, Elizabeth, my friend." He smiled at her when he spoke, morphing into a roguish troublemaker who was about to set aflame the hearts of London's unmarried female population. "You misunderstand my quandary, for my wish is to remain here in

Bryden. Or, at least close enough that I can visit all of my friends every day if I so desire."

Elizabeth was unsure if she kept her emotions off her face, but she attempted to keep her voice even. "Then, I do not understand the problem. You shall be rich regardless, and if you choose to be rich in Bryden, who are we to stand in your way?"

"Alas, I fear my mother will make that very difficult indeed."

"You are a grown man, and she is not God."

"Ah, it is clear you have not met her yet," Sidney said, and they both laughed. "Are you telling me that you would not be swayed into certain choices if you inherited one hundred thousand pounds today?"

She thought of the book, and how it was her path to freedom. She was silent for too long, though, for Sidney said, "You hesitate because you know that, no matter how rich you would become, there would be familial obligations upon your soul."

"That is because I am a woman. What is your excuse?"

Sidney's shocked expression was followed by a laugh. A loud, barking, near hysterical laugh. Finally, when he managed to pull himself together, he said, "Miss Elizabeth Knight. I believe I now understand why you are not married."

"Because no man would have me?" She wasn't laughing now. She felt the arrival of thirty looming in the distance, each month bringing it closer. She found herself glaring at him, so angry that she could not even speak—a man who was not that much younger than herself, for all of his pretending to be young and full of vigor—and...

He had not replied immediately. Instead, he glanced at her and gave her a curious, even kind look. "It is because there are very few men who can handle a wife who is clearly more intelligent and wittier than themselves."

"I believe that is the polite way of saying 'because no man would have me,'" she said. She flicked a softer expression at him, in a pointless attempt to conceal her feelings. He had hurt her with his teasing, and she hated herself for letting it wound her.

"On the contrary," he said, and he said it with great feeling. "I can think of several young men who would have you."

"Are they rich? If so, pray, send them my way for I am at leisure this entire spring."

He tripped in a puddle, splashing mud on his expensive boots, and hitting the hem of her pelisse. "Oh, I apologize! I was not watching my steps well enough. Oh, I made a mess on your outfit."

"It is only a little mud, Mr. Sinclair. *Sidney*," she said, correcting herself at his annoyed look. "And, besides, I cannot be cross with you, for I am in need of your list of rich men so that, if the worst befalls us all, I shall at least be able to find a governess position."

She had meant it as a joke, but his expression turned solemn. "Will that be your fate? If…" He did not need to finish the thought. It was upon everyone's minds, with her father the way he was. "Is there no money for you?"

Three thousand pounds.

In a flash of folly, on the lane currently devoid of all other people to bring an end to their intimate discussions, Elizabeth blurted, "I have secret plans to ensure our protection."

"How secret are these plans?" he whispered, as if the trees and squirrels could overhear them and report back to their superiors.

The whisper made her yearn to share, to trust him, to allow herself to sink into his voice. To convince herself that she was special, protected, and safe in that moment, in the lane, filled with muddy puddles.

But she had learned long ago that she was not safe. Not now. Not ever. Not so long as men could stand in her way. Mr. R had been a painful lesson, but he was not the only one. The Royal Occult Society would ruin her, and sleep well at night having done so. And would not a man of Sidney Sinclair's family have connections there?

"I did not mean to force a confidence," he said, interrupting her deliberations. He stopped walking to bow. Rather deeply. "Please accept my apologies, Miss Knight."

"I took no offence," Elizabeth said. "And, sadly, my secret affairs are not as exciting as yours, for I do not expect an inheritance from afar to arrive on my doorstep. However, I am, of course, always open to that possibility. A lady must be flexible."

Sidney Sinclair snorted.

"I fear this conversation has taken a gloomy turn, and I confess I cannot be so myself in the presence of such a rich man on such a fine February day."

"It is cloudy," Sidney said.

"And it is not raining nor snowing, so indeed I decree it to be a fine day. Now, since you declare you wish to remain in Bryden, then I suspect your first duty is to find appropriate lodgings."

"Do you know of any respectable properties for sale?"

"In fact, I do!" Elizabeth said.

"Indeed?" When she nodded, he said, "Well! Elizabeth Knight, you seem to be all manner of surprises today. Tell me all about these grand houses you wish me to waste my money on. Perhaps I shall buy them all!"

MR. SINCLAIR HAD business with Vane Park's steward, as well as the housekeeper. Maria and Henry both clearly had too much brandy at their ball, and were not the best company. After laughing at them both for acting like her sisters (who clearly also had too much of the Thornes' good brandy), Elizabeth decided to leave before Mr. Sinclair concluded his business under the guise of wanting to return home to assist her father.

The sun was finally peeking out from the grey clouds, and with the absence of wind, Elizabeth found the walk back home to be rather enjoyable. However, her ghostly companion, who travelled with her everywhere in the pendant about her neck, had other plans.

"Why did you avoid waiting for Mr. Sinclair? He would have accompanied you." The ghost did not appear, but she spoke clearly through the pendant all the same.

"My dear Mrs. Egerton, it is a fine day, and I am very capable of walking unaccompanied." Elizabeth considered ending the topic there, but decided a lie of omission was still a lie. "It is not that I dislike Mr. Sinclair's company, but rather I am finding it rather difficult to trust myself around him today."

"Trust? Does his newfound wealth tempt you to flirt?"

Elizabeth chuckled. "No indeed, I was not tempted into flirtation, I assure you.'

"Perhaps it is this age of decadence, but in my time, what the two of you were doing was indeed called flirting."

Elizabeth was indignant at the accusation. A flirt! How dare the ghost imply such a thing. "I can, and have, been accused of many things in my life, Mrs. Egerton, but a flirt has never been upon my ledger, I assure you."

"The lady doth protest too much, methinks."

"It is a sad state of affairs in the world if a lady cannot be polite to her own father's curate."

"He will not be that for long," Mrs. Egerton said. "It appears the world has bigger plans for your Sidney Sinclair."

"He is not *my* Sidney," Elizabeth said. She did sigh, however. "I confess I shall miss his society."

"Your family is respectable, he is a gentleman," Mrs. Egerton said. "And besides all of that, he plans to settle in the neighbourhood."

Elizabeth waved at the passing cart, headed to Vane Park. The labourers must think her mad for constantly walking about the countryside talking to herself. "Mrs. Egerton, I do believe you are a terrible influence upon me."

"I am certainly not."

"I nearly told Mr. Sinclair about the book. When he told me about his good news. A part of me longed to tell him, to share the secret. Even if the secret was mine own."

"Do you not trust him?" she asked.

"On the contrary, Mrs. Egerton, I do. I truly do," Elizabeth said.

"Has our stoic Miss Knight finally found a man worthy of her attention?"

Elizabeth smiled at the two maidservants on the other side of the path, a basket in each hand, heading to Vane Park. The lane had been blessedly empty when she and Sidney had made the walk.

Sidney. How easy they had slipped into that. She frowned.

"There are a number of men worthy of my attention, I assure you."

"Then why do you remain unmarried and unprotected?" The ghost pressed.

Elizabeth took no offence. Mrs. Egerton came from an age where love wasn't in the equation of marriage. Some women did find love, of course; after all, they were still women. But for many, love was a luxury best kept in books and poetry.

"As I have told you before, I will only marry for the deepest affection. And, affection on both sides. I will not marry a man who disdains me, nor I him." She pondered her words to Mr. Sinclair and said, "I believe I would make an excellent governess, do you not think?"

"What a waste that would be," Mrs. Egerton declared.

"Then, perhaps we should turn our attentions to using the occult to have a distant relation die and leave me one hundred thousand pounds."

"Do not forget the shillings and the gold clock," Mrs. Egerton said. Then, she asked, "What is the going rate for melting down gold? Perhaps we could divert the clock to your house and no one be the wiser."

"Oh Mrs. Egerton!"

Chapter 4

February 11, 1811
Monday

The Knight household survived the aftermath of the ball. The young people who'd consumed too much wine, brandy, and cake soon found themselves on steady feet once more. Elizabeth had been enjoying the quiet solemnity of the rectory, but all good things must end.

The morning proved to be rather cold, so Elizabeth relocated downstairs, where it was warmer, with a heavy blanket in one hand and her writing desk in the other. One of the day maids—one of the many nieces of Miss Sims—brought her a steaming tea pot wrapped in a cloth to conserve the heat longer.

Fortified with hot tea, Elizabeth began the task of catching up on months of occult work. She was not grievously behind, but the goings on about Bryden had made dedicating time to the occult difficult on a regular basis.

She decided the most obvious place to start was with her recent letters, since some of the ongoing questions had been answered. While she could not work with Mrs. Egerton nor Miss Gibbs, their healing expert, in the broad daylight of the rectory's main floor, she could consult books, memory, and even common sense to work through various puzzles.

Elizabeth began writing answers to Miss Susan's occult inquiries. Several times, she left the warmth of the hearth to march upstairs to flip through her precious occult books, to find answers, to consult a ghost, and oftentimes discovered even more questions.

The pressing issue was the range of Miss Gibb's locket. Mrs. Egerton had successfully been bound to a rather pretty locket that Elizabeth wore daily, allowing the ghost to see all that her wearer saw. While Elizabeth rarely went any distance of note without the autograph books—the books where lady occultists willingly bound their souls to its pages for future generations—testing was necessary, and it was highly irregular for even the most well-read lady to carry a book into a ballroom.

But Mrs. Egerton had attended last week's ball perfectly, without any disruption in her ability to see. In fact, without Elizabeth's commands or knowledge at the time, Mrs. Egerton did her own independent attempts to break the spellworking, including transferring herself from the locket at Elizabeth's throat in Vane Park all the way back to her autograph book in Bryden Rectory.

She added Mrs. Egerton's account to the letter:

Mrs. Egerton informed me the process was successful, and nearly as fast as the blink of an eye. What is more astounding, I believe, is that she possessed the ability to send herself back to the locket under her own will without any instruction or command from us. This leads both myself and Mrs. Egerton to conclude that whatever ethereal powers of the occult allow Mrs. Egerton's spirit to remain with us sees not only her autograph book as her home, but also now the locket.

Sadly, the many books we do have do not record all that much useful information regarding the nature of the autograph books. Mrs. Egerton made several disparaging comments about men and the nature of book publishing when I inquired, so I do believe that we are to struggle on our own for this. After all, I cannot write to the Royal Occult Society and ask them for their assistance!

Oh, how I wish the occult was merely a simple mathematical formula and not filled with both the whims and peculiar bits that make each of us our own unique persons. I would find it vastly easier if all that was needed was to add a combination of items, say a word or two in Latin, and then the working…worked! Alas, we must deal with the realities of the world in which we live, and in this one the occult is as whimsical as the lady occultists who hide within the pages of history.

On went her letter, with her various theories about why Miss Gibbs' locket could not be out of sight of the autograph book in which her signature and spirit resided. In fact, Elizabeth had to accept that one possible theory was simply—and frustratingly—that she did not have the same relationship with Miss Gibbs as she did with Mrs. Egerton. Therefore, the nature of the workings did not replicate.

And, more frustratingly, it could be as a simple as her needing to spend more time with Miss Gibbs, to get to know the ghost better, to understand the complexities of her own nature. Elizabeth was easy around Mrs. Egerton, who did not steer her toward sin. Miss Gibbs…

Elizabeth sometimes wondered if Miss Gibbs could kill a man and sleep well that night without a whisper of guilt upon her soul. Perhaps it was merely her airy, open nature mixed with the dark realities of healing abilities. Perhaps it was merely Elizabeth being cautious, shocked, or both.

Or, as Elizabeth wondered in secret without a soul knowing, not even Mrs. Egerton, perhaps she was merely terrified of the knowledge that healing could kill. That something all people eventually wished and prayed for existed, but that it had a high price attached, higher than any Elizabeth had ever conceived.

So it made her fear Miss Gibbs, or at least not trust her. Elizabeth sat with that thought, newly formed in her mind. She pulled out her occult journal, where she made notes and random thoughts for later dissemination. She wrote out her feelings that came to her mind, about how she rarely called on Miss Gibbs over the autumn and winter, despite how many people were afflicted with the sickness. How she rudely ignored the ghost's suggestions to target the sickness toward the politicians of the country, for, as she once said, "what good are any of them if they do not allow a woman into their ranks."

She'd laughed off the notion, but now sitting here on this cold, dreary morning, she found herself wondering if perhaps Miss Gibbs had been completely serious. Or, was this yet another attempt to ensure Elizabeth understood in her very soul that healing was a dangerous path that could lead to grievous consequences, and that a lady would have to live with those costs upon her conscience. For the laws of the land would not catch her out, but God would know her heart. And she would know what she'd done.

But every coin possessed two sides, for would not a lady who allowed one to perish when she could direct an illness to a stronger individual also be committing the same sin? Or would she be playing at God in that case, and that would also be an evil?

It was easy during the outbreak not to use Miss Gibbs' talents, for there was too much sickness, too much risk. Very few were safe. That had surely been the right choice. In her heart, Elizabeth knew that. However, in an isolated case...What was the right path? Was there ever a right and good path, or was even the very knowledge of such abilities pushing a lady to sin against her own conscience, if not against God himself?

Thankfully, Elizabeth was rescued by the post lest she sink into the despair of deep religious thoughts. She excitedly opened the letter from Miss Thorne, apparently newly arrived in London.

> *I have yet to relocate to your aunt's house, but it does not signify anything of use as London is as dreary as Bath at present! Your poor aunt continues to suffer from the weather, but she is kept company by the newly arrived Miss Keats. I plan to visit her daily, and Miss Keats has been an excellent addition to our little society, and you must come to London to meet her.*

I know I am welcome at your aunt's home and require no formal invitation, however with her malady at present and the fact that an old school friend is due to arrive from Ireland any day now, and my mother is throwing a ball on Thursday, and a dinner party next Monday—no doubt to break up the mind-numbing tedium, for even she complains about the state of London society—so in any case, daily visits are all I can manage at present. And a daily walk with Miss Keats, where we discuss all manner of things. Rest assured we do even spare some thought for the occult!

My poor mother is beside herself that I remain unmarried and dedicated to the occult. If Miss Keats had an unwed brother, I believe she would be mollified with the false hope that I might turn my direction there, but alas. My father has declared he is ready to offer adoption if Mrs. Spencer would be willing to take on the expense of looking after me. He said so at dinner last night, mostly to rile up my mother and to give her something new to complain of (for even I confess one can only listen to the complaints of boredom for only so long). My mother still has hope I shall catch the eye of an earl, but I continue to be resistant to the charms of men at present.

Now that I mention the charms of men, I must regret to inform you that our Mr. Osborne still has not proposed to Miss Susan, and we are all quite at a loss. My cousin, your Mr. Thorne, complained of it to my parents and even they are now asking daily what is holding up the man. Miss Susan is out of mourning. There is nothing to hold them back. He has his fortune. He has secured her affection. What else is there to be done? Why wait?

My mother has suggested perhaps Mr. Osborne wishes to purchase an estate before proposing, but that is ridiculous if true! He could not continue his business if he bought some dismal country estate where the only thing left to do with his time would be to sit about drinking too much port and learning how to shoot. And what would poor Miss Susan do in the country if she were not with us? Is there a property in Bryden he could purchase? At least she would be close to friends then. I shall suggest that when he comes to dine tomorrow with my parents.

Yes! My parents have invited a shopkeeper in lowly trade to sit at their table. Oh, how the world has changed indeed! My grandmother had to take to her bed over it. Never mind that the shopkeeper in question is richer than most of the people who dine at her own table!

Perhaps it is our Miss Susan, and not poor Mr. Osborne who is the hold out. I have attempted to inquire, delicately of course, but she is more tight-lipped than you!

Pray, come to town and fix this dullness.

Miss Alice Thorne

The second letter in her bundle was from Miss Susan. Elizabeth settled in to enjoy the other perspective on the proposal of marriage situation. Curiously, it was dated for the following day from Miss Thorne's, so clearly there had been a delay of some kind.

My dear Elizabeth,

Alas, there is so much I must convey in this letter that I will be unable to clear my name from Miss Thorne's wild tales about my supposed courtship with a certain distinguished bookseller of our mutual acquaintance.

Now, to the main purpose of this letter. I wish to give you a little hint that Mrs. Spencer's lungs are bothering her again. Please do not be alarmed. We are assured it is not infectious or at risk of turning putrid. It is merely the old complaint. Her physician has recommended an extended period in the country air, to clear the London smoke from her lungs, but she has refused.

I worry her refusal to follow the doctor's instructions is due to her hosting us ladies, especially myself. I have offered to find a position, and to move from the house, but your aunt becomes quite unreasonable when I bring up the subject. My dear friend, pray guide me. You know her better than any other living person. Should I ignore her protests and find employment with a good family? I am certain Miss Thorne, or even your Maria Thorne, could find me such a place. Or, should I believe Mrs. Spencer's words and remain?

I trust you completely and know you would not tell me falsehoods, so I rely upon you my dearest friend to assist me, for I fear it is my heart—and not just my affection for your aunt, but my affection for another person, I confess it to you now in this letter—that leads me to hesitate.

Oh, your aunt has entered the room.

I have included in this letter extensive notes. Miss Thorne insists I include a shilling under the seal for you, for her parents have just released more funds to her. She danced two dances with an eligible bachelor the other night, so she is flush with ready coin! There are days I feel sorry for her poor parents; I swear she does this to them on purpose.

Your aunt says to write that she wishes me to hint strongly that you are needed in London. First, for her health, and second for our general disposition. This rain is making us all moody. What gayness we would have, and we would get so much more research done I am certain.

Oh, and she reminds me of another bit of business. Mr. Grant asked me to pass along to not be alarmed if you hear the Royal Occult Society is sniffing about once more. They are attempting diplomacy this time, but none of us will be taken in, I assure you. According to Mrs. Spencer, they even attempted to re-hire Mr. Grant, who flatly refused them. He stated he has been considering purchasing a property in Wollerton or Eastmore, or perhaps even Bryden.

Now, and you will laugh at this, for your dear aunt was rather alarmed at this bit of news. Not that Mr. Grant isn't an excellent man, but he —and you must forgive what I am to write—is not a good match for you. Again, he would be the luckiest of men to catch you, but forgive me if I am wrong, but you have never shown any interest in that quarter. However, he assured Mrs. Spencer that this was not about a young lady, but rather that he has been considering leaving town for some time now (which your aunt knew), but mostly he'd said it to mislead the Royal Occult men.

So I tell you all of this in case you hear news about your upcoming betrothal to Mr. Grant.

A flutter of activity came down the stairs, and Elizabeth stopped reading her letter to call out. Her three younger sisters dutifully arrived in the doorway in warm pelisses and bonnets, but without their boots yet. She glanced down at Cassie's feet, and noticed her worn wool stockings.

"Where are the three of you headed? It only stopped raining ten minutes ago," Elizabeth said.

"We're going shopping!" G announced.

"Papa said it was fine as long as we didn't track mud in on the carpets," Cassie said. "So we have decided to be quick about it, before the rain started again."

"Well, be off with you then," Elizabeth said while making a shooing gesture.

Isabella came in to ask if she could join Elizabeth to do some quiet sewing, and of course Elizabeth agreed. After all, she teased, the drawing room wasn't for her singular use. Elizabeth had assumed Isabella might wish to discuss a subject that was best to have with the girls out of the house, but her stepmother silently settled near the window, for the best light to do sewing, and so Elizabeth turned back to her letters.

She needed to write Mary. While there was still so much hurt on Elizabeth's part, Mary's honest attempts to rebuild the bridge between them had meant a lot to her. Writing to her was still awkward, it was still forced, but Elizabeth did it now with less trepidation. It was the best that could be expected, given their history.

My dearest Mary,

Please accept my apologies for not replying directly to your letter dated the seventh, as there was no real news to report until the ball. As I understand it, the girls have all written their long and detailed accounts of the ball, so I can now sit to compose my own letter to you, which I hope will have far more sense. I shall also skip the details of lace and silk, for G informed me this morning that her letter to you took up six full sheets! Goodness, where would we be if we did not have helpful neighbours to deliver our mail for us!

So with those details already given, I wish to dedicate this letter to the situation at the rectory and to throw myself upon your sisterly assistance. Now, please, do not alarm yourself, and do not suppose you must drop your own life to come here. In fact, what I desire is quite the opposite. May I persuade you to invite one of the girls to come stay with you until Easter?

Now, as to why I have requested this. I hate to speak so frankly about our own father, but the style of living here has become oppressive with fear and worry. I truly live in daily apprehension he will forget a burning candle, and even Isabella has used her condition as an excuse to stay up well past a godly time to comb the house to ensure he has not left a candle lit.

Mr. Collins and Mrs. Green have been consulted on the sly during their visits and have spoken with me outside of the house, under the guise of walking into the village. I dislike all of this sneaking about, but that is how we live now. Despite Isabella's difficulties, they both feel it is wise to have her up and moving about, as it is impossible for her not to fret. Likewise, on a more practical level, her out of bed means she can assist easing and distracting our father's fits of temper.

My dearest Mary, I feel such pain writing the above, and had to pause several times before convincing myself not to cut up this letter and begin again. I know there is no maliciousness on the part of our father, and I take as much comfort as I can from that. However, it is so painful to see him in such a state. Mr. Collins fears it is his heart; that he has all of the classic signs, and for some, it comes with unpredictable fits of temper. As our father will not take any medicines, since he is "as fit as any man" we must all endure.

So these are my thoughts. Cassie has been invited to London, to stay with the Baldwins until Easter. There is hope in that quarter, if I might be so bold, and our father agreed in a moment of clarity, so we are packing her off to London this week with Mr. and Mrs. Parsons in their carriage.

Therefore, if you could take Thea, I will attempt to send G to London with Maria. From there, I plan to beg Cousin David's excellent wife to extend Cassie an invitation in London, as to not overstay her time with the Baldwin's. Maria has then offered to take Thea and G in turns back and forth to her London home. This will allow someone to be here with Isabella, but the rest of us will receive some respite from home.

I say the rest of us because poor Isabella will not. I plan to stay behind as long as necessary to assist Isabella, and I pray she makes it to her confinement safely. We just heard yesterday that Mrs. Campbell died with a stillborn, and Isabella has been very distressed by the news.

I think Charles moving to Ashbrook to take on the curacy will also be of great assistance, as the girls will no doubt all wish to take turns improving his house and garden. I will not force anyone to visit where they do not wish, of course—you know my feelings on that situation—but I suspect the girls might enjoy playing at being the mistress of Charles' home on occasion, sending out invitations, ordering linens no one can afford, and bossing him about.

Please write back with your thoughts on this matter,

Eliza

On went the letter writing for over an hour, with worries about the girls being trapped in the rain, for the wet returned with vengeance. However, a note eventually arrived with Julia, who'd also been caught in the rain, that the Knight girls had been invited to the Parsons' for both the afternoon and dinner. The invitation also extended to Elizabeth, and the offer of a carriage to transport her both directions was offered, but she sent a note with the delivery boys who'd arrived with Julia that she would decline the invitation, as she was snug and dry at home. She did wrap dry clothes for the girls, though, and sent those with her reply.

With that task done, Elizabeth returned to her London letters. First, to Miss Susan, hinting that her assistance in getting Aunt Cass to do anything recommended by her physician would be of great comfort. She also added in some hints that having Miss Susan married to such a man as Mr. Osborne would give Aunt Cass equal relief.

Then, to her aunt, she wrote that Miss Susan worried in the way all dependent woman worried, and to extend her a little grace. A woman like Miss Susan struggles under the weight of charity, even if freely given, and longs to be considered useful. So, for Miss Susan's own sake, would Aunt Cass please let the woman be useful. And would Aunt Cass please listen to at least some of her cautions and wishes regarding her health, so that Miss Susan would feel she was being of use.

She finished the letter and found herself grinning.

"My dear Eliza," Isabella said, startling her from her thoughts. "You've been staring at that letter and grinning for some time now."

"I believe Mary is right," Elizabeth said as she packed away the writing things.

"Right?" Isabella asked dubiously.

"That the occult has made me bold and saucy," Elizabeth said.

The ladies broke into laughter and soon, letters were abandoned and Elizabeth assisted her stepmother with her sewing. Shortly, however, Mr. Knight rushed into the drawing room.

"Ladies! Come quickly, you are needed in the kitchen!"

"Whatever is the matter?" Isabella asked as she got to her feet.

"You must see!"

They arrived in the kitchen to a frantic Julia, filled with apologies. When asked what was the matter, Mr. Knight directed them to a covered dish. With a flourish, he whisked away the cover to display a bright purple dish within.

"What on Earth is that?" Isabella asked.

"Chicken stew," Julia said mournfully. "I did not know that the purple carrots bled so much. I only ever had added them to beef before this!"

"But Elizabeth! Taste it," her father urged, handed her a spoon. "I promise you shall enjoy this scientific experiment."

Bewildered, Elizabeth accepted the spoon and when she had blown on the stew to reduce the temperature, he instructed her to close her eyes. She did, and the stew tasted as any other stewed chicken would taste.

"It tastes excellent," Elizabeth said.

"Now, taste it again with your eyes open," he said, urging her to go in for another spoonful.

Elizabeth laughed, unsure of what her father was attempting to accomplish. She did as he asked, though, and then exclaimed, "It tastes different when I can see the purple!"

"You see, Julia!" Mr. Knight exclaimed. "I said it was your eyes tricking you! It tastes like stew when we cannot see the purple."

Isabella insisted on having some next and declared with laughter that, indeed, the purple stew tasted different than when unable to see the stew. Finally, Julia was urged to try, and she let out a little giggle when she conceded her eyes had played a trick on her taste.

They all had a spoon each now, all testing the stew over and over, digging into the warm pot, laughing as they confessed the stew was excellent, but tasted more excellent with closed eyes. Mr.

Knight roared with laughter at his bright pink potatoes and declared they must keep some back for the girls to sample when they returned home.

"My dear, this is the best entertainment I have had in weeks!" Mr. Knight declared to his wife. "Extraordinary! Julia, you are a treasure and, if you come to my study, I shall give you a shilling for this! It was well earned."

And, he left them, urging Julia to follow behind him, for she was owed a shilling and he said he did not like to carry open accounts.

Unfortunately, his good mood was short lived, for the morning brought the kind of terrible news no one wished to read on an empty stomach.

Chapter 5

February 12, 1811
Tuesday

THE KNIGHT FAMILY were seated together at the breakfast table when the sound of approaching hoofbeats pulled their attention away from the excellence of the hot muffins Julia had successfully baked that morning. As Elizabeth was closest to the window, her father urged her to report.

"Oh! It is Tomas! What is he doing here so early in the morning?" she said.

As good news seldom arrived with such haste, Elizabeth was already at the door before Tomas dismounted his horse. Coin and letter exchanged, and the obligatory offer of food from the kitchen, which Tomas declined with a tip of his hat.

Elizabeth flipped the envelope over, relieved to see there was no black seal preparing her for terrible news from London. She'd had quite enough of that. The others had left the table and were approaching her, looking for news. She said it was addressed to her, in Miss Alice Thorne's handwriting.

"Well, don't just stand there!" her father declared. "Come back to the dining room and open it!"

She walked back to the room, though did not take a seat. Two coins fell from the letter as she opened it. She did not bend to pick them up. Instead, as she read, she stumbled her way to the nearest chair to brace her courage.

My dear friend,

No one has perished. I feel I must state that at the beginning so that your nerves will be quieted on that score. However, I do write this letter on the urging of your aunt's personal physician, as well as all of your friends, and even Sir William and Mr. Grant. We are all grievously concerned about your aunt, and there is no easy way to put this but that we request your presence in London immediately, as you are the only person we feel can assist.

Your aunt's lungs have taken a terrible turn. The weather in London has been incredibly damp, and your aunt suffers grievously. All attempts to relocate her away from London have failed, and the physician now fears this latest cough fit last night might cause scarring if it does not abate. Scarring! I had no idea one's lungs could become scarred, but he insists it can be so with someone who has weak lungs like your aunt. Her breathing has taken on the wheezing sound she occasionally develops, only it is unrelenting now. Not even laudanum works! In fact, it only made her breathing worse and, for one frightful stretch, we all took turns to stir her while she slept, for she frequently stopped breathing in her sleep! Sometimes for several seconds until she finally would gasp and cough. The physician has instructed she only be allowed hot water and brandy. Nothing else can be trusted.

The only person we are all convinced she will heed is you, my dearest friend, and we all beg you come to London immediately to assist. I have included two guineas in this letter, in case you must travel by post. As I have no notion of the cost involved in such a scheme, I erred on the side of too much money. However you arrive, I beg you come quickly.

Elizabeth looked down at the floor; the coins were not there. She spotted them upon the decorative table, the one with Augusta's favourite vase. Now filled with dried lavender. She had no idea who'd picked up the coins, but the look of worry on Cassie's face said it was probably her.

On went Elizabeth's thoughts, a jumble of the present, past, and future. Her aunt often suffered from poor lungs, and London's terrible air did nothing to improve her situation. She also greatly disliked laudanum and rarely took it unless there was no other option for relief, so she must've been in a terrible way if she agreed to it. And then for it to make her stop breathing! To be reduced to drunkenness for comfort!

"I must go to London," Elizabeth announced.

She did not move, her letter still in hand. There were so many details to consider. Firstly, how would she even get there? They did not own a carriage. Her father would never allow her to travel post, but even if he did, she could not leave until tomorrow at the earliest.

"Oh!" She blurted. She looked up from her letter staring at the faces watching her, a mixture of curiosity and concern. "Mr. Sinclair plans to go to London tomorrow on business. I shall beg room in his carriage."

Isabella stood and said, "With your permission, I shall go to Mr. Sinclair and ask him on your behalf. I am certain he will—"

"She is going nowhere," Mr. Knight said. When all eyes turned to him, he said, "Who is Cassandra Leigh to any of us?"

"Papa," Elizabeth said. "She is my aunt. I must go."

"You are needed here."

Isabella drew in a breath and said, in a steady, but firm tone, "My good sir, there are more than enough of us to take over Elizabeth's duties while she goes—"

"I have spoken," her father said. "Do not contradict me, woman."

"Husband, might I have a word with you in your study?" Isabella asked.

"Whatever you wish to say to me, you can say in front of your daughters."

Isabella opened her mouth, but Elizabeth gave her a swift shake of the head. No, she would fight this war on her own. "Sir, it is my Christian duty to—"

"You will not lecture me on Christian duty, miss!" Mr. Knight shouted, slamming both fists on to the dining room table. One. Two. Three. His face was an unearthly red, and Elizabeth genuinely feared he would clutch his chest if he continued to distress himself in such a manner.

He screamed—the sound a man only made when falling down a flight of stairs—and backhanded his tea cup until it went flying across the room. It shattered and all of the ladies jumped. Three servants were heard rushing from various directions, but steps slowed when Mr. Knight shouted, "There will be no more talk about London!"

G was standing on the other side of the table still. Cassie and Thea were near Elizabeth, frozen in terror. Isabella was standing, her hand gripping her chair's back. Elizabeth watched the servants slip back out of sight, all avoiding Mr. Knight's wrath.

She could not blame them. Her father had never, not in his entire life, behaved in such a manner. He had fussed and complained, and shouting was a requirement to be heard in a household of young women. But not like this.

A memory hit Elizabeth's mind: when her father had thrown the sewing to the floor. How shocking it had been. She stared at her father, red-faced, panting, sweating, and reality struck her. It had not just been the illness that had done this. This had been building for some time, and they did not notice for it was a little here, a touch there, a sprinkle on top.

But today? She could not lie to herself. This man was not her father. For all of his faults, and for there were many, he would have been embarrassed to see this man carry on in such a manner.

So Elizabeth ignored her racing heart when she asked, "Might I take Thea with me?"

"Where?" Her father demanded.

Elizabeth was not a gambler, but her father's moods were such that, at times, he might immediately forget the topic at hand.

So, she placed all of her coin upon the gaming table and said, "To London, sir. Cassie shall be travelling tomorrow, and I know there is no extra room in Mr. Parsons's carriage for me, and I believe you would prefer if I did not travel with Mr. Sinclair alone in his carriage, being an unmarried man."

"Mr. Sinclair is a gentleman!" Mr. Knight declared, as if that answered all questions.

Elizabeth's heart pounded so hard now she had spots in her vision. Her hands shook, so she put them behind her, hiding the letter and the evidence of her distress. "Indeed he is. But, we must not allow rumors to propagate. No, indeed, sir. I believe I should bring Thea with me. Might I have your permission?"

"Where do you want to take her?"

"To London, sir. Tomorrow, when I leave."

Her father sat down to the table, in his usual seat. He opened his newspaper, the stack he received from James Fitzharding every fortnight.

Anger filled Isabella's face, and Elizabeth lifted a hand, just enough for her stepmother to see. It was time to stand up to this changeling illness that had overtaken her father's good sense.

In the calmest tone she could manage under the circumstances, Elizabeth said, "I hate to disagree or disobey my father in anything, but it appears I must. I shall be going to London, with or without your permission, sir."

Her father flipped his paper down to glare at her, a look she did not recognize. It was not the annoyance of a father staring at a daughter. It was of a man who hated. He opened his mouth to speak. "I ordered—"

"Excuse me, sir, you clearly do not understand. I shall be thirty years of age this September and I am old enough to make my own decisions. Now, I can either take one of my sisters with me in the carriage with Mr. Sinclair, or I shall travel alone with him. Or perhaps I shall travel alone on the post. If necessary, I shall walk to London. Either way, sir, I shall be in London by tomorrow suppertime."

Malice filled her father's face, and Elizabeth feared he would hurl himself at her. She was frightened to her core. A man in such a state, so clearly dispossessed of sense, could not be trusted. At this time, she could not rely on her intuitions of him being her father, but rather of an injured animal, feral and terrified. She must do as her instincts told her.

"If you leave, there will be no home for you to return to," Mr. Knight snarled.

"Albert!" Isabella snapped. Elizabeth had never heard her use his Christian name before. In fact, she'd never heard a single person ever use it before now.

"Do not speak to me in the familiar, wife," Mr. Knight said. Sweat was beading along his hairline and brows. He began coughing, nothing extreme, but it was an odd sound. Like he struggled to get enough air.

Her sisters looked between her and their father with terror in their eyes. Leaving them would make life more difficult, more of a struggle, but she must do her duty to her aunt.

She might have raised her voice slightly when she said it, but she wanted to think she maintained some dignity. "Then I am to Mr. Sinclair's, to throw myself upon his mercy."

"If he assists you, it will be his last job as my curate, you can tell him that," Mr. Knight shouted after her.

Elizabeth turned to stare at her father. "Ah. Then you have not heard the news, sir."

"What news?"

Elizabeth shrugged, like a common maid.

"What news!" Her father roared.

Elizabeth did not answer. She turned and walked out of her house. Without a shawl. Without a parasol. Without even a spencer to protect her from the cold February morning. Even as she walked across the field to Mr. Sinclair's house, she could hear her father at the door, shouting at her like a common labourer shouting after his wife.

Her father was ill, of that there was no denying. There was no predicting his moods. No determining how to cool him. No matter the previous insensitivity her father occasionally showed, and his penny-pinching ways, he had never, in his life, been intentionally cruel. And when pressed with information, he had always listened to his daughter. It might have taken him time to come around, but he was always rational.

The man shouting from the rectory's front door was not her father. He never tolerated such foul language in his presence, and spoke sharply to any of his parishioners who used such base manners. Whatever was happening to her father, whatever was causing his swollen hands and feet, his red, puffy face, was also affecting who he was, as a person, as a father, as a husband, as a human being.

She would be kind, tolerant, and compassionate, but only to a point, she decided. There were some things she would not do, and leaving her aunt in distress when her own assistance was gravely needed was beyond that point.

She arrived at Mr. Sinclair's door shaking from both the weather and the distress of home, and was greeted by a shocked housekeeper.

Mrs. Perkins stared at Elizabeth before rushing her inside with, "My dear Miss Knight! You must be freezing! Whatever possessed you to venture outside in such a state?"

"Mrs. Perkins, I beg you. Is Mr. Sinclair at home? I am in need of assistance."

"Yes, yes, come. Mr. Thorne is visiting, but come in all the same."

"I do not wish to interrupt, but…" Elizabeth's teeth chattered. "I apologize, I…"

Mrs. Perkins took the shawl from her own shoulders and wrapped it about Elizabeth's cold form. Warm from the housekeeper's own body, it sent immediate shivers through Elizabeth as it chased away the chills.

"Now, they have tea in there already, but I fear it might be getting cold. I'll get you a hot pot. The last thing we need is you getting ill," Mrs. Perkins called out to one of the various maids and instructed her to bring a fresh pot of tea and to send someone with a warm blanket.

"I do not wish to be a bother," Elizabeth said.

"What is all of the commotion?" called out Mr. Sinclair from another room.

Footsteps. A man's. Growing closer. Elizabeth's heart pounded and she shivered harder, even though she was here to throw herself upon Mr. Sinclair's mercy.

"Miss Knight! Whatever is the matter!" Mr. Sinclair declared. "Did you come here like that? You are shivering."

"That girl is taking too long. I shall find Miss Knight a blanket," Mrs. Perkins said. "Sir, would you be so kind to get her in front of a fire?"

"Of course!" Mr. Sinclair said.

"Is that Miss Knight?" Mr. Thorne called out. More of the heavy footsteps of a man coming closer.

Quickly, she whispered, "Mr. Sinclair, I have come to throw myself on your kindness."

"What has happened? Can you not say it in front of Mr. Thorne? Come, quickly. In front of the fire."

"Miss Knight!" Mr. Thorne's smile vanished. "What has happened?"

"We need to get her into the parlour first, come," Mr. Sinclair said, his hand upon her arm.

Elizabeth struggled to control her emotions. She fought against making a scene, despite having already made one by arriving in such a grievous state. She was barely into the room when she blurted, "Sidney, are you still leaving for London tomorrow?"

She winced at her use of his name; she immediately noticed Mr. Thorne's interest. She never even called him Henry, and she had known him for years and saw him as a second brother. Nevertheless, she must press on.

"If so, I pray, nay I beg you to allow me to accompany you lest my father banish me forever for taking the post."

Sidney—for, in the intimacy of his home, she saw him as thus now—motioned for her to be seated and pulled off his own coat to wrap about the front of her. Clutching the warm garment to her body, she began to relay the situation, pausing for the arrival of Mrs. Perkins and a thick patchwork quilt. A moment later, the maid with a new pot of tea, steaming hot. A cup was poured and thrust into Elizabeth's hands. She accepted gratefully.

Elizabeth continued her tale when the maid left the room. Once she detailed the final indignity of her departure, her eyes welled with tears, and she accepted a handkerchief from Mr. Sinclair.

"Please do not hate my father," she found herself saying as she dabbed her eyes with one hand, balancing the delicate cup and saucer in the other. "He is not himself."

Mr. Thorne said, "You never met my uncle Graham, but ask my cousin, Alice, the next time you write to her. Kindest man you'd ever know. But then this one winter he became a completely different man, slowly at first, and then he attacked one of the grooms. I don't think the man had ever raised his voice in his entire life. They had to pry a pitchfork out of his hands before he hurt someone." He took a sip of his tea. "That's when all of his servants admitted he'd been acting odd, just small things. Then, all at once."

Sidney nodded. "My family also has a similar tale, though it was from when I was a boy, so I don't remember it."

It comforted Elizabeth and she told them so. But then she sighed, and said, "Nevertheless, though, I *must* go. I must."

Mr. Sinclair reached a hand toward her, but quickly pulled back. "Of course, there is no debate on the subject. Mrs. Perkins? Mrs. Perkins!"

As Mr. Sinclair left the room to call out to his housekeeper, Mr. Thorne smiled at her and said, "You must not worry so, Miss Knight. We shall fix it all."

"You did not see him, Mr. Thorne," she whispered. "You would not have recognized him."

Over her shoulder, she heard Mr. Sinclair speaking to his housekeeper. "Mrs. Perkins, would you be so kind as to accompany me to London tomorrow with Miss Knight? She is urgently needed in London, and her father is uneasy with her travelling unaccompanied with an unmarried gentleman."

"I would be happy to accompany Miss Knight!" Mrs. Perkins said. "Besides, sir, there are a great many things we will need once you move, and with your permission, I can begin that task once in town."

The deal was struck, and Mr. Sinclair returned to his seat by the fire. "There, Miss Knight. All is fixed."

"But what about my father?" she whispered.

"Your father's moods, forgive me for saying this, come and go with such rapidity that he might have already forgotten the argument," Mr. Thorne said.

"Thank you. Thank you so very much." Then, a flash of selfishness hit her as she turned to Mr. Sinclair. "So, you shall be leaving us for good then?"

"Mr. Sinclair has a secret," Mr. Thorne said with a grin.

"Oh, she is well aware already," Mr. Sinclair said.

A curious expression came across Mr. Thorne's face. "You said you told no one."

"Those were not my exact words, Thorne," Sidney said, and he smiled at Elizabeth. "I believe I said I have told no one outside of those who most needed the information."

In any other circumstance, Elizabeth would have accused the man of being a shameless flirt. But, thankfully, that was not the case here. "Did you take my advice then?"

"Indeed I did! I have purchased Rose Cottage from Mr. Thorne, and the deal has been struck this very morning."

"Maria does not even know yet!" Mr. Thorne said with a laugh. "And a good bargain I gave him, too. The cottage and enough land for him to easily earn five hundred pounds. Double if he can convince my neighbour to sell him a parcel on the other side!"

"That's right, Miss Knight! You shall pass by my own snug little cottage every day on your way to visit Mrs. Thorne!" Mr. Sinclair said. Then, he sobered, "Please, for my sake, do not accidentally break this news to my mother if you happen to meet her in London. I fear I must be the one to do the unwelcomed task."

"I do not know your mother, so it would be very rude of me to drop such vital information into her lap without a proper introduction," Elizabeth said with a soft laugh.

He smiled at her, holding her gaze. She joined him in the smile, so much relief flooding her that he would not be leaving Bryden. Well, she would have to look at the map as she could not remember if Rose Cottage was in Bryden proper or if it was on the other side of the imaginary line putting it into Wollerton. Nevertheless, the lane to his house would be along the road to Vane Park. She could see him every day, if she wished.

It wasn't until Mr. Thorne abruptly stood that Elizabeth realized she'd been staring into Mr. Sidney Sinclair's eyes for far too long. Nothing was meant by it, of course; it was simply the knowledge she would not lose her friend. A woman like her needed all of the powerful friends she could gather.

"Well, Sinclair. Which of us has the duty to talk sense into Mr. Knight this time?"

"Mr. Thorne..." Elizabeth began.

"I should do it," Mr. Sinclair said, standing.

"I believe we should both go," Mr. Thorne said. "Ah, we must announce to him your good fortune, and in the midst of that, I am certain we can persuade him to allow Miss Knight to take her journey."

Sidney nodded to himself, clearly thinking. "Miss Knight? Remain here at present until I either return or send word. I shall say you are consulting with my housekeeper over…over…the female touch to Rose Cottage. Yes, that would be perfect. Mrs. Perkins? Might I trouble you to take care of our Miss Knight?"

Mrs. Perkins came into view and smiled. "I would love to sit with Miss Knight, if she will have me."

"I would be so very grateful for the company," Elizabeth whispered.

Chapter 6

February 13, 1811
Wednesday

ELIZABETH FOUND HERSELF fighting surprise the next morning when Mr. Knight gleefully waved his farewells to his daughters. He'd even tried to give away G while they loaded the carriage, saying it was unfair that three would be in London while a fourth lingered in the doldrums of the countryside. But Mr. Sinclair reminded Mr. Knight that G was expected at Maria Thorne's house that day.

"A bonnet-mending party, if I recall," Sidney said.

"And you wish that over town?" Mr. Knight asked G dubiously.

Georgiana Knight, who had been saved most of their father's ire thus far, had offered herself up as the sacrifice for her escaping sisters. She smiled, widely and broadly, and lied to her father's face in a way that Elizabeth had always struggled to do. "Why, Papa! Three days of dinner parties at Vane Park is worth more than pompous strangers in London! Think of the bonnets, Papa!"

Mr. Knight stared at his daughter with warranted suspicion, but he gave his blessing for her to remain. The previous evening, Julia had apparently fed him for an hour straight in the kitchen while she cleaned, raiding their pantry stores of anything ready-to-serve. He'd eaten himself ill, then promptly went to bed. Julia whispered that he had wanted cake, biscuits, and other sweet things, so she had convinced him to eat a little meat with everything, a little cheese, a little of the leftover potatoes or the creamed celery.

"Have I done correctly?" She whispered; the poor child terrified of her master's moods. And, having only just lost her own mother, Elizabeth was very aware of the girl's silent suffering.

Elizabeth had told her she'd done properly, and instructed her to do so again if necessary for it had put their father into an excellent mood. All traces of the previous day's argument were gone, and back was the acerbic, curmudgeon father she knew, and indeed loved, as difficult as he was at times.

And so that was how Elizabeth found herself halfway to London, in a carriage with Thea and Cassie. A hired carriage, in fact, since Mr. Sinclair wisely decided that three Knight girls locked up in a carriage together for twelve hours would result in arriving in London with fewer Knight girls than from which he'd left with. Speed was a necessary consideration, borrowing the horses at each stop.

As it was, the poor man had to ride alongside the carriage for the entire trip, in the depths of winter. And, again, not even on his own trusty mount. Instead, he also switched to fresh horses each time the carriage stopped for the same.

Elizabeth gave her sisters the forward-facing seat, and feigned sleep whenever possible. Cassie had been meant to travel with the Parsons', and was disappointed about the change in conveyance to London. She tried not to complain, but brought up the young Mr. Baldwin's name repeatedly.

"At least you have friends in town. I have no acquaintances," Thea lamented. "I shall have to return with Mr. Parsons in four days. Even Isabella said I could not bother Aunt Cass for long."

"I shall ask Miss Baldwin to invite you to stay, at least for a fortnight, if Aunt Cass cannot take you," Cassie said.

Aunt Cass was not their aunt, it was true, as she was related to Elizabeth and Mary's mother. However, in a large family, such matters were frequently ignored. She was Aunt Cass to two Knight children; therefore, she was Aunt Cass to all.

"Perhaps Mr. Sinclair will escort me back home," Thea said in that dreamy tone she reserved for when talking about him.

Elizabeth tried not to laugh at her sister, for no young lady wishes to have her secret affections mocked. Or, in Thea's case, her open affections. Alas, she did not succeed.

"Elizabeth! Are you pretending to sleep?" Thea demanded.

Elizabeth did not open her eyes when she said, "I am mere months away from becoming an old maid, ladies, and if I wish to pretend to sleep, it is my God-given right."

Thea's dramatic sigh was exactly what Elizabeth wished for. "You aren't *that* old."

"Tell me," Elizabeth said, eyes still shut. "What are your thoughts about being thirty and unwed?"

"Elizabeth, stop teasing her!" Cassie protested. "Or we shall never get any peace the entire trip."

Thea made a shocked sound, which brought on another snort-cough by Elizabeth. That only seemed to enflame Thea's raptures because she spat, "Everyone knows you have your eye on Mr. John Baldwin."

"Thea!" Cassie snapped.

On that, Elizabeth opened her eyes and found her sister's face a bright crimson. "Do I need to speak to you about the intentions of young men?"

Cassie gave Thea the meanest of looks, one that only a sister could give another. Then, to Elizabeth she said, "I find him very agreeable."

"Does he find you likewise?" Elizabeth asked.

This sent the other two sisters into a tizzy of argument, protestations, and declarations. So much so, Mr. Sinclair pulled his horse near the window and motioned for Elizabeth to open it. She did so and he shouted to her over the sounds of the horses and the carriage, "Is all well within?"

Elizabeth laughed. "My dear sir, if we arrive in London with the same number of Knight girls in here, I will consider it an act of God."

That made Mr. Sinclair throw his head back in laughter and he advised her to carry on, lest he add his spoon into the mix and cause the cake to be too salty. That produced a dreamy sigh from Thea once the window was closed. "He even knows about cooking!"

"I am not certain I trust an Englishman's cooking," Elizabeth mused.

"Do you not like Mr. Sinclair?" Cassie asked. "He's often looking in your direction."

Thea nodded glumly. "I have not noticed him looking in *my* direction, except if you are there."

That did not match Elizabeth's own experiences with Mr. Sinclair. She pondered on it for a moment, considering if he did look at her "often" as Cassie said. She found herself having to concede that perhaps he did, but she was quite certain it was not for any matrimonial reasons. As the eldest, men often looked in her direction when Isabella or her father were not afoot, as she directed the tone of any setting.

"Well?" Thea demanded.

"Well what?" Elizabeth asked, pulled from her contemplation.

"Do you like him?" Thea asked.

"What an odd question. We are currently riding in a carriage paid for by Mr. Sinclair's own purse, and not our own. Indeed, he is undertaking his journey on horseback, in the cold. It would be very ungrateful for me to say a bad word about him."

"But do you *like* him?" Cassie asked, drawing out the question to force meaning into it.

Elizabeth found herself very uncomfortable with two pairs of inquisitive eyes staring at her. It was an incredibly inappropriate inquiry for a younger sister to make of an elder one, and more so with one of them wildly in love with the man in question.

"Girls," Elizabeth said with a smile. "I do not wish to be in competition with my sisters."

Thea groaned loud enough to drown out the sounds of travel. "Why will you not answer the question?"

"I have!" Elizabeth protested as she glanced out at the tall figure on horseback. He caught her looking and smiled. She rolled her eyes before returning the smile. That made a wide, toothy grin form on his face before turning back to being observant as he rode. Seated backward-facing meant that she often saw Mr. Sinclair's face when he allowed his horse to fall behind a few paces, to look at her, and smile. He had been smiling a lot at her on this journey.

A terrifying thought filled her heart.

"Elizabeth?" Cassie asked. "If we have offended you…"

"I am not offended," she said, still looking at a very excellent gentleman, to whom she found forced to admit—to herself, for indeed her sisters did not need to be informed about her heart—that she had grown attached. Not love. No. Certainly not that. But a companionship, a comfort, a routine. The quiet knowledge that there was one person on this Earth who seemed to always see her private thoughts.

"Then why are you quiet?" Thea asked.

"I was only looking for gossip," Cassie said.

"Girls, we cannot always control who we like, who we do not like, and we certainly do not control those we love, and who return that affection. Time and circumstance change all of those, and far too frequently for my taste." She smiled at her sisters. "As for Mr. Sinclair, at present, I find no fault with his person. Only his ridiculous collars."

"I think he looks very fashionable!" Thea protested and began a defence of Mr. Sinclair's entire wardrobe.

Elizabeth turned back to the window, smiling and nodding at the appropriate times during her sisters' detailed accounting of Sidney's closets.

Sidney.

It had been a mistake to allow that familiarity into her heart. She felt it now. Memories of a man she once called Nathaniel when none other were around. The terror she felt, now witnessing her own affections slowly, inexorably, inescapably moving in the same direction. And while her sisters did not know yet about Mr. Sinclair's one hundred thousand pounds (and a few shillings), she did, and she felt the loss of his society. Oh, he bought the pretty little property from Mr. Thorne. A little land, with the prospect of a little more. But that would not satisfy him or his family. Unmarried men of consequence do not stay put. She would lose him.

Her father would be dead soon, and she would remain. They would lose their home. They would be scattered to the winds, to this house or that, reliant on the fortunes and goodwill of others.

"And how he ties his cravat!" Thea said dreamily.

"Mr. Baldwin has taken to tying his in the same manner," Cassie said. "After I pointed out how dashing it looked upon Mr. Sinclair."

"Oh Cassie! He must surely be in love with you!" Thea declared. "Do you not think, Eliza?"

Elizabeth was caught, lip trembling, as she found herself confronted. She had let her guard down. She had believed her own teasing, that a woman on the cusp of becoming an old maid did not reduce herself to such trivialities. The simple question. Such a simple question. Did she like him? A question she'd been asked a thousand times before. One she'd answered without hesitation. A question that made her heart sob today.

"Elizabeth, are you all right?" Cassie asked.

"You are pale," Thea said.

"Are you certain we did not offend?" Cassie asked. "We were only teasing you, since you are always so harsh on Mr. Sinclair."

"Oh, a little motion sickness, that is all. I found myself staring at the trees, and, well, you girls have heard the lectures about that."

"Often from you!" Thea said.

"I believe I shall attempt to sleep for real now, if you both do not mind," Elizabeth said.

Elizabeth accepted a small pillow from Thea to lean comfortably against the carriage window. She closed her eyes and tried to chase away the sight of Sidney riding alongside them. She would have to guard her feelings now. That much was obvious. She did not wish to be humiliated when Sidney moved on to a rich woman.

She did not like how melancholy she felt at that prospect.

Chapter 7

IT WAS LATE in the afternoon when the carriage finally arrived in front of Aunt Cass' steps, having made excellent time without delay when changing horses. Mr. Sinclair had left on foot for his mother's home with polite wishes for Aunt Cass' health, and the coachman's assistant had tied the horse to the back of the carriage while the men unloaded their baggage. They would return Mr. Sinclair's luggage once the girls were settled, before returning the carriage and horses to the nearest post station.

Once outside the carriage, Elizabeth leaned backward, as much as her stays would allow her. Cassie merely stretched her arms out in front of her. Thea began cracking every single joint in her body until Elizabeth told her to, please, for the love of God, wait until she was in the privacy of her own bedchamber.

Thea turned an ear toward her shoulder, and a loud, painful sound echoed from the girl's neck. At Elizabeth's reproachful gaze, Thea promised to stop, though her impish smile said she was tempted to crack another joint. She turned solemn, reminding her sisters to be silent upon entering the house. There was no knowing the state of her aunt's health.

Elizabeth's knock at the door was not noticed, so she opened the front door herself to look inside. She had expected the hushed tones of servants doing their duties as silently as possible.

She had not expected several raised voices, and maids standing about looking concerned. James the Butler turned with surprise on his face as she smiled at him. He bowed deeply.

"I do not wish to leave London!" That was very clearly Aunt Cass, though her words were slurred, despite the volume.

James began accepting her gloves, then hat. "Your arrival is most welcome, miss."

"Do not speak to me in that tone, Sir William!"

"Do not raise your voice to me, Cassandra!"

"Ah, she is not alone?" Elizabeth asked.

"You are not my husband, nor shall you ever be!"

"I would not marry you if you were the last woman on Earth, Cassandra Spencer. Now take heed to my words!"

"I would rather be dead!"

James gave an exasperated sigh. "You are very welcome, indeed, Miss Knight. And your sister, too. Very good to see you, Miss Cassie. Why, Miss Thea! Hello to you, too! I did not see you. Have you grown since last summer? I believe you are taller than last I saw you."

"Indeed I am!" Thea said gleefully, then checked her volume. Not that it mattered anymore. "I had to let down the hems of my new gowns."

"Oh excellent!"

More shouting. Another male voice she could not immediately identify, but sounded familiar all the same. "May I inquire who is upstairs?"

"Half of London, miss," he said. "Might I be so bold as to suggest you bring some sense to that room?"

Elizabeth decided to keep her pelisse on, as she would have the maid shake it out later. She instructed her sisters to remain downstairs, and politely asked the butler to arrange tea and cake for the girls. Cassie declared she was in desperate need of a moment's privacy, then Thea said she, too, needed to tend to nature. Sally, Aunt Cass' maid, had been hiding around the corner, and she was called to escort both girls to the servants' quarters, as their rooms were not yet prepared.

Which was unlike this house, but considering the language coming from above, perhaps the maids wisely decided to attend the downstairs chores.

Each step brought Elizabeth closer to hearing the full argument. New voices entered the fray, and Aunt Cass' remained clear, greatly distressed, and in fact Elizabeth would argue very put out and at the end of her patience.

Elizabeth successfully slipped into her aunt's bedchamber unannounced and unseen. Sir William, her aunt's next-door neighbour argued fiercely, and in Elizabeth's opinion, with an air of intimacy one's neighbour should not have. Mr. Grant and a man Elizabeth didn't recognize were arguing off to the side. Cousin David stood in the room, as well, though he currently had the good sense to exercise silence.

"Sir William! I do not wish to leave London!" Aunt Cass finally shouted.

"My dear aunt, you are becoming hysterical," David said. "I believe we might require a sedative if you continue—"

Aunt Cass turned a withering gaze upon David, one so fierce he stopped speaking mid-sentence.

Elizabeth cleared her throat. "I apologize for interrupting this male jolly making."

"Elizabeth!" Aunt Cass exclaimed and she vaulted from her chair. She did not push the men out of her way, but she glared at them until they grew the good sense to move from a lady's path. She caught her niece into an embrace. "What are you doing here?"

"Our mutual friends begged me come to London, and I shall tell you all of the particulars about the journey later." She looked about at the men gathered in the room and said, "Clearly, it was required. Now, why are all of you gentlemen teasing my aunt so?"

"Cousin Elizabeth, this is not the time for feminine—"

"For the love of the Savior, not now, Mr. Leigh!" Mr. Grant said. "Miss Knight, I am so relieved you are here to bring some sense to this house."

"I am always happy to bring sense to disorder, Mr. Grant," Elizabeth said. "How may I be of assistance?"

"Tell them to leave me alone!" Aunt Cass said.

"You must insist she go to Cornwall," David said.

"Try to convince her to go to Bryden," Mr. Grant said.

"No one has ever improved after a trip to Cornwall, David!" Aunt Cass said. "Find me one person whose spirits or health have improved, and I shall declare you have found a liar!"

"My dear neighbour, calm yourself!" Sir William said. "There is nothing wrong with Cornwall!"

The strange man spoke, and Elizabeth got the impression he was a physician of some sort. Not Aunt Cass's regular, though. "If you persist in this, I may have to administer..."

Mr. Grant stepped in front of Aunt Cass. "I recommend another course of action, sir."

Elizabeth held up her hands. "Gentlemen! Please. Let us speak like there are ladies in the room. Raised voices will not help one's cause in this matter, I assure you."

"Grant, who is this young lady?"

"The person who can get you what you wish," Mr. Grant said.

Elizabeth smiled sweetly. "Indeed I am. Now, if the wish is to excite my aunt and to work her into a fit that brings on a coughing episode, and perhaps even a fever, perhaps heart pains? Then, I congratulate you, sirs, for you are on that path. Now, if you wish my aunt to remove herself from London's questionable air, and indeed I cannot blame anyone for wanting that, then gentlemen? I recommend you cease bullying the lady."

"Women do not know what they want!" the physician exclaimed. "Mr. Leigh, I believe we should retire..."

"Sirs," Mr. Grant interjected. "Any conversation you wish to have about Mrs. Spencer's well being shall be done in my presence, or I shall be forced to banish you from this house."

"You have no such authority!" David Leigh said. "I am her only living male relation."

Elizabeth decided to gamble in a very unladylike manner. "If pressed, I shall be forced to involve my father. I am certain he will object to forcing any medical procedure upon my aunt."

"Your father is wholly unconnected to our aunt, Cousin," David said.

"The man who married one of my sisters and one of my cousins is wholly unconnected with me?" Aunt Cass asked pointedly.

"I am certain he would do his Christian duty for his first wife's sister and step in to assist her," Elizabeth said.

Elizabeth decided her words were not a lie, and felt no guilt for them. Her father's current situation might make his interest in this task wane, but there was a time, and not that long ago, that such a letter to her father would have brought him to London. He would have done it, she was certain. The man did know his duty. So, this was not a falsehood.

Mr. Grant cleared his throat. "Mr. Leigh, consider that bringing Miss Knight's excellent father into this will also bring her sister's husband, Mr. Fitzharding of Ashbrook. I know him well enough to state with certainty that he will claim himself Mrs. Spencer's closest living male relation by the nature of his marriage. Do you agree, Miss Knight?"

"Completely," Elizabeth said, relieved to have support.

"What they are saying is to get out!" Aunt Cass shouted.

"My dear woman..." the physician argued.

"Get out of my house, sir!"

The terrible, rather loud, physician left and the peace was easier to achieve. Sir William was soon also convinced that yelling at Aunt Cass would not produce the results he wished to see, something that Elizabeth resisted stating he should have known, having been her neighbour all of these years. Cousin David gave way when Elizabeth asked him how he thought his dear wife would react if she heard of him yelling in the presence of a sick woman.

Elizabeth asked, "Where is Mr. Lane? I expected to find him, not some assistant."

"Putrid fever," Sir William said. "Have pity on the poor lad. Your aunt is the most stubborn woman I have ever met."

"Do not forget I knew your poor wife, Sir William," Aunt Cass said.

"Yes, and that was why you were thick as thieves for her entire life," Sir William retorted.

"We ladies must stick together against the tyranny of men," Aunt Cass said.

"Tyranny of men!" Sir William declared. "Do you hear such nonsense, Miss Knight?"

"You must not take these things to heart, Sir William!" Elizabeth declared.

"I am only trying to help the woman, what good it will do!"

"If I wished a man to boss me about, I would have married again!" Aunt Cass shot back.

Elizabeth glanced at Mr. Grant, who gave a vigorous shake of the head, warning her not to become involved.

"As if any man would want you!"

"I recall a number of them pounding upon my door before my dear George was cold in his grave," Aunt Cass said.

Sir William threw up his hands. Actually threw them in the air! Like a common worker. He said, "My dear Miss Knight, it is good to see you and your good sense. Lord knows we have been lacking it." He near shouted that last line.

"Are you still in my house, Sir William?" Aunt Cass shouted back.

"Would you like me to walk you to the door, Sir William?"

He waved her off. "No, girl. I know the way."

Aunt Cass coughed, a wheezing, dry sound. She took a sip of brandy. "Oh, do not give me that look. The brandy is all that keeps my cough at bay. Mrs. Cook mixed it with boiled water, honey, and spices."

"It adds an excellent scent to the room," Elizabeth confessed.

"Indeed, but I admit after having six or seven of these in a day, I feel rather fuzzy about the edges."

Elizabeth laughed. "Oh goodness! No wonder you are short tempered with all of these men!"

"I would be less tempestuous if they were not so pushy!"

"They aren't wrong, though, my dear aunt," Elizabeth said.

"What is this? Conspiracy?"

"Concern," Elizabeth said.

"Why? Everyone is waiting for me to die to get their hands on my money," Aunt Cass said.

Elizabeth knew it was the brandy talking, so she ignored the comment and said, "On the contrary. If we wished you to die, we'd all insist you remain in London."

Aunt Cass attempted a scowl, but burst into laughter. "So that is your plan in coming here? To force me into the country?"

"I am here to improve your spirits, and to assist Mr. Grant with whatever good sense he requires from me, and to visit with my dear ladies of the occult, and renew all of my old acquaintances." Elizabeth glanced at her cousin, David. "And perhaps finally be able to visit my cousin and his new wife for more than a few minutes in a room."

"You are always very welcome at my home, my dear cousin!" David exclaimed. "How could you think otherwise?"

"You are a married man now, sir! I cannot barge into your house and disrupt your poor wife's plans!" Elizabeth said.

"My dear! You are family! There is no barging amongst family!" David said.

"You must like all of your relations, sir," Mr. Grant muttered darkly.

"Enough!" Aunt Cass declared. She pushed herself up. "Enough! I am tired of men in my bedchamber. Out! All of you! We will gather in the drawing room like civilized people."

DOWNSTAIRS, ELIZABETH WAS greeted by Miss Alice Thorne and Miss Susan, who had both been entertaining the younger Knight girls. They were unable to engage in a proper greeting—with gossip and the occult—but they acquitted themselves very well. There were the usual exchanges —the state of the roads, the weather in the country, the odd odor of London's air. Who was dead, who was with child, who survived. All of the usual polite conversation.

Aunt Cass came downstairs within a quarter of an hour, dressed, with her hair in a simple cap. She accepted a cup of tea and requested "something decent" to eat.

"Aunt, you should be careful! Your digestion is, no doubt, in a delicate state," David said.

Mr. Grant groaned, but dutifully filled up a small plate with various slices of cake and sweet delights. "Sally says Mrs. Cook is preparing a cold meal in case the ladies are hungry from their journey."

"Oh yes please!" Thea said, being the first words out of her mouth that weren't a scowl at David.

"One can only eat so much cake," Cassie agreed from the corner, where she was busy writing letters of arrival to her friends.

"There is no point in offering my opinion, for ladies never listen to me," David said glumly.

"Do not be offended by such trivial things. We ladies are tougher than you men think," Elizabeth said.

He made a sound of disbelief.

"Surely, your own wife! I would wager a shocking amount of money that she is as tough as any man."

"Elizabeth! How can you say such things! And about my own wife!"

"I was complimenting her!"

"By calling her a man?"

The ladies in the room all chuckled.

"My dear cousin! I did not call her a man. I simply said she is as strong as any man, in her character, in her resolve, in her constitution, and in her own intelligence. And if that is considered an insult by modern society, then pray, I hope I am insulted every hour of the day!"

"You are impossible!" David said.

"Perhaps so, but ask your wife when you return home. See what she says," Elizabeth said.

"Oh niece, enough! Pray, leave the poor man alone," Aunt Cass said. "You will have Mrs. Leigh removing to Naples to get rid of us at this rate."

"I hear the weather in Italy is excellent for the lungs," Mr. Grant said before popping a thin slice of cake into his mouth.

That seemed to break Aunt Cass' resolve for she said with a sigh, "Mr. Grant, I shall consider removing to the country if you can find me somewhere civilized to live."

"What part of the country interests you the most?" he asked.

"If I am forced to leave my house and all of the comforts of town, then I would prefer to be within easy distance of Elizabeth," she smiled at the others, "and all of the Knight girls."

"Oh! Aunt Cass?" Thea said. "I apologize for interrupting, but I did not wish to forget. I brought the shawl you had made for me. I will show it to you once I have my bags organized, so that you can see how well it suits my gowns."

"Do not unpack too quickly," Cassie said, "for I am writing to Miss Baldwin to announce our arrival and inquire if there is room for you to visit for a night or three."

Thea's squeal startled Mr. Grant, who jumped enough that his tea spilled on his trousers.

David stood up and said, "I believe that is my invitation to take my leave. As my dear Charlotte has said on more than one occasion, when a young lady squeals in delight, a man's presence is no longer welcome."

"Oh cousin! You are most welcome," Elizabeth said.

However, David would not be persuaded to stay, and indeed he was smiling broadly enough to announce there was no malice in the remark. "Ladies. It was a pleasure to make your acquaintance once more. Cousin Elizabeth? Always a pleasure. Grant, I shall see you about, no doubt. And Aunt? Pray, for my sake, at least pretend to rest."

"I shall do as I please," Aunt Cass said, but she was smiling when she said it. "But I promise that, if Mr. Grant can find me a suitable abode, I shall *consider* taking it."

"That is all I ask," David said. He bowed once more, "Good day, ladies."

Mr. Grant put down his own cup and stood. "Well, I am to the country tomorrow, apparently. Miss Knight? Would you like me to call upon your father?"

Thea looked at Elizabeth with wide, shocked eyes. Cassie was off in the corner, so Elizabeth could not see her expression, but she assumed it was similar. Hers did not offer such emotion. Instead, she smoothly said, "I fear my father has been quite under the weather, as he continues to recover from this autumn's illness, so I worry he would be poor company. Also, I would not wish to distract you while you go about your business."

The final goodbyes and promises to write with news over, Mr. Grant departed. The door closed and Aunt Cass sighed. "Finally. We are rid of all of those men."

Alice exclaimed, "Your aunt has been besieged!"

Miss Susan said, "Mr. Osborne came to visit earlier, and even he said it was too masculine here for his tastes."

"Goodness," Elizabeth said with a chuckle. "It must've been terrible! Now, tell me all of the news! Cassie has to write to her friends, so she is too busy to talk, and Thea is near starving, so will be busy eating all of the cake and will not be able to answer any questions."

Thea attempted to chew her food faster, which only made the others laugh.

Elizabeth felt her shoulders immediately relax. She was safe.

CASSIE AND THEA retreated to bed early; both were exhausted by an excellent supper and the journey, plus the prospects of more excitement the following day. With Aunt Cass safely to bed to rest, her brandy-addled nerves starting to ebb, Elizabeth stayed up with her occult companions. The servants were instructed to go to bed, that the ladies could very well handle putting a log of wood on a fire as well as any other human being. So the three ladies were set up in the downstairs drawing room, with a nice fire, cooling tea, and cold delights. They laughed and chatted, and teased Miss Susan about a certain bookseller.

Finally, Susan begged for mercy. "Oh Elizabeth! Must I endure this teasing from you, too?"

"I beg your pardon, my dear friend," Elizabeth said between sips of her wine. "I mean no harm, I promise you. I am merely frustrated by the entire situation. What is taking the man so long? Does his mother not approve?"

"Oh, on the contrary!" Alice said. "I have it from his mother herself that she approves the match, and why not? Our Susan is the best creature in England, even if she doesn't have a farthing to her name."

"Thank you, Alice," Susan said dryly. "There is little a lady loves more than to be reminded of her poverty."

"Do not take that tone with me, Miss Susan Markson!" Alice said sternly, though she was laughing. "In fact, Mrs. Osborne told me if this foolishness of lingering without an offer of marriage continues, she will step in and begin giving hints."

"And pray, what about my own wants and needs in this?" Susan said with a laugh. "Perhaps I do not even like him, and I have merely been polite this entire time."

"Oh please," Alice said. "If you liked him more, you would become such a scandal that Mrs. Spencer would have to turn you out of doors without so much as your bonnet."

"Ridiculous," Susan said. "But enough about me, I grow weary of the subject. What about you, our dear Elizabeth? Are there any new men in Bryden that have finally turned your eye?"

"Alas, ladies, I must report that Bryden continues to suffer from a shortage of rich, handsome, and charming single young men. My three requirements for happiness."

"You are impossible!" Susan said. "It is bad enough that Miss Alice here refuses to marry, much to the disappointment of her family, I assure you."

"Now, I will confess there is a gentleman who has turned my mind to marriage," Alice said.

"There is?" Susan and Elizabeth said, in complete amazement.

"A Mr. Faust," she said. "He recently turned seventy, with no heirs. He is a good friend of my grandfather, and I have been very tempted to ask my mother to arrange a match."

Elizabeth stopped sipping her wine to glance at Susan, for she was uncertain if this was a joke, or if her friend was serious. Susan had turned to Elizabeth with a quizzical expression of her own.

Alice continued with, "I have come to believe that a rich, childless widow is, by far, the best circumstance for a young woman."

"Oh, be sensible!" Elizabeth exclaimed, realizing her friend was teasing. Then, in a somber voice, "Pray, how much money does he have?"

"A very respectable two thousand a year," Alice said.

"Oh, I'd be tempted if it were four," Elizabeth said.

"You would not!" Susan said. "What about this Mr. Sinclair? Is your sister still in love with him?"

Elizabeth successfully kept her face serene. The journey in the carriage and the realization of her growing…comfort in the man's presence had shaken her. But she would not let it show. "Yes, and I am sorry for it, as I do not believe he returns the affection."

"Oh, the poor girl," Susan said.

Alice nodded. "Is there anything worse than being in love, and being unseen at the same time?"

"He is very attentive to her, but shows no special treatment," Elizabeth said.

"Does he show attention in any other quarter?" Alice inquired. Innocently. Without design, Elizabeth was certain.

However, Cassie's voice echoed in her mind. *He's often looking in your direction.*

"What was that look?" Alice demanded. "Do not lie to me, Miss Knight, I recognize when a lady is keeping secrets from her friends."

"Oh, I was merely thinking about my poor sister during the journey here. She glumly spoke on the very subject, how his attention never turns to her, no matter how much she wishes it."

Elizabeth found herself lying more and more since the occult came into her life. She had always prided herself on openness, on truthfulness. But the secrets of the heart were supposed to be secret, and she would not expose herself to ridicule, the village old maid flirting with the most sought-after young man in all of England.

Her friends stared, neither believing her words, if their expressions were to be read correctly. But they were still ladies first, and neither pushed a confidence, for one of the most important qualifications for being a true female friend was to know when to push, and when to restrain one's curiosity.

Thankfully, Elizabeth was rescued by a gust of wind. She invited Mrs. Egerton to join them, who immediately appeared in the room wearing an excellent hat, and a rather stiff dress that was, no doubt, fashionable for her time.

"Ladies! Surely there is more to speak of than men, abominable creatures they are."

"Mrs. Egerton! We have been speaking about more than just men," Elizabeth said. "I must defend my friends. And, I must say, not all men are terrible."

Mrs. Egerton made a disapproving sound. "We should call on Miss Gibbs."

Miss Gibbs appeared, and looked about the room with a wide grin. She looked at Alice Thorne's gown and exclaimed, "Yellow!"

A blur of yellow gowns. Sometimes sleeves, sometimes without, until the ghost decided upon a short-sleeved gown with long gloves, yellow silk, with blue embroidery and ribbons. Her bonnet was likewise yellow and blue.

"I do love this naked fashion!" Miss Gibbs said.

"You are very properly dressed, Miss Gibbs," Alice said.

"Not for our time," Mrs. Egerton said. "You would not wear that on your wedding night."

"Not if I had to marry someone like your husband," Miss Gibbs said.

"Matilda!" Mrs. Egerton gasped. "Not in front of the unmarried ladies, if you please."

Miss Gibbs waved a dismissive hand. "They've been to the country."

"Nevertheless, it is undignified to discuss such delicate topics over tea!"

"And, pray, when are young ladies to learn of such delicate topics if not over tea?" Miss Gibbs demanded of her friend.

"They are to learn them on their wedding night from their new husbands," Mrs. Egerton declared.

Miss Gibbs made an undignified sound that elicited chuckles from the assembled ladies. "As I recalled, you learned the details from your sister first."

Mrs. Egerton sighed. "Miss Gibbs, enough. I have yet to properly greet our lady occultists."

"Oh, I have missed you both," Susan declared. "You are most welcome."

"Indeed, it is so unfair that Miss Knight gets you all to herself," Alice said.

"That is unfair! It is not my fault I live in the country," Elizabeth said. "There is nothing stopping either of you from moving to Bryden."

"Except possibly my mother," Alice said.

"Do you have your father's permission then?" Mrs. Egerton said.

"Oh, my father's only hope is for me to be happy in life," Alice said. "He'd probably let me buy an estate, but my mother would never allow me to live alone. Unmarried! Can you imagine the scandal!"

"If I recall, your father was so enraged at Henry for teaching you Latin that he made you go stay with your brother!" Elizabeth said.

Alice laughed. "Cecil and Papa have had a falling out, so I am, once more, the favourite Thorne child."

"What about your mother?" Elizabeth asked, now laughing.

Alice leaned forward. "She and Sophia had a falling out at Christmas. I am free as a bird."

"My dearest Sarah, I have a brilliant notion!" Miss Gibbs burst forth, interrupting Alice.

"Are you considering the Wynn sisters?" Mrs. Egerton asked.

"Indeed!" Miss Gibbs said. "Think of it! Our ladies could write to each other with the speed of conversation."

A dubious expression overcame Mrs. Egerton's face. "Are they ready?"

"You allowed me to come forth into their lives!" Miss Gibbs said with a boisterous laugh. When hushed, reminding her of Aunt Cass' situation, she moderated her tone to a loud whisper. "If they are wise enough to handle my direction, they can handle the moods of two sisters. And I so adore them."

"They did not feel the same way about you," Mrs. Egerton said.

"Oh pish," Miss Gibbs said.

"Who are the Wynn sisters?" Elizabeth asked.

"Evelyn Patience and Violet Prudence Wynn," Mrs. Egerton said. "A fine example of why virtuous names should never be given to anyone."

"Mrs. Egerton!" Susan said with a laugh. "Pray, do not influence our judgment of these ladies before we have even made their acquaintance."

"Did you bring the autograph books?" Alice asked of Elizabeth.

"I brought one with me," Elizabeth said. "We still have not mastered the art of Miss Gibbs' locket enough for my comfort, and

I never travel without their book. The other two are locked away. One at Vane Park, in a steel box, and the other in my closet, also in a small, steel box, hidden away."

"You are willing to keep the books out of sight then?" Alice asked.

Elizabeth sighed. "There was a house fire in Bryden before Christmas. No one was severely injured, thank the Lord, but they lost everything they owned. I have come to fear such an event, and decided to separate the books."

With her father's memory, the fear of burning to death in her bed was real. But she did not share that thought.

She also did not add that she'd placed her rare book in a metal box, and that the box was also place inside another. Nor that she had written several business letters to London, inquiring on the best method to preserve a book in case of fire. They instructed her to wrap the books in the highest quality heavyweight cotton she could find, which would protect from smoke and dampness. And to air out the books every two weeks for at least an hour, and then to change the cloth to a clean, dry one.

"But, pray, how will these sisters assist us?" Elizabeth asked, changing the topic away from her anxieties of fire. "Not that I require all lady occultist ghosts to have a purpose, I assure you!"

"Oh, the sisters love to write letters!" Miss Gibbs said. "One would stay in London, and the other straight to Bryden."

"But that means they would always be apart," Elizabeth said. "That does not seem very kind to them."

"Yes, which will make them significantly more tolerable to be around," Mrs. Egerton said.

"Those two women have never gotten along a day in their lives, I do not care what they say," Miss Gibbs said in a hushed, gossipy tone.

"That is very sad to hear of sisters fighting in such a manner," Susan said. "Will they agree to assist us?"

Mrs. Egerton pondered. "They will complain if forced to be in contact with one another for trivialities, so for non-occult work, I would recommend short notes or letters of emergency."

"I cannot see them objecting to any letters concerning the occult," Miss Gibbs added.

"I agree," said Mrs. Egerton.

"Then let us get started!" Miss Alice declared.

"It is eleven o'clock at night!" Elizabeth said with a laugh.

"And I have had four cups of tea!" Alice said. "I shall not sleep for hours."

Elizabeth sighed and said, "Well, I suppose I should get my autograph book."

Chapter 8

February 14, 1811
Thursday

THE NOISE OF a busy household coming to life stirred Elizabeth from sleep. The ladies had stayed up until the small hours of the night, until finally wine and exhaustion overtook them. Elizabeth was surprised, though, to find the curtains already opened, and morning light pouring into the room. A small fire was crackling, chasing away all traces of dampness. And a basin of water was set out for her, along with a clean chamberpot.

Elizabeth was startled to discover the time was ten in the morning, and she hurried about her morning chores. In her aunt's house, undress was acceptable, so she did not summon a maid to properly lace her stays. She tugged on a heavy gown, one of Augusta's old garments that they'd done alterations on to fit Elizabeth.

She was wrapping a shawl about her shoulders when Sally the maid knocked, entered, curtsied, and said, "My dear Miss Knight! A letter has just arrived. Your sister will be here within the hour."

"Which sister?" Elizabeth asked.

"Mrs. Fitzharding!"

"Oh, good God," Elizabeth muttered.

With Sally's assistance, Elizabeth's stays were properly laced now. One of the maids had already shaken out all of Elizabeth's clothes, so she picked the wrinkle-free simple blue gown. It had a decent neckline, making it appropriate for the breakfast table. Sally offered the shawl, but Elizabeth shook her head. Instead she asked for the gauzy fichu in her luggage, a triangular work of art, delicately embroidered, and wrapped that about her neck. Finally, Sally pinned the ends together with a brooch that had been a gift from Maria Thorne.

Elizabeth was tempted, however fleeting, to request a cap for her head, instead of properly doing her hair. But appearing at the table wearing a white frilly cap would have sent Mary into fits of hysteria, unwed and dressing like a spinster? Goodness. The world was not ready for that. So Sally combed, braided, and pinned Elizabeth's hair up in a simple style that would economize on time, but not bring shame to the household.

Elizabeth made her way downstairs to find she'd been the last to arrive at the breakfast table. She offered apologies for tardiness, and took her seat at the table. One of the footmen offered hot chocolate, and she happily accepted.

"I would have allowed you to sleep as long as you wished, but with Mary visiting," Aunt Cass said. She waved a disapproving knife before plunging it into rather soft butter. "I do not approve of visitors before one in the afternoon, I have said this time and time again, but there is no telling that girl anything. How did you sleep my dear?"

"Like the dead apparently!" Elizabeth said with a laugh. "I did not even stir when my fire was lit, nor when my curtains were opened. I'm quite ashamed of my tardiness this morning."

"Nonsense!" Miss Thorne said. "One of the maids had to wake me."

"And me!" Miss Susan said.

"And me!" Aunt Cass said.

"I do say, Aunt, you look quite cheerful this morning," Elizabeth said. "Quite an increase in colour in the cheeks, I would wager."

"I find myself much improved." Then, Aunt Cass leaned forward to loud whisper, "Though, I suffer from a terrible head from all of that brandy." She laughed and said, "I suppose we should invite David and his lady to dine sometime next week. And a good dinner, too, not a simple family meal. Perhaps we can entice Mary to join us, and possibly Sir William as well, provided he ceases being a bore."

"Are you and Sir William not getting along, aunt?" Elizabeth asked.

"We have been neighbours for so long that I fear we occasionally forget we are not, in fact, married to one another." That made Aunt Cass laugh. "I think old age is finally catching up to us!"

"You are barely forty!" Elizabeth said. "And Sir William cannot be that much older."

"He turns fifty next month and acts like he is the king of all he sees," Aunt Cass said.

From there, the conversation at the table settled into the usual gossip. They did not discuss the occult, beyond the basics, as the footmen were in and out, along with the various deliveries and young boys that came with crates and boxes and letters. They discussed Miss Thorne's family—a large family with plenty of news to fill an entire day—and how she was to return to them that afternoon.

"I am to return to my parents' roof for a few days," she said. "But I shall not be a stranger. Oh, and we did not tell you! Miss Keats is still in town, so we must formally introduce the two of you."

"Oh, how exciting! I long to meet her," Elizabeth said.

Miss Keats had been a distant member of the Ladies Occult Society, the little name they gave their informal studies. Elizabeth had written to her at one point, but poor Miss Keats laboured under a sister-in-law who would not allow any discussion of the occult in her home. However, with the departure of that wife and her brother's discovering of another who did not care two pennies what Miss Keats did in her private time, the young lady reached out to Elizabeth, begging forgiveness and asking to participate in occult studies.

She'd been in town twice since the summer, and Elizabeth had been unable to visit both times. She was determined to meet Miss

Keats in the flesh on this visit. But first, she had to eat breakfast for Mary's imminent arrival would be upon them.

Cassie and Thea made their way downstairs as Elizabeth began filling her plate. Mrs. Cook had no notion of Thea's arrival, so came out to apologize for not having a table appropriate to her unique needs. However, Thea smiled and said she was very happy with the buns, as well as the eggs, and dried fruit.

"I eat very little," Thea said.

Mrs. Cook frowned down at the young Knight girl, no doubt asking herself if Thea's cheeks were more hollow than last summer. Elizabeth thought they were, but said nothing beyond encouraging the consumption of more bread and butter. "Well, we shall attempt to tempt you whenever you are here to dine."

"Please do not trouble yourself, though!" Thea said, remembering her manners. "For, I might have an invitation to stay with the Baldwins, and if I do not, I shall have to return home on Sunday."

Aunt Cass looked up from her own plate. "Travel on a Sunday? I always thought your father disapproved."

"Mr. Parsons is needed in Bryden on Monday," Elizabeth said.

Mrs. Cook assured Thea that, as long as she was in the house, she would have an excellent dinner and one well beyond cake and bread. "Now, I will just point out to you that the eggs in the white sauce are very wholesome and to your needs. I only used butter, I assure you! No lard or bacon. I will not stand for trickery!"

"I have complete trust in you," Thea said very properly. "And I remember how excellent the stewed eggs were on my last visit."

Elizabeth saw Thea's face fall and she inquired into the reason.

"If I go to Miss Baldwin's house, her cook will not know and I will not be able to trust anything but the bread and jam."

"If you are invited, I will send a note to their cook, with some of your favourites and how to make simple adjustments that will not offend anyone's senses," Mrs. Cook said. "If you wish, miss."

"Oh, please Mrs. Cook!" Thea said, her face brightening.

Elizabeth mouthed a thank you to Mrs. Cook, who gave her a little inclination of the head. Thea did not notice, for she was loading up her plate with the hardboiled eggs that were covered in a thick white sauce with specks of parsley. Thea added four rolls to her plate as well.

The others knew not to draw attention, for Miss Thea did not regularly eat heartily and Elizabeth's letters frequently contained her worries for her sister.

With Mrs. Cook's departure back to her domain, Elizabeth found she had a hearty appetite herself, and took the cold ham, hot buns, and the freshly baked bread. She also added a couple of Thea's eggs at her urging, and helped herself to some of the stewed dried fruit, which she dipped her bread into until a spoon was required. She found she also had room for smoked kippers and a third bun with jam.

They were still lingering over their teacups when Mary arrived. She was invited in to join them, intermixed with Thea and Cassie leaving the table to hug and gleefully greet their sister. Mary attempted to shoo them away, but was worn down. The three embraced and Elizabeth sipped at her tea from her seat at the table. Mary met her eye in the midst of the cheerful embracing, and gave an exasperated sigh.

Taking it as a hint to intervene, Elizabeth said, "Girls, allow Mary to retain some of her dignity. Mary, come join us. The chocolate will not be wise, I fear, but I believe the buns will not disagree with you."

"Is Mrs. Fitzharding not allowed chocolate?" Alice asked.

"Alas, it brings on the most terrible head pains," Mary said. The footman pulled out an empty chair for Mary, who sat. She reached to accept a bun, and accepted the butter from Aunt Cass. "I do not believe it is the milk, nor am I convinced it is the sugar. I fear it may, in fact, be the cocoa itself."

"Oh, that is dreadful!" Alice said. "How did you discover it was the chocolate?"

"Mr. Sinclair, our father's curate? You must know of him." When the others nodded, she continued, "Well, his sister has the same affliction as I do, and we have been corresponding for months now, as we attempt to find the source. We have both sadly concluded certain foods cause it. Now, there are some discrepancies, but there are foods that bring on the pain for both of us. And, sadly, chocolate is one of them."

The conversation turned to the frustrations of medicine, and how comforting it must be to Mary to have another who intimately understood her malady.

"Speaking of health," Mary said, and Elizabeth could see Aunt Cass brace, "I have heard from our cousin David how they attempted to browbeat you into leaving London. Is this true?"

"For a city of a million souls, news travels rather fast," Aunt Cass said. "Is nothing secret?"

"Not for long, Aunt," Mary said. "I came to visit my sisters, of course, but also to offer up my estate, for your comfort, at any time. My husband and I have discussed it, and we do not approve of these men attempting to shove you off to Cornwall. Goodness. And think of the current tenants! They have a lease! Indeed, it would be in very bad manners to ask them to move lodgings solely because you have a cough."

Elizabeth held her cup to her face in a veiled attempt to hide her laughter.

"Oh, Eliza, for the love of God, stop that cup trick. You are terrible at it," Mary said.

That sent the table into giggles.

"I am quite serious in my offer, Aunt."

"Oh Mary," Aunt Cass said with all warmness. "You are so kind. I could never accept an offer to invade your home, but I appreciate that you offer to rescue me all of the same."

"It would not be an invasion!" Mary protested. "Your servants could come with, or stay here! Whichever you preferred. We plan to be in London for at least a month. And country air is so much better than town."

Aunt Cass smiled. "I confess my health is improved greatly with the addition of you to my table, and I promise that, if my cough does not improve, I shall consider the offer. But, I should warn you, Mr. Grant has been dispatched to the countryside today to find me a house to rent."

Mary did not hide her surprise. "Will you quit London all together then?"

"It mostly depends if he can find a house that meets my standards. Despite me being an easy mistress, I am a stickler for my comforts, Mary, I assure you I am. And I will not quit this house until I find the exact same one. I might even end up purchasing another house, just so that I can knock down the walls and rebuild it in this style."

That seemed to mollify Mary, and conversation turned back to gossip and news when a letter arrived for Cassie. She announced it was from Miss Phoebe Baldwin, who invited Cassie to stay with her for a month. "Oh, and she extends the invitation to Thea! Mrs. Baldwin says, 'the more Knight girls, the merrier my house will be.' Those are Phoebe's exact words! Aunt Cass? Elizabeth? Do you mind?"

"Take your bags now and leave us, if you must!" Aunt Cass said, but she was laughing. "I would never stand in the way of young ladies in search of society."

Excitement overtook the dining room, which could not be contained. Thea and Cassie rushed upstairs to repack all of their trunks, and Mary announced she'd brought her carriage, as she had a number of errands to accomplish and inquired if Aunt Cass needed anything at the shops. Inquiries to the servants were made, and it happened there were several tasks—thread, a new package of metal needles and dress pins, several new boot laces, and picking up a repaired brooch—and Mary said she had a similar list for herself.

Sally oversaw the household coin purse since Aunt Cass' housekeeper had formally left, and she passed Elizabeth a collection of coins. Then, made a little joke that she would take exact accounting.

Elizabeth laughed and said, "My dear Sally! Do you think I would steal from you?"

Sally turned a bright red and curtsied low. "Forgive my forwardness, Miss Knight! I was only teasing, the way I do all of the young maids when they ask for coin. Please forgive me for being pert."

"I thought it was quite humorous," Elizabeth assured her, realizing the poor maid was genuinely distressed by such familiarity. "I shall bring back a thorough accounting of every farthing, I assure you, Miss Sally!"

"Elizabeth, for the love of God, stop teasing the servants!" Mary called out as she put on her bonnet. "Cannot you see you have frightened the girl senseless!"

"Then I apologize to you, Sally, and to you Aunt Cass for frightening the servants so," Elizabeth said.

Aunt Cass waved her hand. "Go away with you. I shall go take a rest for a few hours, as I feel the pressure in my lungs once more. Alice? Susan? What plans do you have today?"

Alice was to return to her parents, and planned to bring Susan with her, and they promised to seek out Miss Keats to determine when she was free for a visit. That made both Aunt Cass and Elizabeth very happy.

"Should we have offered the girls the carriage?" Mary asked when they were outside.

"Mr. Baldwin no doubt plans to bring his carriage around for them," Elizabeth said.

"Ah," was all Mary said.

They got into the carriage together, silent awkwardness lingering. Elizabeth's heart ached with the distance of the gulf between them. However, she found herself happily agreeing to come with Mary on this trip, and Mary seemed to have offered the invitation with genuine affection. Each attempt to shrink the distance would be hard work, on both sides, but Elizabeth hoped each effort would improve their sisterly relationship.

Unable to take the silence any longer, Elizabeth said, "I did not know you planned to stay in London so long. I had thought you wanted to oversee the improvements to the curate's house for Charles."

Mary drew in a deep breath. "I confess I found myself in need of some distance from my family."

Elizabeth was unsure of what Mary had meant at first, and asked, "Is it Charles?"

Mary waved a hand. "Oh, on the contrary. He improves daily, and I do not only mean as a return of previous spirits. He is turning into a proper gentleman."

Elizabeth did not offer a reply to that, but she hoped it was true. She had also noticed a change in him, and hoped it was permanent. "Oh. Papa?"

She nodded. "Did you know he rides out to visit us still?"

Elizabeth was surprised. "No, indeed I did not. Surely not lately? It's been raining."

Concern spread across Mary's face. "I did not wish to write, to inform you, for I feared the girls or Isabella would see, and cause worry. But, yes, even in the rain."

"He was gone all day about a fortnight ago. Was he with you?"

"For part of it, but his disposition became…" Mary struggled to find words. "I asked my husband for assistance managing his temper. It feels as though each time I see him, he has worsened."

"If it had not been for Mr. Thorne and Mr. Sinclair, I fear he might have locked me in the attic to prevent me from coming to London."

"Is that an exaggeration?" Mary demanded.

Elizabeth gave a small shake of her head. "We have all become fearful of his outbursts."

"Can anything be done to help him?"

"He will not let them. He insists there is nothing the matter. But he cannot even put his boots on some days, his feet are so swollen! Surely you have noticed."

Mary nodded. "At first, I thought it was riding in the rain that had made his fingers swell, but no. James says he has seen it before, and believes it is my father's heart."

James Fitzharding, Mary's husband, was about the same age as their father. A good man, a *rich* man, and in whom Elizabeth trusted unreservedly. She nodded and said, "Mr. Collins and Mrs. Green both agree, but what is to be done?"

"How is Isabella? The truth, if you please."

"Does she not write?"

Mary rolled her eyes. "She writes to me of the weather, the state of the roads, and what new sewing project she has taken up. Nothing of substance."

"Well, she is with child again, and with such a husband. How do you think she fares?"

"Elizabeth..."

"But it is true! They have always been a terrible match, I make no apologies for saying what is upon everyone's mind, but now?

In her situation, with this? I would not be surprised if she loses this one, as well."

"She married our father to be safe," Mary said, a hint of the old accusations in her voice. "She has very little money, and becoming the wife of a rector was a good, safe marriage for her."

"As James was for you." Elizabeth immediately regretted her words and said so. "That was not my place to say."

Mary pondered for a moment before asking, "Do you imagine that I despise my husband?"

"He is a very good man in company," Elizabeth said.

An impish smile formed on Mary's mouth. "He is very good company in private, as well."

"I shall take your word for it, since I have no knowledge of what he is like when company is not underfoot," Elizabeth said. To mend the fence, though, she said, "But I am very pleased to hear he is not putting on airs for me, being one man in public and another in private. I could not abide that in marriage."

Mary waved politely at someone on the street. "Like any man would satisfy you."

Since Mary was turned away, now eyeing the stores and people, Elizabeth had the time to compose a serene face. When Mary turned to look at her, to see if she had anything to say for herself, Elizabeth smiled. "I am certain there is a man or maybe even two, who would convince me to settle down."

"Well, he does not live in England," Mary said sourly. "Oh, there's our first shop ahead."

"Mary, must we quarrel?"

"We are not quarreling!"

She and Elizabeth laughed at the small family joke of squabbling over squabbling. The carriage came to a halt, having found a convenient location. And so, for two hours, the sisters gossiped and shopped like there were no barriers between them, no history, no hurts. Just the quiet comfort of the shorthand that comes with being family.

Chapter 9

ELIZABETH RETURNED TO an empty house. Miss Alice Thorne left a note stating she'd stolen Miss Susan for company to survive a "dull" afternoon of visiting relations at her parents' home. Aunt Cass had decided to visit Sir William next door to test her health. Elizabeth took it as a good sign that she was well enough to even think of such a scheme, and that Sir William would tolerate her back in his house, for all of the shouting between the two of them.

As well, four letters had arrived by express for Elizabeth while she'd been shopping, and were offered to her on a platter. One from G, one from Isabella, and two from her father. She decided to read Isabella's first, for that would have the most important news.

My dear Elizabeth,

Your father and sister have mentioned to me that they were writing you letters, so I am taking up my pen to provide as unbiased of a summary of events as possible, to help guide your own replies. I am sending mine by express, in hopes that it arrives before theirs and you are prepared.

Elizabeth's nerve gripped at that line, for it was too often the harbinger of worries.

> *Your father's moods have been greatly improved since you have all removed from the house. Please do not let this pain you, for he has quite forgotten the scene surrounding your departure. He is convinced the removal of the three of you to London was his own scheme, and has been feeling very pleased with himself. I have discussed this with Georgiana, and we have concluded it is best not to remind him of unhappy events.*

Elizabeth attempted to draw some comfort in this. Her father's behaviour was terrifying, and this was just another reminder that it was not him. This was whatever the illness had done to him. She must remind herself of that, while protecting her family at the same time.

> *G relocated to Mrs. Thorne's house about an hour after you left yesterday, which has the poor girl rushing back and forth between there and here, to get my frequent opinion on matters. I have told her she does not need my permission for every decision, but I fear she struggles with her new independence.*
>
> *Which says to me that she needs more of it.*
>
> *However, I wish to bring up a subject that is perhaps a little delicate for a letter, but I wished you to be prepared. Mrs. Thorne purchased far too much of a fine white net, and wishes to have a gown made up for G in it. However, G wishes the petticoat to also be in white, and we all fear G standing in front of a candle at a ball.*
>
> *I have given my permission for her to have pantaloons made up. Now, I know your objection to them, and indeed we will ensure they are the most proper things ever. Just the simple style, two separate leg coverings, and a white ribbon to tie both at the waist. We will also not tell your father.*

And, indeed, you know that I have worn them! They stop the chafing upon my legs, and you know that has been a great comfort. They will not turn G into a wanton lady, I assure you. I know you, Elizabeth, I know your objections! But Mrs. Sims says the netting is so thin that she cannot see another path forward for G's dignity. And, as I understand it, it will also help the gown fall properly.

So I beg you to support me in this. I prefer not to take my stepmother privilege over you, but G so rarely asks anything of me of this nature. Pray, do not be angry with me.

Elizabeth barked out a laugh. All of this anticipation and fluttering of nerves and the expense of express post…over pantaloons! She chuckled at herself, grateful to have privacy for she was embarrassed enough without company to witness her foolishness. No, a pair of pantaloons would not lead Georgiana down the wayward path, to a life of debauchery before falling prey to a London bawd.

Oh, perhaps Elizabeth was just a little more old-fashioned than she would like to admit, enjoying her long sleeves and covered neck. She loved warmth, and more so with every passing year. Fashion was fleeting; warmth never went out of style. But she was not Miss Georgiana Knight, the youngest of a large brood desperately yearning for a little independence.

She skimmed Isabella's letter, to ensure there was nothing more of note; there was not. She opened G's next, to glean if there were other lurking shadows awaiting an elder sister's careful attention. G's enthusiasm of being at Vane Park, without any sister present to check her, with Mr. Henry Thorne's ready coin and Maria's open accounts at the shops…well, a youngest sister could not be more content.

G said Mr. Thorne insisted her letters be sent express, so not to be alarmed. G breezed past the issue of the pantaloons with the skill of an ambassador at court. Elizabeth could not help but chuckle. There was a small concern about matching jewelry, so Elizabeth began a letter to Isabella with the usual pleasantries, and then to address the pearl cross pendant first. They had still not dispensed all of Augusta's jewelry, so she would take it upon herself to ask her sisters if they would consent to it being given to G.

Elizabeth smiled at the maid who brought her tea and a plate of food for her to pick at—cold ham, pickles, jam, and rolls—and then began carefully crafting a letter to give her support of the pantaloons. She considered for some time, until finally deciding that she would confess a secret of G's own mother: that, after successive children and the physical changes that brought, Augusta Knight took to wearing them herself. After all, there was no great impropriety, especially as they would not be joined in the manner of men's attire.

Her hesitation was due to how it had been Elizabeth and Augusta's secret, that how mortified she would have been to discover Elizabeth had shared the intimate detail, and in a letter, no less. Sadly, Augusta Knight was no longer in the world to speak to her own daughter on the matter, so it fell to a stepmother and an elder sister in unity of purpose: dressing G in such a manner that did not expose her to the world whenever in front of a candle.

Once done that delicate writing, Elizabeth left the letter unfinished to read the two letters from her father. This first one was dated before she'd left Bryden, and did not appear to have been sent express. It surprised her to discover he'd written to her in London before she'd even left!

It was soon evident he'd written that letter when she'd left for Mr. Sinclair's. It most likely went with all of the morning post the next day, and he'd forgotten about it. A letter full of violent protestations about hangings of disobedient daughters who will burn in the depths of hell with Satan where they belonged. Her father had never been the type to dwell on such things, having been the type of rector to focus on guilt and the disappointment of God, parents, and society.

Despite the harshness, the cutting remarks, and the sadness of it all, it did not touch Elizabeth's heart except for the simple sad strangeness of it all. He did not even have the same penmanship, just sprawling, angry, jagged words that were often difficult to read through the ink blots.

She opened the next, preparing for more of the same.

My dearest daughter,

I heard from Mary this morning, who says London's roads continue to be intolerable. How fares your aunt? If I understand correctly, Mary planned a visit upon your arrival, so perhaps this might appear on a silver platter during that meeting. If so, pray give your sister my regards. And tell Mrs. Spencer I pray for her speedy recovery. No one wishes to be sick, but a cough is the worst affliction for you cannot do the simplest of tasks! It takes your breath away at the smallest activity.

We are all suffering here from various maladies, and the absence of our G has both been useful for us—for we can suffer in silence—but I confess I said to my dear Isabella just this morning as I took my tea that I find myself missing the bustle of so many ladies in the house. A man grows used to feminine company, I have found, and the absence of it is more keenly felt.

That hit Elizabeth harder than anything else. Not the fire, not the brimstone, not the tales of the hanging of poor, unfortunate women who stole their bread to survive. No, this shook her to her very soul. The changeable nature, that from one letter to the next, he was a completely different man.

Her father was always a complicated man, who did not easily show his feelings of delight or affection, not even with those closest to him. He'd had an old-fashioned way of thinking, that silence in a lady was a virtue. Mrs. Egerton, at times, had the same notions, which always amused Elizabeth greatly as the ghost particularly was not the type to exercise silence.

A sudden appearance of memory, of when Cassie first came out. Her father complained women's clothing should not be so close to nudity, and how odd he found the entire concept of fashion. They all teased him, until he finally declared, with a big laugh, that he was raised to believe women should be fully clothed and silent at all times. That brought on further abuse from the gathered girls who…

Elizabeth inhaled deeply, pushing away the tears that wished to form. She would not reduce herself to sobbing in the drawing room for all of the servants to behold. It would disrupt their day, their work, and their duties, for they would feel obligated to care for her. No, she would hold herself together with dignity. She would not grieve the rapid loss of her father's mind, not for the world to witness. She would be as a lady should be.

Her hands betrayed her, though, and she put down the letters. To sit serenely. To breathe. In. Out. *Calm*, she told herself. *Calm.*

When the inevitable moment came, she would write to Mr. Grant, requesting he arrange the public auction of her book. She would not ask Charles. Nor James Fitzharding, despite him being her brother-in-law and a good man. She would not ask Henry Thorne, or Sidney Sinclair, or Alice Thorne, or Cousin David. No. She would be independent. She would do business, as if she were a man. Within the confines of dignity at all times, of course, but a lady could do business through the assistance of a man, and she could hire Mr. Grant.

She hardened herself more. She would pay Mr. Grant to assist with any of the legal matters, as well as the banking and investments. She would use her current inheritance from Uncle Edward, plus her savings, to support her sisters. With the sale of the book invested, that should net her close to one hundred fifty per annum. Her sisters had little money; that was all tied up in Charles' future to protect them. Isabella would receive some money from her marriage articles.

They would struggle, but they would not starve. They would be the pity of their neighbours, and Aunt Cass would no doubt double her already generous gifts. She could best help by taking in a sister or two, to lessen the food costs at home, and to expose her younger sisters to society as much as possible, to find them husbands to protect them.

With Isabella a widow—no matter her youth—she could lead their household of ladies without needing Charles' presence to preserve their reputations. They could afford to keep Julia, and perhaps take in one of the village girls to live with them as a maid-of-all-work. Well compensated with good hours, though. Elizabeth would insist.

In theory, Elizabeth could earn a decent living as a governess or a Sunday School teacher, but alas, Mary would never allow that. It would shame the family too much to have her turn to earning her bread in such a manner. Of course, her working as an unpaid governess for Mary would be very different, but she would do whatever was necessary to …

"Elizabeth?"

Elizabeth was shaken from her thoughts by the concerned faces of Miss Alice Thorne and Miss Susan. "Oh! I did not hear the door. I thought you were to stay with Mrs. Thorne."

"I forgot something so we decided to walk back, but never mind that!" Alice grabbed her hands. "My dear, you are shaking like a leaf. What is in those letters?"

Elizabeth sucked in a sob, and gripped Alice's hand tightly.

"I shall have the footman fetch you a glass a wine," Alice said.

Susan had already escaped the room to issue the order. She returned only a moment later to hand the goblet to Elizabeth. "Please, tell us whatever is the matter. Is there distressing news?"

Elizabeth held the glass in her hands and whispered, through a cracking voice, "Will you promise, when the time comes…and I am poor…that you will not abandon me."

The reality of the words broke Elizabeth's resolve. She buckled over sobbing, knowing her life would soon never be the same. They would lose their father's income. They would have to leave the rectory, the place she had lived for all of her life. They would have to find accommodations, and rather quickly, and there was almost nowhere within their income. They would most likely be split for months, while they attempted cheap lodgings.

"When we are living above the butchers because we cannot afford any other place," Elizabeth said as she tried to gain control.

Two sets of arms wrapped about her. Not asking. Not pushing. Just offering the comfort and society of two women who would not ridicule her for a lapse in propriety.

Within moments, she collected herself, sucking in breaths to bring stability to her turmoil. "I apologize."

"Nonsense," Alice said. "Besides, your aunt would never allow you to starve in the hedgerows. And if she did? Well. I would simply insist on my father finding me some frail old man to marry so that I could be a widow within a year, and then I could safely establish myself as a haven for your family."

"That is not what she needs," Susan said with gentle rebuke. "My dear friend, I understand poverty all too well. We will do all that we can to protect you and yours. Besides, you will have Mrs. Knight, so we will not need to marry off poor Alice to be made into a respectable widow for your household of ladies.

"All the better then for I detest the idea of being shackled to a man," Alice said. "I shall only sing the songs of Aphrodite and Sappho."

"There are no songs of Sappho," Susan said, though she was smiling. "And surely you would not say such things if I were to become shackled to a man, to use your words against you."

"Oh, you know that is not the same!" Alice cried out. "Be reasonable! You know the reasons for my disposition. I simply prefer the society of women, you know that. And, indeed, so do all of you or else you would not be here!"

Elizabeth found herself laughing, even as she wiped away her tears.

"Regardless of your disposition, I just want Elizabeth to know I understand her worries. Indeed, I would take a position immediately if Mrs. Spencer would allow it, but alas she has threatened to make me her lady's companion every time I bring up the subject."

"What need of you for money?" Alice declared.

"A great many things, I assure you."

Elizabeth laughed, as she wiped at her tears. "The two of you are impossible!"

"Ah, but you are smiling now," Susan said.

"Indeed, I believe we should take this skill of ours across England. We shall cure all of the young ladies of the country out of their melancholies and tears," Alice said with a laugh.

There was the rustling at the door, and then Aunt Cass' voice. "Please, do not distress my aunt. Pray, if pressed, I choked on my tea."

So when Aunt Cass walked into the room, Elizabeth was pretending she'd been coughing, which had caused her eyes to water, and the two friends were teasing her excessively. Aunt Cass seemingly did not notice the deception, or perhaps chose not to. "Goodness! You have been in town but a day. What warrants so many letters?"

Elizabeth took the opportunity to tell of the news about the pantaloons, which brought shock to Aunt Cass, and laughter from the other two. "I will not understand this current fashion of being barely dressed!" Aunt Cass declared. "Look at the three of you! Bosoms everywhere! If fashion continues, you shall be nothing more than bonnets and a bit of netting!"

"Oh, be reasonable, Aunt!" Elizabeth said. "I am certain we would also wear a shawl in winter."

That brought on laughter, until finally Aunt Cass was distracted into telling of her visit to Sir William's.

"I would never let the man know, for he would get the wrong idea, but if I were to marry again—which I absolutely will not, allow me to be clear on that, for no man would agree to the marriage contract Mr. Grant would bring forth on my behalf—but if I were to become feeble of mind enough to consider another husband, Sir William would not be the worst choice."

"Praise indeed," Elizabeth muttered.

Aunt Cass made a dismissive gesture before accepting her own letters on a platter. She flipped through them until she said, "Oh, this appears to be Miss Keats' handwriting. Perhaps her family has finally done with her company and now we can see her? Surely I can use the excuse that I am not well enough to visit as a means to skip some of the proprieties. What do you think?"

"Oh surely Miss Keats would understand, and being invited to this address would not offend any of her family, I assure you," Alice said. "Even my own parents are rather proud of my frequent visitations here."

"Visitations!" Aunt Cass cried. "You have your own room!"

That sent them all laughing once more, and Aunt Cass penned a quick letter, with tidbits from all of them, inviting Miss Keats the following day to engage in a day of occult studies (and tea, of course) and would love her assistance for the entirety of the afternoon and for her to stay for dinner and supper, if her family could be persuaded to spare her.

The letter was dispatched with one of the maids, who was to head to market to find "anything fit to eat," in the words of Mrs. Cook. They chatted about what they should study when Miss Keats visited, and how Elizabeth had been very tardy with her letterwriting. She apologized profusely, stating that she was very busy at the rectory, especially now with three younger sisters all out in society. She did not speak of her father; Aunt Cass knew very little, and she preferred to keep that knowledge to herself as much as possible.

Aunt Cass did hint, however, that Mr. Knight had been suffering a grievous illness throughout the winter, and thus they must be kind to her. The ladies apologized, stating they had not meant any offence, and would never force letterwriting upon a fellow friend.

Soon, Aunt Cass found herself weary from visitation and declared she would take to her bed to be well-rested for dinner. Susan and Alice said they would leave soon, as they would need to get ready for dinner eventually.

"Ah, there is time yet. We are on London time," Aunt Cass said. "None of your country dinner hours here!"

That made Elizabeth laugh, who said her poor stomach was sick of cake and sweet things, and needed a heavy meal before five in the afternoon, which brought declarations about the backwardness of the countryside. Elizabeth took it in good humor, however, and settled to finish writing her letters. Likewise, Alice decided they "needed" occult materials for Miss Keats' visit, and that they could make a stop at a certain shop before walking to her parents.

"But we do not even know if Miss Keats will be here tomorrow!" Susan protested. "Not to mention, we do not even know what we need until we need it!"

"Susan, if you do not wish to see a certain bookseller, perhaps you must inform your friend," Elizabeth said. "Otherwise, we shall all find your words very peculiar."

"I do not wish to bother the man," Susan said.

"How would visiting his shop be a bother?" Alice asked. "If what Elizabeth says is true, and you do not wish to see him…"

Susan sighed. "I shall fetch my good hat then."

Alice winked at Elizabeth as poor Susan was manipulated out of the door and toward the man of her heart, no matter how stoic she pretended to be. Elizabeth declined, however, stating she truly did have a great number of letters to write, and that she had no immediate need for anything at the shops, having done her errands with Mary already.

Alice and Susan promised they would return the following afternoon to dedicate at least three hours to their occult studies before closing the door behind them, off in search of single men.

With that, Elizabeth turned back to her own family obligations, and the issue of the pantaloons. She re-read Isabella's letter, confirming she did not miss any hints or warnings. Her father's angry letter must have been accidentally tangled with the rest of the post, and he had forgotten of its existence in the morning. She would not alarm Isabella with it. She would simply destroy the letter.

Pen in hand, she began writing to Isabella. However, she'd only gotten half of a letter written when she was interrupted by a knock, and a very familiar gentleman's voice. Polite. Confident. Elizabeth was smiling when she stood.

"Charles!" She declared. "I had not expected you!"

He stood at the drawing room door and bowed. "I only just arrived, and stopped at Mary's first—only because she was along the way here. I did not play favourites with my sisters, I promise."

In the shock of not expecting him, she blurted without formality or good grace, "You look so much improved! Even from Christmas!"

She had not meant to sound so forceful or surprised, and Charles' cheeks blushed. "Yes, I've put on more weight. You do not need to make a fuss about it."

Except, she did wish to make a fuss, and the kind that only a sister could make. Charles had been ill, and perhaps enough time had passed to stop worrying, but worry they had. And afterward, his bad behaviour had intensified, and the harsh words and judgment did not help. With the reflection of time and space,

Elizabeth found herself wondering if it had been the illness still gripping him. Was it overgenerous? Perhaps. But illness currently gripped her father's mind. Why could it not do the same to her brother?

And, between herself and God, this is what she needed to tell herself so that she could continue to love her own brother.

So, with a kind and quiet voice, she said, "Oh, it was not a criticism. It looks good on you. You look nearly back to your old self."

"I can fit my old clothes properly again," he said, and had a diffident tone.

"Come, sit," she said, motioning toward some of the empty chairs. She called for a footman, and requested fresh tea, and an assortment of nibbles.

"Oh, thank you," Charles said, picking up one of the stale slices of cake. He took a bite and declared, "I'm starving. I'd not eaten all day, with the travel. I didn't want to risk it, and…well…if I'd said anything to Mary, I'd have never been set free until I was sick from food."

Elizabeth laughed, and said she understood. And she did understand; Charles lived off boiled potatoes and carrots mashed together for most of his illness, and she knew he would always be careful now. The fear of food. Well, if she could accommodate Thea's notions on what was and was not food, she could do the same for her brother. Elizabeth kept reminding herself of that, over and over, to make the resentment and anger subside. And it was working, for she found herself happy to see her brother.

"I came to tell you that I have been accepted for a second curacy position in Post Hills. They are very aware that my first duty is to Ashbrook parish, but as they are such a small village, they would be very happy if I could run a service after any duties at Ashbrook on Sundays, and to visit the poor two days per week. I have agreed, and they have offered twenty-five pounds per annum, which is a fair sum given I would not be available in the village all of the time."

"Two curacies! How wonderful for you," Elizabeth said. "It will not be too taxing on you, I hope?"

"I had hoped to take the curacy in Bryden, but Sinclair is still there," Charles said. Then, he added quickly, "Do not think I am criticizing the man. The opposite, in fact. My father's letters…well, it does seem like he respects him, at least, and listens to him more often than not."

He waved off her concerns as they thanked the footman for bringing in a pot of tea. A fresh platter of food arrived as the tea was poured. This new platter contained substantial food, including cheese, slices of bread, pickles, warmed butter, and smoked kippers. A second tray arrived, though, and that one contained a delightful assortment of the tiniest sweets imaginable.

"Yes, our father does listen to Mr. Sinclair."

A third tray arrived. This one with French rolls, caraway buns, the tiniest bowls of various fruit preserves, dried fruit, roasted nuts, and a bowl of cut up cold potatoes and carrots in the centre.

"I am constantly amazed that Mrs. Cook can produce three trays of food within five minutes." Charles looked at the tray closest to him. "I will be offered potatoes and carrots for the rest of my life, won't I?"

"Yes," Elizabeth said. "And, as your eldest sister, I advise that you eat them, sir, lest we worry."

Charles chuckled. Then he grew somber. "Elizabeth…"

"Oh, Charles, must we?"

"Elizabeth…"

"How were the roads?"

"I do not wish to speak of the roads," Charles said with irritation now. He cleared his throat and stood. "I wish to speak of what is between us."

She set her cup down. "My dear brother, it is impossible to move past something if someone continuously brings it up in conversation."

"I believe silence is how resentment festers," Charles said.

"I believe the refusal to bury something in one's mind is the root of festering evil," Elizabeth said. But she sighed and said, "Very well. Say your piece."

"I did not come here to fight," Charles said.

"We are not fighting!" Elizabeth said. Then, with a smile, she asked, "Do you need my forgiveness?"

"No," Charles said. "For I shall never earn that."

"Charles…"

"Good God, Elizabeth! Allow me to be the villain I know I am!"

There were times in Elizabeth's life that she needed to be the eldest sister. To set aside her own hurts and pains, and to support her family. "What I see is not so much a villain, but a young man who became lost. And in those woods, he found trouble, but did not know how to extract himself. Who regrets a great many things. Who is now finding his footing once more. That is what I see."

Charles looked away from her. When he managed to speak, his voice cracked. "I will never forgive myself."

"What is her name?"

He looked up sharply from his tea. "Who?"

"The young lady who has brought on this self reflection?"

Shock. That was the only word to describe Charles' expression. "Who told you about Miss Talbot?"

Elizabeth put a hand over her mouth, but could not hold back her laughter. "Who is Miss Talbot?"

"No one!"

"That does not seem truthful, Charles," Elizabeth said.

"You tricked me! You are impossible!" Charles said. "I came here to apologize to you, to open my brotherly heart and…and…"

"Is Miss Talbot in town?"

"I am not answering that question."

"Ah, she is. Pray, who is her family?"

"I do not have to answer these questions!"

"You might as well to me, because once Mary finds out…"

"You will not tell Mary!"

Elizabeth called out, "Sally?"

"Yes, Miss Knight?"

"Pray, have you heard of a Miss Talbot?"

"A few actually." Sally hesitated until she glanced at the blushing, flustered Charles, and then a candle flickered to light. "Ah! I suspect you are speaking of Miss Talbot of Wellesley Buildings. I have not met her, but I have heard of her. Excellent reputation amongst the servant class, I assure you. I believe she has recently lost her father, a clergyman."

"Ah, thank you Sally," Elizabeth said. She smiled at her brother and asked, very casually, "Is this the same Miss Talbot?"

"I regret this visit," Charles said by way of reply.

"Oh Charles," Elizabeth said, and for the first time in a very long time, she felt like she finally had a brother. "I insist upon meeting her."

Chapter 10

February 15, 1811
Friday

CHARLES DID AN admirable job hiding the identity and whereabouts of his Miss Talbot, but Elizabeth was an elder sister; she knew her brother, and knew how to burrow until she found his secrets. And, like the younger brother he was, he relented, and the information spilled forth: Miss Talbot needed to pick up a repaired watch Friday morning, and he had planned to meet her.

So Elizabeth insisted her brother also take her shopping, which only made him scowl and sigh, but he relented as he eventually accepted there would be no peace until he did. He would not allow her to take his arm, however, which amused Elizabeth greatly, and he used the excuse, of course, that his arm greatly ached from the carriage ride the day before and he did not wish to aggravate it further.

Elizabeth knew that it was because Charles did not wish to be seen linked with another woman, until his Miss Talbot was assured this was a sister and not a rival. But, she said nothing, for she was a strong walker and did not require a man to slow his pace for her benefit. Of course, they arrived on Bond Street with Elizabeth a touch out of breath, given that they had made excellent time on foot in the pursuit of the infamous Miss Talbot.

"I do not see her," Charles announced, gawking about the street as if he were a common costermonger looking for the next customer.

"There is no need to be so obvious." Then, realizing that a grown man, even a brother, might not wish to be scolded in the street, she asked, "Where did she say she was going?"

"She did not say the shop's name. Stupid me, I did not ask. She needed…oh, what did she say exactly? She said she also wished to purchase a new pair of good gloves, since her evening ones were stained. And then Mrs. Talbot asked her to see if a pocket watch had been repaired, but I do not recall the shop's name. But she did say she would be here, I am certain of it. And then I was to meet her. Oh, how foolish of me!"

"There is a clockmaker just around the corner, so it is possible that she is somewhere along here after all," Elizabeth assured him.

A few more steps down the street and Charles' face lit up at the sight of a rather short young lady. He lifted his hand, waving to get her attention, and she turned to walk toward them. Charles walked so quickly that he left Elizabeth behind, not taking notice, either, until he'd exchanged enough words with his Miss Talbot that he turned to his left to find his sister missing.

"Ah, there she is," Charles said as Elizabeth made her way to his side, at a dignified pace. "Miss Talbot? Allow me to introduce my eldest sister, Miss Knight."

Miss Talbot was a plain young lady, but Elizabeth would never hold that against anyone. She wore a very sensible black bonnet, and was dressed appropriately for being on foot in February after a week of rain. Her smile, though? That was contagious, and in the best possible way.

The ladies exchanged curtsies. Miss Talbot gave Elizabeth a wide-eyed smile. "Oh, Miss Knight! I have heard so many excellent things about you from your brother."

"You have?" Elizabeth blurted. At Charles' glare, she amended, "I am always surprised when my younger siblings have anything nice to say about their mean, mean eldest sister. Pray, do you have any siblings, Miss Talbot?"

Elizabeth did not think the girl could smile any brighter, but she did. She had excellent teeth, though, and it made her eyes light up the grey sky. "Alas, it is just myself and my Mama, but the more I hear about life with so many children, the happier I am for my solitude!" Miss Talbot laughed to show she meant no offence. Her expression sobered thought, as clearly a thought overtook her. "Oh! I assure you that Charles, I mean Mr. Knight, has never said a mean word about you, not even. So much so that I believed he must've thought you had spies! For what brother is so kind. But, perhaps our Mr. Knight a cut above other men."

It took all of her good breeding and Augusta Knight's years of shouting, "decorum!" in the household for Elizabeth's face not to flicker nor for her eyes to glance at her brother. Instead, she smiled, sedately, kindly, elegantly. "Indeed! It is good to know young ladies hold my brother in high esteem. Pray, has he stated which of his sisters is his favourite?"

"Elizabeth!" Charles muttered.

Miss Talbot's eyes flicked between the Knight siblings, a little uncertainty before her smile returned. "I can assure you he is a very diplomatic brother, and that he has equal esteem for all of his sisters."

"Oh look!" Charles blurted. "Elizabeth? Thorne's over there. I didn't know he was in town."

"He did not say anything when we spoke on Tuesday," Elizabeth said.

"Would you like to speak to him? I can wait here, with Miss Talbot, if she doesn't mind the company?"

"Oh, no indeed, I do not," Miss Talbot said.

Elizabeth pretended not to have been dismissed, and replied in such a manner to appear that it had been her idea. She hurried off across the street, leaving the young and in love to whisper and giggle like fools. She waved at Mr. Thorne, catching his attention. He was not alone. He had a pretty little thing with him. When he caught sight of Elizabeth, his face did not brighten as usual. Instead, it was stricken, and he turned to speak to the girl. She gave a quick nod, and the happy conversation between them vanished, replaced with guarded expressions.

She found that very curious, but they approached in her direction, so perhaps it was the normal reaction of an older relation to a younger. The Thorne clan was huge—Elizabeth had not met a tenth of them—so this was possibly one of the many nieces.

"Good day, Mr. Thorne! I did not know you planned to come to town," Elizabeth said.

"Only for a couple of days. Thank God there is no rain, and it is not blustering for once," he said. "How does your aunt fare?"

"Much improved, I believe. She has been convinced to consider a move to the country, for the sake of her health. Town's air is too dirty and dreadful for anyone with weak lungs, such as her, but you know my aunt."

"Indeed."

Elizabeth's glaze flicked down to the young thing, who looked surprisingly like Mr. Thorne. The hair was a touch lighter, but not by much, and she had his eyes. Her chin was different, but no. Those eyes, though. She'd seen before.

She glanced at Mr. Thorne's awkwardness, and his eyes. Yes, indeed, she'd seen them before.

Figures and dates and calendars immediately came to Elizabeth's mind, as she calculated the months, and years, of this girl against the length of her friend's marriage to him. And she found her heart souring.

"Amelia? This is Maria's very good friend, Miss Knight. She's from Bryden."

Miss Amelia curtsied, an excellent, genteel curtsy for such a young girl, in fact. She held her hand out, in the modern fashion. And so Elizabeth accepted the gesture, and they shook hands in the style of advanced ladies. That is to say, a gentle squeeze of the fingers, nothing masculine or coarse.

"It is an honour to meet you, Miss Knight. I have heard excellent things about you from my cousin's wife."

No cousin in history looked this identical, but Elizabeth smiled and said, "Oh! You have met Maria?"

"Oh, indeed. She takes me shopping every time she comes to town! She gave me this muff for Christmas!" Amelia settled her tone back to elegant and said, "She is a very attentive woman."

"That is an excellent muff," Elizabeth said. "It goes very well with your bonnet."

"Thank you!" Amelia said with genuine delight.

"Amelia, my dear, pray, would you be so good as to run into MacIver's shop and fetch me some boiled sweets? I promised my mother I would bring some back for her." He dug out a few coins. In a stern voice, he said, "Remember to buy some for you, too."

She gave him a big grin as she accepted the money. To Elizabeth, her expression became guarded once more, but she gave a pretty little curtsy and said, "It was lovely to meet you, Miss Knight."

"And the same, Miss Amelia."

Elizabeth's smile faded as soon as Miss Amelia disappeared behind her. She waited, staring at Mr. Thorne with an unguarded expression.

"It is not what you think," Mr. Thorne finally said. "She turns eleven in a month."

That put her at ease, knowing that Mr. Thorne had not been unfaithful to her friend. She knew it was common enough, but she would never forgive him for such an action. "She is very small for her age."

"Yes, I suspect she will take after her mother…is that Charles?"

Elizabeth glanced over her shoulder and said, "Ah, yes. He just arrived in town."

In a panicked tone, he said, "Please, I beg you. Pretend she is my distant cousin. I will tell you all, but…"

"Thorne!" Charles said, interrupting them. "It is good to see you."

"Charles! It is good to see you. I did not get the opportunity to see you at Christmas, with all that went on. You look well!" Mr. Thorne said. "And pray. Who is your walking companion today?"

Introductions were made, and Miss Amelia returned with her treats. Mr. Thorne introduced her as his distant cousin who had recently lost her father.

"Oh, I am so sorry," Miss Talbot said. "I know how that feels, young miss. I recently lost my own, too."

"Was he a good man?" Miss Amelia asked.

"Indeed he was. And I miss him daily."

"I miss mine," Miss Amelia said with a glumness that made Elizabeth's heart sink. "But Mr. Thorne talked to the school, and they will allow me to stay until I move to the country. I have been there since I was eight, and I really like it, so staying will not be so bad because I have so many friends there."

"Well, Miss Amelia, I would be very honoured to count you as a friend. And, as a friend, you are very welcome to write to me at any time, even when you are at school or in the country, when you need the ear of someone who understands missing a good papa," Miss Talbot said.

"Oh thank you, miss!" She looked at up Mr. Thorne. "May I?"

"Yes, yes," Mr. Thorne said. "I do not see any harm in writing an upstanding lady such as Miss...Miss…"

"Talbot, sir," Miss Talbot said, curtsying again.

"Yes, my apologies," Mr. Thorne said.

"Thorne, where is she staying? Because, if she's at your house, I don't mind if we take her about for a walk, so she can talk with Miss Talbot for a bit. We can bring her back," Charles said. "The weather is fine enough today for it, I think, and we will promise not to tire her out."

"Oh please do," Mr. Thorne muttered. At Miss Amelia's sad eyes glancing in his direction, he quickly said, "Oh, I was teasing my dear! Only good natured! I am an old man and not used to the energy of such a young lady."

"You aren't *that* old," Miss Amelia said. Then, with a face of concentration, she asked, "How old are you? Fifty?"

"Please take her away, Charles," Mr. Thorne said with a laugh.

Miss Talbot laughed and said, "I believe a little female company might be exactly what Miss Amelia needs today. What do you say to that, young lady?"

"Oh please, Henry! Please?"

Mr. Thorne, a man infamously who could not say no to a woman with big, pleading eyes, relented, and his charge took off arm-in-arm with Miss Talbot and an amused Charles Knight.

"I believe they have stolen her from me."

"I believe they did," Elizabeth said. She chuckled. "I am certain she will do fine."

"Her, I do not worry about in the slightest. I worry for all the young men in about five years." Mr. Thorne sighed. "Walk with me and ask your questions."

"I do not wish to pry," Elizabeth said, as they began down the busy street.

When they reached a stretch of the walk where no one claimed an acquaintance with Mr. Thorne, he said, "She is my natural daughter, to answer the question I know burns in your heart to ask. Her mother died two summers ago, and her father—or her mother's husband, I should say—died two months ago."

"Oh, the poor thing," Elizabeth said. "Oh, is that why you came to town at Christmas?"

He nodded. "I had hoped to have her moved into Vane Park by now, but she wished to remain with her friends. I spoke with the school mistress—all of my sisters attended the same school, so I have complete trust in their direction—and they recommended that Amelia stay in school until Easter, but that she should live with me here, in town, whenever I can be spared here to ensure, well, to speak plainly, that she can tolerate me as a replacement for the parents who loved and raised her."

"And if she cannot?"

"One of my sisters has a widowed friend in Liverpool with no children, and she has offered to take Amelia if necessary, to ensure she has a place to live." He stared at Elizabeth and said, "If she were to go there, I would support her financially for all of her life, if necessary. Rest assured, Miss Knight. Whatever you think of me in this moment, I have not, and will not, abandon that girl."

Elizabeth was quiet for a moment, waiting for people who knew Mr. Thorne to pass alongside them. Then she said, "I would have thought less of you, if you had."

He sucked in a deep breath. "I know I not the first man of means to have a child, such as her. And there will be a time when I will acknowledge her properly. For now, though, I believe the fiction is best."

Elizabeth did not pry into that decision making, but she did ask, "When did Maria find out?"

Mr. Thorne gave her a curious look. "My dear, I told her when I asked her to marry me."

Elizabeth stared at him in utter amazement. Her friend had said nothing. Not even a whisper. Not even a hint. Henry Thorne's gambling was no secret, but even that he'd been tiring of, and …

No one had told her of Miss Amelia. It hurt her, far more than it should have she was quite certain. The existence of this girl did not impact Elizabeth's life. However, she found it was the principle of it.

Mr. Thorne must have misinterpreted her silence, for he said, "For all of my faults, ma'am, and I am assured you are aware of most of them, excepting the exact details of your special book, I do not keep secrets from my wife. And even then, I told her some were very rare and left it at that."

"I now understand your reluctance to lie to Maria about the book," Elizabeth said.

Henry Thorne nodded. "I did not wish a marriage built on lies. I would not have her marry me if she did not know of Amelia, and I would not marry her without her acceptance. Do not be cross with Maria. I had asked her to keep Amelia secret."

"Did you believe I would judge you?"

"In truth, I did not want your father to know," Mr. Thorne said honestly. "At first, it was merely because I did not wish to be lectured about virtue from the pulpit. But, as time went on, I simply did not want *her* judged for the sins of her father. She is such a bright girl. Loves reading. She gets that from her mother."

It was not appropriate to inquire into the girl's dead mother, especially not in the middle of a busy street, so she smiled, complimented Mr. Thorne's daughter repeatedly, until the conversation turned to Miss Talbot.

But throughout her walk with Mr. Thorne, Elizabeth felt an odd stirring in her heart, a confusion that such a secret would be kept from her. Even if Mr. Thorne had asked for secrecy, Maria never kept a secret from her.

Until now.

Chapter 11

ELIZABETH ARRIVED HOME in time to enjoy a cup of tea and a small sample of delights with her aunt in peace before her friends returned to turn their minds to ethereal matters. Not that Elizabeth wasn't looking forward to it —indeed, she was!—but she felt out of the habits of regular study. And, the revelations of the morning preoccupied her so much that even Aunt Cass asked what plagued her mind.

"I think I shall like Charles' Miss Talbot," Elizabeth said. This was not a lie. It was not the whole truth, but she had to accept her life was one of half-truths now if she were to protect herself.

They chatted about if Charles was finally ready to settle down, and the finances of his marriage. Aunt Cass made a face and said she would be expected to gift them a thousand pounds or two, of which Elizabeth laughed.

"No one would dare be so bold as to demand you give the couple your own money!"

"They may not demand it, but I am certain many will think it." Aunt Cass tapped her finger on the table. "I will have to check my accounts, but I do believe I promised Augusta I'd settle five hundred on Charles if he ever managed to attract a woman."

"Five hundred!" Elizabeth exclaimed. "This is the first I have heard of it!"

"I come from a generation when private agreements made between family members were kept private," Aunt Cass said.

"Then, I shall keep your secret, too," Elizabeth said.

"The last thing we need is him rushing into marriage."

Elizabeth choked on her tea, and gave her aunt a good-natured chiding.

Aunt Cass ignored her and passed a letter from Miss Keats that had arrived while she was out with Charles. She could not visit until Tuesday—and she had a family obligation that evening as well—but that, if they would like a morning visitor, she would be very happy to spend Tuesday morning and part of the afternoon with them.

That put Aunt Cass into an excellent mood, who decided she was well enough to host a dinner party on Monday. Dispatches were sent to Cousin David and his lady, Sir William, Mary, Charles, and the girls along with the Baldwins (who, since they were hosting two Knight girls, deserved a dinner invitation as well).

Surprisingly, it only took an hour for the first replies to arrive. The Baldwins and Cousin David were both engaged at the same dinner party that evening; however, they suggested other dates. So, Aunt Cass happily went about making those arrangements for a second dinner just for them.

Letters arrived from Thea and Cassie, both detailing their excellent friend. Miss Phoebe Baldwin, and her family. Thea's letter had more details about Mr. John Baldwin, thankfully, and she promised Elizabeth she was keeping her sister on the straight and narrow path. That made Elizabeth smile. Poor Thea. Being the chaperone could be a challenge, but maybe that was exactly what Thea needed.

Alice and Susan arrived just as Aunt Cass's cough became bothersome, but she waved off concerns to call for the "useless" doctor, and said what she needed was one of Mrs. Cook's healing draughts. An egg mixed into warm milk, a sprinkle of excellent nutmeg, a little rose-water, and a large spoon of honey. That would set her up, she was certain.

Sally arrived with the draught within mere minutes, as Mrs. Cook apparently already had milk warming for her buns, and was happy to comply with the request. Aunt Cass accepted it, advised the ladies to keep the noise down, and reminded them where her good bottle of sherry was located. With a wink, she ascended the stairs, teacup in hand.

That left Elizabeth, Alice, and Susan with an excellent bottle of sherry, a selection of edible delights, and hours to work on their occult studies. After the usual exchange of news and gossip, Mrs. Egerton and Miss Gibbs were summoned to offer their own unique ideas.

"Why, you have barely been in each other's presence in months!" Miss Gibbs replied. "I suggest drinking the entirety of the sherry and then inflicting Mrs. Spencer's cough on a worthless politician."

"Which one do you have in mind?" Alice asked.

"I'm certain they are all worthless," Miss Gibbs said in her cheery manner.

"But what of your locket?" Elizabeth inquired. "I feel quite terrible that we have yet to increase its range, or that you are expected to stay with me at all times."

"Pish!" Miss Gibbs said. "I am always very happy to be of use! If I am not needed for a week, or a year, or a decade? What do I care about such things! My only aim is to be useful. And to have a glimpse at the latest fashions."

"Be sensible!" Mrs. Egerton admonished her ghostly companion. "We have the opportunity to bring the sisters forth."

"What good will that be," Miss Gibbs complained. "They are so grim."

"But said you liked them!" Elizabeth declared.

"Oh, I do! They are dreadful though." Miss Gibbs added that last bit in a whisper before laughing.

And so the ladies quickly turned their minds to the task of summoning. While the three had very little time thus far to sit together to work, they had been pondering the question of the summoning, so began by comparing their thoughts on the subject. As with Miss Gibbs and Mrs. Egerton, the personalities of the sisters would make the summoning unique.

The sisters' summoning was intertwined, their autographs both cutting across each other, as if in conflict. The reverse reflections of their autographs likewise had various conflicting images. There was no unity or symmetry. It was as if they were thrown on the page together without thought, which Elizabeth knew was not how the autograph books were composed.

"Mrs. Egerton?" Elizabeth asked as Alice failed at the third summoning attempt. "Are the sisters the kind who people say there are no two individuals closer, or … more like myself and Mary?"

"There is some animosity between them," Mrs. Egerton said with great caution.

"They hate the sight of the other!" Miss Gibbs proclaimed. "Even Miss Knight and Mrs. Fitzharding can be forced into a carriage for a half hour without a scene."

"I protest!" Elizabeth said. "Mary and I have been…in disagreement, I admit, but we have made great strides to return sisterly affection between us."

"Perhaps you will model that habit for them," Mrs. Egerton muttered.

"Should we not attempt this?" Susan asked. "If we will be making it more difficult for them…"

Mrs. Egerton waved a fan in the air, despite not having had one in hand a moment before. "They will be happy to assist with your letter writing, I assure you."

So, the ladies went back to their work. It soon felt familiar, and whatever hesitation or awkwardness Elizabeth felt mattered not, for the comfort of distraction overtook her mind. Gone were the worries of her father, replaced with the excitement of a new challenge. Of work, of female companionship, of usefulness.

Another two hours went by, and Sally came to ask the ladies if they wanted an informal dinner. Aunt Cass requested hers to be sent to her room, and so there was no need to bring out the dinnerware if they did not wish it. The dining table was strewn with various scribblings, an autograph book, and various occult texts that permanently lived at Aunt Cass' house.

The ladies agreed to an informal dinner, with the dishes placed on a side table as to not dismantle their work.

The footmen assisted, and soon they were serving themselves eel pie, kidney beans, cabbage, and fried smelts. "Mrs. Cook says to tell you there is plenty of cold ham still in the pantry, from the meal two days ago, and there are more potted shrimps that must be eaten, a pickled tongue, and there are some potato rolls from last night. So, pray, if this is not enough, there is more to be fetched!"

The ladies assured the servant that the meal was plenty, but they promised they would send word if they needed anything. From there, they continued their work, the decanter of sherry reducing as the evening went on.

Two hours later, Elizabeth was instructed to re-read the autograph book's passage for the sisters aloud for the third time in a row. It was then they all agreed—living and not—that the ladies had been completing the spellwork properly. However, there was no hint of the sisters, not even a breeze or a giggle. Not even the softest sigh of complaint. Just mere silence.

"I do not understand what they are about!" Mrs. Egerton finally declared. "This is ridiculous and degrading. And they should know better."

"Do you suppose they are napping?" Miss Gibbs asked. "They were quite fond of doing so in life."

Mrs. Egerton's glare could've melted wax. "They are dead. How much more sleep do they require?"

"Are we perhaps offending them in some manner?" Elizabeth asked. "Are there too many of us? Or, conversely, not enough? Do our outfits offend them?"

"What is the matter with your gown?" Miss Gibbs inquired. She looked down at her own pretty thing. "I find these to be quite fetching for my figure."

"You look like a half-dress trollop," Mrs. Egerton muttered.

"All the better to catch a husband," Miss Gibbs said with a wide grin.

Susan looked down at her plain, but very serviceable gown. "What is wrong with our clothes?"

"Mrs. Egerton was scandalized by my gown upon our first meeting," Elizabeth said.

"What were you wearing?" Alice demanded, now, too, offended. "I think you dress rather sharply."

"Well, thank you my dear. It is good to know I have ladies in my life to defend me against fashion-hating ghosts." Elizabeth laughed.

Mrs. Egerton interjected, "I was merely shocked. Goodness, look at you all! You're barely dressed!"

"They're practically as bare as a newborn babe!" Miss Gibbs said, in a hushed, scandalized tone. Then she looked down at herself and said, "Still, we must not apply the fashion of our youth to these modern ladies. Though, I have overheard Mrs. Spencer say that she agrees the gowns of her time were far superior, and our hats never to be outdone by today's youthful fancy. And do not forget the wigs!"

Mrs. Egerton blurred, to return into view wearing a curly grey wig, with a severe black hat with a white lace bow perched on one side of her head. "This was true elegance."

"You look very fine indeed," Elizabeth assured her.

"I prefer my own hair," Alice mused.

"Young ladies should not contradict their elders," Mrs. Egerton snapped.

Suddenly, two new ladies appeared in the room.

They were all startled in various degrees at the appearance of two new ghosts. The ladies wore the fashion of Mrs. Egerton's era, which made sense given all four ghosts were of the same occult group. That was where the similarities ended. The black-hatted lady wore a sack, as the gown was called, if Elizabeth remembered her history properly, and it was a severe one at that. A plain brown gown, with only white stitching upon the stomacher.

Her companion, who looked similar in the way that sisters did, wore the exact same style of gown, but in a bright yellow silk, with yellow ribbons in her hair instead of a cap or hat, and various delicate details sewn across the gown and stomacher.

"Well?" the black-hatted one demanded.

Elizabeth stood to curtsy. Good manners rarely offended a person, and from her limited experience, rarely offended ghosts, too. "Welcome. My name is Miss Elizabeth Knight. My companions are…"

Black Hat waved her fan in the air. "Yes, yes, no one cares about such introductions these days. Where am I to be, for I have no want of being in the sight of this … this… trollop!"

Yellow Gown made a shocked sound and said, "How dare you!"

Black Hat: "You stole him!"

Yellow Gown: "It is not my fault he preferred me!"

"Um, ladies?" That was Elizabeth.

Black Hat ignored her. "We had a legal contract!"

Yellow Gown threw her hands up and declared, "What purpose do legalities serve when it comes to happiness?"

Black Hat gasped in shock. "You mock the law, madam!"

Mrs. Egerton rolled her eyes. Miss Gibbs turned to one side to give Elizabeth a massive, toothy grin, one so wide and vulgar that the ghost summoned a fan to hide behind.

"Oh, of course Sarah would give me that look," Black Hat said with disgust.

"Ladies, perhaps we should—"

Mrs. Egerton was not afforded the curtesy of finishing her sentence. Yellow Gown began hurling insults at Black Hat, which brought Miss Gibbs into the mix, and then, finally, Mrs. Egerton attempted to bring the voice of ethereal reason. This only brought the argument to a fevered pitch.

After several increasingly uncomfortable moments of Elizabeth attempting a polite disruption into the arguments of life that clearly had not dimmed in the candlelight of death, she lost her patience.

"Ladies! Enough!"

All four ghosts turned to Elizabeth, and she felt her face flush with heat. She sucked in a breath, curtsied politely, and began introductions in a civilized manner. "My name is Miss Elizabeth Knight. My uncle was once the proud custodian of the autograph books, which he has passed on to me. These two ladies are members of our little occult group. Miss Susan Markson and Miss Alice Thorne. And this is my aunt's home, Mrs. George Spencer, who is recovering from illness, so has taken to her bed while we work."

"It is very excellent to meet such a polite young lady," Black Hat said. "Unlike *some* people in this room."

"Do not start, Evelyn!"

"Do not *Evelyn* me! You will address me as Miss Wynn, or lest I remind you we are no longer sisters. Those were your words!"

"For the love of God, Evelyn! That was…Pray, Miss Knight? What year is it?"

"1811."

"Good God, no wonder fashion has changed so much. Gracious Redeemer, you all look naked. Oh, hello Sarah! At least you are wearing clothes, unlike these ladies."

"Hello, Violet," Mrs. Egerton said. "Don't bother with the gowns, but you must give the new bonnets a try."

"They are divine, even if it's impossible to see properly in them," Miss Gibbs added.

"Hello Sarah," Evelyn said. "It is good to see you again."

"And it is good to see you as well," Mrs. Egerton said. "Now, should I assume the two of you waited until we began bickering for you to arrive?"

"Good God! I tried to get her to appear because we were clearly awakened by these lovely young ladies, but Evelyn wouldn't have it."

"That is a falsehood!" Evelyn said. "I merely said that we should discuss the proprieties of the situation, but you wished to run head long just like you always—"

Elizabeth sighed as the sisters argued for another few minutes. Finally, she interrupted. "Mrs. Egerton says you can both assist us with letter writing."

"Indeed," Violet said. "I shall go to another room to begin immediately. Anything to have some peace."

"Try not to walk into any single young men, for you might have to marry them," Evelyn said.

Violet whirled on her sister. "He is dead, Evelyn! Dead and buried! What more can I do to make you happy?"

"You stole my betrothed!"

"He never said he'd loved you!"

"You never gave him the chance!"

"No one had enough time for you to make up your damned mind!"

Elizabeth cleared her throat. "Ladies. Ladies. Shall we focus on the letter writing? I am so happy to meet both of you."

"Now, now, Miss Knight," Miss Gibbs said. "Lying is a sin."

Elizabeth glared at Miss Gibbs. Now was not the time nor the place. She turned back to the sisters. "With your consent, of course, we have found it useful to work on travelling amulets. Would that be agreeable before we attempt the letter writing? As I live in the country, and am very far from London most of the year."

That set the sisters off again, and finally Elizabeth turned to Mrs. Egerton and said, "Mrs. Egerton? I am going to the kitchen, to inform the maids we will accept any cold thing tonight for a light supper. Please, I beg you. Speak to your companions to cease this bickering."

"Not even the grave can shut these two up," Mrs. Egerton muttered. Then, in a louder voice, she said, "But I shall attempt it, all the same. For you are a very worthy young lady to take up the mantle of lady occultist, and I do not wish you to be offended."

"Now see, Evelyn? You've offended them," Violet said.

"Me!" Evelyn gasped. "You have been rude to these strangers!"

"Me? I have never been rude a day in my life!"

Elizabeth stepped out of the room and the bickering immediately quieted, no doubt both under the harsh glare of Mrs. Egerton's disappointment and her ghostly lectures.

She almost pitied them.

Chapter 12

February 18, 1811
Monday

A SUCCESSION OF mild, but annoying, head colds descended upon their acquaintance, including Alice Thorne and Susan Markson. They opted to stay with Alice's parents—who were also stricken—to protect Aunt Cass' health. Poor Miss Keats also sent her apologies that she could not make her appointment the next day, for she was feeling very poorly from her own cold and had no wish to spread her misery.

That left Elizabeth and Aunt Cass to enjoy a quiet breakfast together in the dining room with no obligations for hours, which Elizabeth found to be soothing to her weary nerves. She had been busy since arriving in London, all the better to keep her mind occupied.

But at night?

At night, she lay awake, thinking of her father. Thinking of if the worst should happen. Thinking of if Isabella was not spared. Thinking every what if her scared mind could conjure. Then the dreams would come. Of happy times. Of bad times. Of times that she wished did happen. Of times that never could.

Then, to get up in the morning and smile and be cheerful.

So she enjoyed the quiet conversation of Aunt Cass over a hearty breakfast. Smoked kippers, hot rolls, cold rolls, cold sliced mutton, jams, stewed fruit, and pan cakes (complete with the nutmeg grated on top and not mixed in, as was Elizabeth's preference). There was no hot chocolate this morning, as the pots were in service, but Elizabeth would never think to complain of such a thing. But Mrs. Cook came to the dining room personally to apologize, of which Elizabeth assured her there was no need at all. Indeed, it was an extraordinary show for Mrs. Cook, a woman who was not young, and who had been up half the night cooking.

"Indeed, Mrs. Cook! You made pan cakes! Oh, how extraordinary a treat for me, especially since our poor cook is just seventeen and she has lost her additional helper."

"If only you lived closer. I would be very happy to teach your girl," Mrs. Cook said. "Pray, remind me before you leave, Miss Knight, to send along instructions for your maid. I suspect all she needs is a little encouragement and direction. Well, speaking of girls, I have three in my kitchen right now who, God help us, act like they have never seen an onion in their lives. I must go before they burn down half of London. That's all I need today!"

And with that declaration, Mrs. Cook hurried off. Aunt Cass sighed, when she was certain Mrs. Cook was out of hearing. "I have attempted to convince her to let me hire more permanent help, but she refuses."

"She is only worried, ma'am," Sally said. "Begging your pardon for interrupting."

Aunt Cass waved her off. "Oh, I know she probably has some notion in her head that I will let her go and turn her out into the streets, as if I would ever do such a thing. I have even offered to pay her a proper annuity, to allow her to move in with her sister, and enough to make her retirement very comfortable. But she will not. Says she would worry too much about me."

"Have mercy on the poor woman, Aunt! It must be so difficult for a woman of her age and class. She has worked her entire life, and probably would not know how to sit still for an hour."

"A woman of my station should have triple the servants I do, but…" She sighed. "I am so snug here with my little family that I worry about disrupting the balance. But with my housekeeper now off to take care of her dear sister's children, I find myself already disrupted."

Sally was still in the dining room with them and she curtsied when she asked, "Might I be so bold as to offer a suggestion?"

"It is just Elizabeth here. There is no need to stand on formality in this house," Aunt Cass said. "You are not offended if we discuss business at the dining table like men, are you, my dear?"

Elizabeth laughed. "Indeed not! I shall help myself to another roll, though, with some of this excellent apricot jam."

"It is the last jar until they are in season again, miss," Sally said. Then to Aunt Cass, she said, "Ma'am? My suggestion would be to offer Mrs. Cook the position of housekeeper but I know she has already rejected that notion."

"I have offered it to her thrice, with Mrs. Dover's departure, but she refuses."

"Why?" Elizabeth asked.

"She says making excellent buns for my table is her calling in life and she has no skill or patience for doing the books, or paying servants, or looking after silly young things who flirt with the footmen," Aunt Cass said. To Sally she asked, "Did I leave anything out?"

"I believe those were her exact words, Mrs. Spencer," Sally said. "So, my proposal, forgive the forwardness, is that instead of another temporary kitchen maid, I believe we should bring on the twins permanently as chambermaids. They are old enough now that I cannot see their mother disapproving of the employment. Then, we can bring on a maid-of-all-work permanently as well."

"Sally…" Aunt Cass said. "You know my feelings on that."

Elizabeth shared many of them, though in the country it was a little different. In town, a maid-of-all-work was worked until her fingernails bled, her knees were bruised, and she collapsed on the stairwell after sixteen hours of hard scrubbing. Only to be called upon to do it all again in the morning. They were paid nothing, five pounds in town, and many were not even fed anything beyond half a loaf of bread.

In Bryden, they earned about the same but were fed better, and they were cleaning significantly smaller homes. Or, sharing work amongst other maids. And with a small village, abuse of the poor maids was greatly frowned upon, since it could bring the attention of the rector—her father—and no one wished to have the harsh glare of her father lecturing them about their Christian obligation not to abuse the maids.

Sally curtsied. "I know your feelings, ma'am, truly I do. But consider, if I might be so bold, that a woman of your position does not need to pay anyone according to custom, but rather your conscience. And, if you choose not to overwork the girl, then what does it matter? And, begging your pardon ma'am, Mrs. Cook should not be scrubbing the pots, and I have said so, but she will not listen to me. She says I do not clean the pots properly, in any case."

"Is there anyone in London who will meet her approval with regards to the pots?" Elizabeth asked with a laugh.

Sally curtsied.

"Sally, out with this scheme of yours," Aunt Cass asked.

"I have a childhood friend with a sister…"

"Is this the friend who was seduced by the sailor?" she asked.

Sally nodded gravely. "She will begin her lying in any day now."

"Has the scoundrel married her?" Elizabeth asked.

"He is long gone, miss," Sally said. "Men like him do not stay to see the trouble they make for ladies."

"She cannot work in her condition," Aunt Cass said.

"No, indeed. She is very fortunate in her situation, for she lives with others. The women of the household have taken in sewing and ironing, along with other children, and they are well set up. However, her sister who has lately brought forth a son is in need of employment. Currently, she assists with the infants, but she has previously worked as a maid-of-all-work and wishes to return to that profession. And with my friend in her situation, she can easily take over acting as a wet nurse any day now."

"Was this poor sister also seduced?" Elizabeth asked, shocked at the abuse suffered by the hands of men.

Sally seemed to hesitate, but said, "She is properly wed, miss. I assure you."

Which did not answer the question to Elizabeth's satisfaction, but at least the poor creature was protected.

"What about lodgings?" Aunt Cass asked.

Sally shook her head. "No, indeed, that will be unnecessary. They have an excellent housing situation, sharing with his mother and hers, along with my friend, several other family members, with children. They are about forty minutes by foot from your door, if I recall my last visit."

"And what does this friend expect for salary?" Aunt Cass asked, serving herself more coffee.

"Her last employment, before her lying in, paid her five pounds per annum, so I am certain she would be happy with that."

"Five pounds," Aunt Cass muttered. "No wonder my friends complain they cannot find good help these days. Five pounds, indeed. James? James?"

"Yes ma'am," James said stepping into the room.

"Sally here has a scheme to get Mrs. Cook's hands off the scrub brushes." Aunt Cass filled him in, and then asked, "What is your opinion?"

"As a maid-of-all-work, she can do any small tasks about the house to spare those who are needed elsewhere," James said thoughtfully. He was an older man, having been in service his entire life. He seemed to think on his own words, before nodding. "The twins are old enough now that we should offer them a proper position, as well, if I might be so bold. Then, with this new miss, who is older and one assumes steadier given she is now a mother, she can get the kitchen scrubbed, the pots cleaned, tend the pickles, run the errands Sally is too busy to run, all of that."

Sally curtsied. "I do not mind."

"Nevertheless," Aunt Cass said. "Without Mrs. Dover, I must make some changes about the house. James and I have spoken of it…"

The butler bowed deeply.

"What do I pay you now, Sally?"

Without hesitation, she responded, "Nineteen per annum with laundry, lodgings, and unlimited tea and access to the larder, I might add, ma'am. None of my friends have that, I assure you."

Elizabeth saw Aunt Cass glance at James who gave a slight incline of the head. She did not know what had been discussed, so she simply sipped her tea and waited.

Aunt Cass thought for a moment, then nodded. "I shall move you to the position of housekeeper, with the salary of one hundred pounds per annum, and your access to the kitchen, and laundry, of course."

"Ma'am!" Sally protested. "That is for a steady woman, not for me!"

"Are you not a steady woman?" Aunt Cass asked with a laugh.

"But I cannot earn more than Mrs. Cook!" Sally protested. Then, remembering herself curtsied and said, "Begging your pardon, Mrs. Spencer, but I could not accept earning more than her."

"Indeed not, that is why I plan to adjust her salary from eighty to one hundred so that she can provide the steady hand you feel you are lacking, but what say you?"

"But…what am I to do with one hundred pounds?" Sally blurted.

"A great many things, I suspect," James said. "Now, with that settled, we only need to bring on Emily and Ellen permanently. I can talk to their mother for you, ma'am, but I am certain she will not see any issue, since they are already here frequently as it is."

"Then, I believe I shall offer a permanent position to the twins to be chambermaids. Let us make it ten pounds each, since they cannot do any of the heavy lifting. They're still too small. Should we leave their brother where he is?"

"Little Tom does not wish to be tied down to one house yet," James said with a laugh.

"Is he still working for Sir William then?" Elizabeth asked.

"Yes, Miss. And nearly every single one of our neighbours. The lad likes to be useful, and he's at that age where he only has two speeds: running and lazing about. So, I say we let him run."

"Then, we can continue on with him. So let us hire Sally's friend as a maid-of-all-work. Nine pounds per annum, with the unlimited tea and access to the kitchen. Laundry. All the usual things I offer. But, hear me, I will not tolerate abuse, do you hear me? I will not abide that under my roof, and I will dismiss any of the household who does. Make that clear to the men."

"Indeed not, ma'am. I would not allow it," James said sternly.

"And regular hours, please. Or, at least a set of tasks that can be completed sensibly in the day. None of this foolishness with servants passing out on the stairs from exhaustion, do you hear me, James? I will not stand for it. If she has to walk over an hour a day here and back, then I want her to have enough strength to do so."

"Of course, ma'am. Very good. Shall I speak with Mrs. Cook?" James asked.

"No, I shall," Aunt Cass said. "It will come as no surprise to her. And, we are to help this poor creature who has married far too young for her own good. Pray, what is the age of the man she has married?"

Sally cleared her throat. "Thirty, if I recall, ma'am."

"Thirty. A man old enough to have better sense," Aunt Cass sneered. "Well, I will not be assisting him. However, to support your friend's sister, I shall make allowances. Can she find a wet nurse before her sister comes to bed?"

"Yes, one of the others living with them," Sally said.

"And, pray, what does this husband of thirty do?" Aunt Cass, rather coldly.

"He is a labourer, ma'am," Sally said.

James made a tutting sound.

"Well, he might as well enjoy it while his back can handle the work, I suppose," Aunt Cass said. "Very well. I shall speak to Mrs. Cook, but tomorrow morning. There is no point to tell her now, for she might decide to retire and leave us all to starve to death."

They were interrupted by a footman holding a tray full of letters. They were to have one new addition to the party: one of Aunt Cass' letters had been from Mary requesting if Miss Talbot could attend, as she was currently staying with Mary for a week.

How interesting, Elizabeth silently declared.

However, her interest waned when she considered her seven letters, all from her father. She sighed and excused herself from the table. When her aunt inquired at the extraordinary letterwriting of her father, she only said that he still suffered grievously from his illness, and allowances must be made. To what, Elizabeth did not elaborate. Only that she wished a little privacy to read her letters, before facing the evening's festivities.

MARY AND HER husband arrived with Miss Talbot and Charles first, and introductions were made all around. Mr. Osborne arrived while they were in the entrance passing their hats and gloves to the footmen. Elizabeth was certain Mr. Osborne was disappointed to discover Miss Susan was unwell.

Mr. Baldwin's carriage arrived to deposit Thea, who was not suffering from a sore throat. More introductions, more gloves, more people laughing in the entrance, while Aunt Cass told them to move inside so that they may close the door.

"And it is good to see you again, Charles! Mary, I was telling Elizabeth just yesterday that I think your brother has finally gained his health back. Look at the colour in his face," Aunt Cass said.

"Indeed, I agree with Aunt Cass, Charles," Elizabeth said as they stood about talking. "It was difficult to tell the other day because you did not remove your greatcoat, but even then I noticed a bit more fullness in the cheeks."

"I told him when he first came to London, but he would not believe me," Mary said. "Oh, but he believes Eliza!"

"It is simply that I knew Elizabeth wouldn't lie to me," Charles said defensively.

"I have never lied to you, Charles!" Mary said.

"I think you look very well, indeed," Miss Talbot said shyly.

The entire group stared at each other, no one daring to speak for fear of laughter and teasing. Charles' cheeks turned red, and poor Miss Talbot turned the colour of beets. As more coats and bonnets and gloves were discarded about, he told them about how he had finally regained his entire appetite, though he was still careful about eating while travelling.

A part of Elizabeth still wondered if the improved attitude and overall demeanor was perhaps the final grasps of his illness fading. She wanted to think that, perhaps, so many of his issues had been out of his control. And now this man before her was the man Charles truly was. She hoped, for his sake.

They had only just removed their outer garments, busy laughing and teasing each other that Mary complained they were gathered like "common workers," for which they all ridiculed her.

Finally, Mary sighed and said, "Aunt? Shall we dispense with formality and simply push all of these people into the dining room? For there is no point attempting any form of ceremony with this lot."

"Mary! We are all family!" Elizabeth protested. "Surely family is the one time we do not need to stand on ceremony!"

"Not everyone here is family," Mary said. Then quickly added, "Yet."

"Mary," Mr. James Fitzharding said.

Mary merely continued to smile as if no one had noticed what she'd said, despite all of the blushing faces about her.

"Well, for my part," Miss Talbot interjected, "I have heard so much about the Knight sisters from Mr. Knight and from Miss Thorne that I shall, if you wish Mrs. Fitzharding, pretend to be family for the night so that that I may engage properly in the family squabble."

"We are not squabbling!" Mary said. She took a deep breath. "I apologize for my tone, Miss Talbot. This is what sisters and a husband do to a woman of sense. Be wary."

That made Miss Talbot laugh, and Charles let out a breath as the noose was removed from his neck for a few more minutes.

Thankfully, the soup arrived. Everyone sipped from the sides of their spoons. Carefully. Elegantly. Silently. The air started to feel like the soup before them: thick. Thea made idle chatter with both Mr. Osborne and Miss Talbot, and that broke the discomfort at times, with everyone pitching in a few words, occasionally a full sentence.

Mr. Fitzharding—James, Elizabeth reminded herself. She must start considering him *James.* Then chuckled at how many people in her life had the same names. James, Aunt Cass' butler. James the husband of her sister. Aunt Cassandra. Sister Cassandra. Honestly, she was shocked how few Marys there were in her life, for indeed she was certain there should be more.

"Elizabeth, what are you grinning about?" Mary demanded from across the table.

"I do not believe grinning is a sin," Elizabeth said between delicate sips of her soup. As Mary's piercing gaze did not leave her, she chuckled and said, "I was merely thinking that everyone in my life has the same name. I have several James, several Cassandras, there are two Charles—three! If we count Miss Sims' nephew. It seems that we only have about ten names in England and then we just reuse them like a fine silk gown until they are rags."

"Waste is a sin," Charles said very gravely. All of the heads of the table turned to face him.

"My dear Charles!" Aunt Cass said. "If my eyes were closed when you spoke that, I'd have wagered a guinea that it was your father sitting there."

"I do not sound like my father," Charles said. "I was merely supporting my sister, and attempting to tease her in the process."

"Charles!" Thea said with a chuckle. "Indeed, you sounded like our father."

Elizabeth nodded. "I thought you were about to scold me and send me to bed without my supper!"

"Oh be reasonable! I would never do that." Then, in a more sullen voice, added, "As if you'd ever listened to Father when he'd done that. You always got your own way with him."

"Me!" Elizabeth said laughing. "The eldest? I most certainly did not."

"You did," Mary said. "You could always talk your way out of things with Papa."

Aunt Cass nodded. "It is true, Elizabeth. When you were a girl, you frequently got your own way in the end."

"I have never gotten my own way in my entire life!" Elizabeth defended herself.

"We younger girls always say if we need something, get Eliza to ask Papa," Thea said.

"These are lies, Miss Talbot, Mr. Osborne. I assure you," Elizabeth said.

"Really?" Charles said. "How many occult books are in our father's house, right this moment?"

"That is not the same," Elizabeth said.

"Father knows you have money hidden in your desk," Charles said.

Fear struck Elizabeth. She put her spoon down so that they would not see it shake. "What do you mean?"

"You had left your account book open. He was looking for you, and saw it," Charles said. "He told me, months ago. It hurt him, I think, that you felt you could not tell him, but I told him that you were always secretive. He sighed and said that was your way he supposed, and that seemed to mollify him."

She couldn't speak, her heart pounding at the revelation that her father knew of her money. That her entire family did. She wanted to control the expression of fear that she knew was upon her face, the wide-eyed stare of one caught.

"I am not secretive," Elizabeth whispered. The best she could manage.

Her response did not bring harmony. It set the table off, abusing her. Finally, James Fitzharding took pity on her and said, in a rather loud voice to get ahead of the hubbub, "So Charles, I've not had the opportunity to inquire. How was your journey here? Mary did not say."

"Oh, the roads were excellent," Charles said. Then, he added, "Well, except for a small patch. We had to dismount the carriage because the rain had washed out a section and the coachman feared we were too heavy. But there were already men filling in the holes, so we were able to get across safely enough."

That allowed the poor footmen to transition the table to the fish course without the Knight children stabbing one another with their spoons.

When the fish arrived, Mr. Osborne announced the mushroom catsup on potatoes to be an excellent combination, and Miss Talbot quickly joined in to agree.

"Oh, then you must try some," Mr. Osborne said. Since Miss Talbot was on the opposite end of the table, a footmen stepped in to accept the dish from Mr. Osborne and then bring her the dish to help herself. "The catsup at Mrs. Spencer's table is always excellent. My compliments to Mrs. Cook, madam. She is excellent at her craft."

Aunt Cass said she would pass along the compliments. Elizabeth, wanting to continue the conversation of little nothings, said she loved boiled potatoes mashed up with a little butter and cream poured over the top, while Charles jokingly made a show of loudly rejecting the boiled potatoes, opting to fill his own plate with fish, bread, and a sampling of all the pickles. Mary irritably said she had not realized he disliked potatoes so much now, and was rather embarrassed that she had served three types when Charles dined with her.

"Oh Mary, I did not say it as a criticism of your table!" Charles said. "I was only teasing myself."

"My own family tells me nothing," Mary said in a sulk.

"I am certain Charles did not mean any slight," Elizabeth said.

"Indeed I did not!" Charles said. "Elizabeth had only mentioned..."

"We all heard the conversation, Charles," Mary said. She sighed and said, "I do not wish to quarrel at my aunt's dinner table."

"We aren't quarreling!" Charles said.

"I believe we're quarreling about not quarreling," Elizabeth said, which cause Mr. Osborne to turn away to hide his mirth. She winked at Miss Talbot, who giggled, and returned to her fish.

"I regret that Miss Cassie suffers with a sore throat," James Fitzharding said. "She would bring us all of the London gossip, I am certain. All you lot wish to do is argue like fishmongers!"

"Husband, I wish you would not encourage such bad habits in my sisters!" Mary said. "And I have never behaved like a fishmonger in my life."

The servants, seeing that this dinner party needed to be broken up as quickly as possible, whisked away the fish course and marched onwards to the main. A game course, which James the butler was tasked with carving, and not Mr. Fitzharding, for as he put it, "Mary dislikes how I do it."

"You cut the pieces too thick," Mary complained.

"Not everyone wants meat cut so thin you can see through it, Mary!"

"Not everyone wants meat so thick you need two men and a saw to get through it!"

"Elizabeth, what is your view on meat thickness?" James Fitzharding asked Elizabeth.

"Elizabeth is going to agree with you, just to spite me," Mary said.

"I have not yet opened my mouth to speak," Elizabeth said. "I was going to say I believe having Aunt Cass' very neutral butler do the job allows for us all to enjoy each other's happy company."

"Oh God," Charles muttered.

"My dear Mrs. Spencer, these Knight children are terrible company!" James Fitzharding said. "All they do is bicker at your fine table."

"It has always been the case, my dear Mr. Fitzharding," Aunt Cass said. "And in front of our guests! Poor Miss Talbot, and poor Mr. Osborne! The two of you must be scandalized by this show."

"I have been on excellent behaviour," Thea muttered darkly into her potatoes.

"Mr. Osborne, would you pass me some of the cheese?" Elizabeth asked loudly, in an attempt to start a new conversation.

"I thought you didn't like Stilton," Charles said casually.

Elizabeth smirked at Mr. Osborne and said, "I've developed a taste for it now that I am old and infirm."

"Oh, I made one comment, Eliza! One!" Mary said.

"Is she teasing you about still being single?" Charles asked.

"Endlessly," Elizabeth said. She accepted the dish of cheese from a chuckling Mr. Osborne. "Thank you, sir. Most kind."

Dinner went on in such a manner that, finally, Elizabeth was relieved to escape the dinner table. Mr. Osborne informed the others he was expected at his mother's for an evening party of cards—Aunt Cass had already been informed and took no offence with him not lingering—and so their party became all family, with one exclusion.

If Mary had anything to do with it, that exclusion would soon end, of that Elizabeth was certain. She knew her sister, and saw her schemes. But she found no fault in having Miss Talbot to visit. After all, what an excellent idea to bring young people together who could not find the excuse on their own.

They did not bother to break in the formal style into women and men, and instead all went together to the drawing room, much to Mary's subtle complaining about how her family had no manners. Aunt Cass laughed, and called for tea. Soon, sweet things arrived with tea and coffee. Mr. Fitzharding took to happily serving everyone, having a grand time of annoying Mary in the process.

Elizabeth checked in on Miss Talbot as often as possible, ensuring she was not in need of a rescue from her sisters, but they were quite engrossed in conversation. Charles hovered about Miss Talbot, though Elizabeth got the impression that he was more concerned about what Thea would say than anything else.

She did manage to have him out of hearing of Miss Talbot to whisper, "I find myself wishing to be better acquainted with Miss Talbot."

"Indeed?" Charles asked, his face lighting up.

"Indeed I do." Then, in a louder voice, Elizabeth said, "Miss Talbot? Miss Talbot. Pray, I do not believe you have told us where your family is from."

"Oh!" Miss Talbot said, blushing. "My mother is from Liverpool, originally, but she moved to Exeter, and that is where I grew up. I was sent to school in London, and that is where I met Miss Alice Thorne, where we have been friends since childhood."

"And, pray? Where do you live now?" Aunt Cass asked.

"Since the death of my father…rather, my father was a parish…that is to say…" She dabbed at her eye. "Forgive me."

"Miss Talbot's father only died four months ago, after a prolonged illness," Charles said. He gave her a smile. "They had been living just outside Cambridge, in fact. But since the death of her father, Miss Talbot and her mother have been graciously enjoying the hospitality of her relations during this difficult time."

"I apologize," Miss Talbot whispered as she accepted a handkerchief from Thea.

"Not at all," Elizabeth said. "I find myself sometimes rather weepy when I consider my own mother, and she has been gone a very long time."

"I occasionally shed a tear for my father," James said near the tea service, "and we famously did not get along."

"Indeed, Mr. Fitzharding?" Miss Talbot asked.

"Oh indeed. I will spare you a recounting of the last words we ever spoke to each other, but I assure you, they were not words of kindness, nor words gentlemen should ever say to one another. And yet, I find myself at times…" His voice had grown unsteady the more he spoke. He cleared his throat and thumped his fist against his chest. "You see Miss Talbot? We understand one another."

"You are all so very kind," she whispered.

"I sometimes worry about what it will be like when father dies," Thea said. Rather loudly into the silence.

Teacups clattered around the room as everyone stared at Thea.

"Well, we don't talk about what is happening to him," Thea said. "And if we are allowed to discuss Mr. Fitzharding's grief, and Miss Talbot's grief, I cannot see why we cannot discuss our father."

"Dearest, his situation is not polite conversation," Elizabeth said.

"Why not?" Thea asked. "We're all family here, are we not? Even Mrs. Spencer, who I suppose is not my aunt, but whom we all call Aunt Cass."

"Thea..." Elizabeth said.

"How poorly is he?" Aunt Cass asked. "Elizabeth, you have said nothing."

"I did not wish to alarm you," Elizabeth said quietly.

Charles asked, "Truly, is he worse than at Christmas?"

Elizabeth said she would fetch that morning's letters from her writing desk that was set up in the far corner of the drawing room. "You might as well read it aloud, since Thea insists we ruin the evening."

"I did not mean to," Thea complained.

Charles accepted the letter. "'My daughter, I cannot abide you gallivanting about the countryside in this manner. Why are you not home, attending your duties? Your poor mother is beside herself. And just because Mary is allowed to go to London does not mean you can. I do not know who gave you permission because I surely did not. What kind of ungrateful daughter are you? I...' I cannot read this."

Mary accepted the letter and glanced at it. "Most of this is completely illegible. 'Ungrateful. Spoiled. Disrespectful.' Well, the usual words us girls have all heard before."

Elizabeth remained silent, though she thought bitterly that those were the words that caused Mary to marry the first man who glanced at her.

Mary read a little more until her voice faltered and her husband requested the letter. She handed it to him, and he folded it without reading and passed it back to Elizabeth. "We do not need to read this aloud. Charles, to answer your question, he is worsening, and by the day."

Charles looked to Elizabeth and she nodded. "That is why G is still home. She is at Vane Park mostly, though I cannot even recall the pretense for which she is there. The rest of us escaped to London, as Aunt Cass' health had been grave."

"I would not call it *grave*," Aunt Cass said.

"Well, nevertheless, we came, and we have left the youngest of us all to face what is happening there," Elizabeth said.

"I cannot go back yet..." Mary said.

"I would not ask you to," Elizabeth said. "Truly, I would not. Sidney, I mean, Mr. Sinclair"—she winced that she slipped up—"has written via Isabella to say that he has been attempting to mediate. I shall write to him and ask him to attempt to stop the letters."

"Who is Sidney?" Aunt Cass asked.

"Mr. Sinclair," James added, in a rather gleeful tone if Elizabeth was any judge.

"I have never heard you call him Sidney before," Mary said.

"He calls her Elizabeth when he thinks we aren't listening," Thea said glumly.

"Theodosia!" Elizabeth said.

"Well! I overheard the two of you talking!" Thea said. "We all talk about it!"

Elizabeth's face burned and she wished for nothing more than to crawl under the furniture.

The others were sensible to remain silent, as Elizabeth searched her mind for the appropriate words to say, both to scold her sister and to defend herself. But it was Mary to speak first. She knew Elizabeth the best, so it was always going to be her to break the silence.

"I thought you didn't like him."

Elizabeth glanced in Thea's direction, and into her big, sad eyes. Thea would not have asked the question, not even in an indirect manner. Of course Mary would, and as much as it pained

Elizabeth to admit it to herself, Mary had the most right of all of them to do so.

Mustering her courage, she spoke with as much truth as possible. "My dear Mary, it is not a question of liking or disliking the man. He is our father's curate. It is only my opinion, but I do believe he has remained in the position longer than his family would prefer—again, this is my opinion, of course—and I believe he has done so solely for our family's sake in this difficult time."

Elizabeth left off the part about him inheriting a shocking amount of money that would steal him from their lives forever, as she felt that would distract from her sermon.

"And he has done this, and gone up against our father, as late as the day before we left Bryden. He hired a carriage to escort us here in sole support of our family. And he knows that, eventually, the guilt will overtake one of us for having left G there, and, when that happens, he shall return to escort us back home."

"Perhaps our father will ease when I am in Ashbrook," Charles said.

"You will be very busy with your duties," Mary said sharply.

"Mary, I already have Elizabeth. I do not require you to mother me," Charles snapped.

Elizabeth turned to her brother. "Do not speak to your sister in that manner."

"See?"

Elizabeth tried not to stare at the manservant behind Mary who was very much trying not to laugh, but his face was contorting into the strangest shapes. Elizabeth started to snicker. She covered her mouth, which Charles started laughing. Soon, they were all laughing, with Mary being the final one to join in. She rolled her eyes, attempted to be stern, but finally gave in. Even the servants did, finally released from propriety.

"Miss Talbot?" Elizabeth said, "Please do not judge our family too harshly this evening."

"On the contrary, Miss Knight! I shall compare all future evening parties to this one, indeed!"

Chapter 13

February 20, 1811
Wednesday

THE CONCERNS ABOUT sore throats, putrid fevers, and head colds ended by Wednesday, with everyone declaring themselves hearty and ready to resume visitations, including the infamous Miss Keats who finally could visit.

The young lady did not disappoint in Elizabeth's estimation. She was a mousy girl, perhaps, but not all were born to be beautiful on the outside. What mattered was what was underneath, and Miss Keats turned out to be a goodly sort. Her sister-in-law even came to the door with her, and stayed for a quarter of an hour.

While Miss Keats and Alice were already exceedingly close friends, Miss Keats was shy with Elizabeth at first, but it only took another hour for the discomfort of new acquaintance to fade in the face of the easy nature of women's conversation. Elizabeth was grateful for such distraction; she had not received a letter from Isabella in several days. She'd only been in London for a week, but also the worry of being away from home was starting to wear on her.

However, the conversation soon fell to discussing the problem of the ghostly sisters, of which Miss Keats had already been well informed by Miss Thorne. Elizabeth turned her full attention to answer Miss Keats' questions until, finally, Mrs. Egerton and Miss Gibbs were summoned to meet Miss Keats, whom they both declared to be "delightful" within mere minutes. Mrs. Egerton specifically approved of Miss Keats' bonnet, but not her bosom, but the young lady took it all in good humor.

"My dear Mrs. Egerton!" Miss Keats protested. "I even wore my highest gown, and my thickest neck covering!"

"London air is more difficult to see through than that gauzy fabric about your throat," Mrs. Egerton said.

"I think it divine," Miss Gibbs said. "I suspect an entire gown of that on one's wedding night would—"

"Miss Gibbs!" Aunt Cass declared. "I must protest such language! In front of unmarried women!"

"Oh, pish," Miss Gibbs said. She turned to the ladies and declared, "Sarah told me all about the act, so I find myself very well informed."

And that was the day they all learned ghosts could blush as deeply as a living person.

Tea and cake fortified the ladies as they laboured to bind three ghosts to lockets: the Wynn sisters, and Miss Gibbs. Miss Gibbs did not take offence that Elizabeth did not summon her as much as Mrs. Egerton, and said so.

After about an hour or so, the ladies decided that Miss Gibbs should not be on her own; instead, be bound to the same hinged locket as Mrs. Egerton that Elizabeth kept about her neck. The reasoning being that Miss Gibbs only ever appeared with Mrs. Egerton and perhaps the original autograph spellworking meant they should be bound together.

Miss Gibbs did not offer any opinion on the occult aspects of it, only to say she found it highly amusing and supported the idea. "Oh, think of it, Sarah! We are to be joined at the hip for all of eternity!" Miss Gibbs declared.

"How extraordinary," Mrs. Egerton said, without her ghostly companion's exuberance.

Throughout their work, however, Elizabeth found it rather difficult to bring focus to Alice, who normally was very dedicated to her studies. She and Miss Keats were huddled at a corner table whispering non-stop and giggling. When Elizabeth glanced at Susan, she only shrugged and smiled. Finally, though, Elizabeth stepped in to break up the feminine conference.

"Ladies! We only have a short time and I would hate to annoy Mrs. Egerton," Elizabeth said. "We have two tasks in front of us. Do you propose we divide them, or shall we all attack at once?"

"I believe myself and Alice should continue our work on Miss Gibbs' locket," Susan said, interrupting whatever was about to come out of Alice's mouth. Clearly it was something different, as Alice seemed rather disappointed. "That will leave Miss Keats and Elizabeth to work with the sisters."

Miss Keats gave a little bob of the head and said, "Yes, I believe that is the wisest course of action, for I fear I am distracting poor Miss Thorne with all of my trivialities."

"Nonsense! I do not find them trivial at all," Miss Thorne said.

"Nevertheless, Alice," Miss Keats said.

Alice sighed the sigh of a woman who could not find an appropriate argument to the contrary. Elizabeth glanced at Susan, who gave her a rather curiously resigned expression. They soon discovered Miss Gibbs' presence adhered to the locket only if they topic on discussion was of interest to the ghost. The healing properties of the occult was anticipated. The nature of dress in town versus the country, and the ever changing fashion for sleeves or no sleeves caused Miss Gibbs to linger in the locket for three quarters of an hour.

"My dear Miss Gibbs! Can you be sensible?" Mrs. Egerton demanded.

"My dear Mrs. Egerton! I cannot change who I am in death no more than I can change the weather!" Miss Gibbs said. With a wide grin, she said, "And I do love the new fashion of nakedness!"

"We are not naked!" Miss Keats protested with a snort. The sound shocked her and she put a hand over her mouth to hide her embarrassment. "Indeed, we are very decent, I think."

"I attended a ball in December and one of the young ladies in white purposely moved a candlestick to a low bench and then stood in front of it, to better show off her figure underneath," Alice whispered.

"How scandalous!" Elizabeth said. Then, "Was she not afraid of burning to death?"

"A woman must be willing to take a risk or two," Alice said, bringing laughter from the others.

"I have yet to meet a man for whom I would risk dying in a gown fire to gain his attention," Elizabeth said. "Perhaps that is why I am still single."

The workings to separate the sisters did not yield any better results. The sisters could, in fact, convey messages from across the room. Elizabeth would whisper a phrase to Violet, who would write it down. Evelyn would then write, and Alice would read it aloud. The message always matched. So, they declared that a success.

Unfortunately, they could not seem to separate the sisters. Elizabeth could not go upstairs and summon only one Wynn lady; she'd always get both. They moved the decorative screen into the middle of the room, to create a barrier between the sisters. However, as soon as they were out of sight of one another, they would both disappear back into the autograph book. Then, they would need to be resummoned, relive their arguments, and start over.

After four hours, the ladies declared defeat and decided to open a bottle of wine. After that, no work was done.

Chapter 14

February 21, 1811
Thursday

Dearest Isabella,

I worry at the silence from the rectory; I have only received a letter this morning from G that was less than a page detailing the rain and news of the old bridge. Please send even a short note to say all is well.

For us, there is nothing new to report, so perhaps that is the same as for you. My aunt's health continues to improve. She has regained most of her colour, and her spirited nature is returned now that she is not reliant upon drink to calm her lungs. I admit to you that I was terrified to hear the news that laudanum caused her to stop breathing! Did you know it could do such a thing? I find myself now terrified of the mixture for all future ailments.

She has been venturing further from the house each day now, with first a visit next door to her good neighbour. Then, to her neighbour across the street. Now, we find her going out visiting daily or for short trips to the shops. She finds the exercise good for her, provided it is not windy or very cold.

Cassie and Thea are doing well. They are comfortable at the Baldwin's, and I have visited them twice since arriving in town. I cannot remember the last time I have been this busy! I swear to you, I have not been this occupied in town since my coming out year! My days are full of visiting, company, running out to the shops for Aunt Cass...In fact, this very morning I turned down three dinner invitations because they were to take place on the same evening!

Pray, do not misunderstand me. I do not complain of the bustle. It has been good for my mind, to keep me from worrying or dwelling. The weather has been excellent considering how rainy this month has been. And, what is more, there has been no wind most days, making a daily walk in the sun quite an invigorating experience.

My occult friends and I have been working hard, in between an outbreak of sore throats (do not be alarmed; all are healed), company, and their own family obligations. Enjoying an hour or two devoted to a book has been very soothing to my soul.

As ever, I send my love, and please advise if there is anything I need to purchase for you.

Elizabeth

Then, with a deep breath, she wrote to Maria. The scene with Mr. Thorne and Miss Amelia took place last Friday. Elizabeth had not written to Maria in that time. She wished to blame the hectic nature of the weekend, and her arrival in town, but that was not the full truth. She had been hurt, and feeling a little hypocritical, given that she'd asked Mr. Thorne to conceal something from his wife.

Enough time had passed for letters to travel between Henry and Maria, and back to her, so she wondered if Maria waited to see

Elizabeth's response. Therefore, she gathered her courage and, after the usual greetings and statements about health, roads, and weather, Elizabeth got to the point.

> *I have made the acquaintance of Miss Amelia. I have found her a delightful young girl, who is a credit to her family as well as the excellent school I understand she attends. I had no idea such a creature existed, as I would have longed to make her acquaintance before now. I look forward to her arrival at Vane Park, and plan to be amongst her first visitors.*

Elizabeth felt this was the best path without displaying anger or hurt. She was hurt, and it had taken her some time to confront the uncomfortable truth of it. The knowledge that secrets were a part of marriage, and that a lifelong friendship did not penetrate that intimate bond between two people.

And the carriage ride. Oh, she wished she could be angry with Cassie and Thea for putting the idea of Mr. Sinclair in her head. He did look at her, and always with delight in his expression. A vainer woman, a younger woman, would have read far more into it than she knew she should.

Then, in a quiet moment, alone, she let her mind wander. What would marriage be like? Not the marriage of a man desperate for another son, but one of mutual respect, interest, and affection. She had once dreamt of such a union, with Mr. Rutherford.

That did not turn out the way of her dreams.

This time, though? It felt indulgent. So for just one moment, that one, precise moment, she let her mind wander. What was it like to wake to a familiar face? She knew Maria Thorne shared her bed with Henry every night for she often made little comments about it. She could not even imagine, not really, how that would feel. To always have someone to rest cold feet against.

"Eliza!"

Elizabeth dropped her pen, splattering ink all over her letter to Maria.

"Eliza! Where are you!" That was Thea, calling out from downstairs like a common worker.

Elizabeth patted her cheeks, finding them warm to the touch. She should not have allowed her mind to wander like that, but she hurried downstairs to find Thea, Susan, and Alice taking off their hats.

"And where did they find you?" Elizabeth asked her sister. "And, your mother would have swatted you with her fan if she were alive right now."

"Ugh. Cassie abandoned me to walk off with Mr. Baldwin," Thea said as she handed her bonnet to the footman. "I can only stay for a moment, she's going to stop by when she's done flirting, but I saw your charming friends and I was so bold! And asked if I could accompany them back to give you a surprise. Why weren't you out shopping today? Why is your face so red?"

Elizabeth laughed, and felt her face grow hotter. "I was so engrossed in my letterwriting that you all frightened me! I jumped so far out of my chair that I splattered ink everywhere."

"Oh no!" Susan said, but she was smiling. "We saw your aunt while out. She is not quite done buying up all of London."

"Then I am very happy she is feeling well enough to overload the courier!" Elizabeth said with a laugh.

Tea was called for as they awaited both Aunt Cass and Cassie's arrivals. Thea happily told them the intimate details of Cassie and Mr. John Baldwin, including his family's connections, his favourite colour, his favourite meal, and how much he was due to inherit beyond his current income.

"He sounds very agreeable if this were a letter," Susan said, "but is he a good match for her?"

"Oh, indeed! They are so rude to everyone when they are together," Thea said.

"How is that a good thing?" Elizabeth asked with a laugh.

Thea rolled her eyes. "People in love are always rude because they only have attention for each other."

Memories of Mr. Sinclair's smile as he rode alongside the carriage, the way he always spoke to her, turning his entire body in her direction. Never just a turn of the head. No, he always turned his entire body to face her. To bow. To smile.

Had she misread him?

No. No, she was listening to the foolishness of a lonely heart.

"And how do you like Miss Talbot? I think she is lovely and so elegant, but I do not like her gowns, but Cassie says I must not say so for she is poorer than we are!"

"Pray, how much cake and tea have you had today, dearest?" Elizabeth asked her sister, which brought laughter from the other ladies.

Thea looked offended. "Not much."

"How much is not much?" Elizabeth asked.

"Just the two slices here, and then some with breakfast, and then I had tea with Mr. Baldwin when he first visited, so that was a few more slices. Then, I had some coffee, too." Thea stopped and then said, "Well, I am very hungry!"

They all laughed about how difficult it must be for Thea not wishing to eat meat, and how Julia had worked so hard to learn how to make soups Thea liked when a knock came at the door.

"Oh, that must be my aunt," Elizabeth said.

But a man's voice, footsteps, and then the butler announcing, "Mr. Osborne, ladies."

Elizabeth and the other ladies stood abruptly to curtsy. Elizabeth smiled at him and said, "Ah, good morning, Mr. Osborne! You find us quite at leisure this morning."

"Excuse me ladies," Mr. Osborne interrupted her, rather rudely if Elizabeth was any judge. He grabbed his hat off his head and held it in front of him, tight-knuckled grip with both hands. It could have been a trick of the eye, but Elizabeth was certain sweat beads formed on his forehead. "I must...Forgive me, ladies, Miss Knight, but I wish to speak with Miss Markson. Alone."

Sally was standing there with a log of firewood in hand, unsure of what to do. She glanced at Elizabeth, and then Elizabeth said, "Ladies. To the dining room please."

Elizabeth was the last to leave, each one of them curtsying to Mr. Osborne as they left the room, as if the man needed the distraction from the very important question they all hoped would soon be coming forth from his mouth.

"We cannot hear if the door is closed!" Alice loud-whispered.

Elizabeth made a shooing gesture, and they all filed into the dining room to giggle and gossip. Elizabeth found a warm, soft feeling in her soul as she thought about what a good man Mr.

Osborne was and how, finally, *finally*, he was asking Susan to marry him.

"Mr. Osborne is quite the dashing gentleman!" Thea exclaimed. "Is he not? I thought him so the first time I saw him."

"I am so happy for her!" Alice said as she pulled out a chair. "Oh, I am so disappointed your aunt missed this."

"I have no doubt they will be very happy together,' Elizabeth said.

Then the door to the drawing room flung open so fast it hit the wall. The three ladies in the dining room rushed to see what had happened, as a wailing Susan rushed by them toward the stairs.

"Susan! Please wait!"

That was Mr. Osborne, chasing her to the bottom of the stairs. He turned and caught Elizabeth's eye. "Miss Knight."

"What has happened?"

Mr. Osborne was glanced back over his shoulder, back to the stairs, back to the wailing sounds of his beloved. "I asked her to marry me, but...she refused."

"Why would she do that?" Thea blurted.

Elizabeth did not wish to chide her sister, but also she had the same question. "Refused?"

Mr. Osborne said, "I do not know what I did to offend her. I thought…Is it too soon since the death of her aunt?"

"Wait right there, sir," Alice said sternly.

"Alice, wait!" Elizabeth called after her.

"Do not caution me, Eliza. I shall fix this," Alice called back as she raced up the stairs.

"Forgive me, but what possible reason did she give you?" Elizabeth asked.

"No reason, miss. She said she loved me, but that she could never marry me. And then, as you saw." Mr. Osborne looked back up the stairs as the wailing increased. "I do not wish to force her to do anything against her will, if that is not her…I do not understand. Forgive me, Miss Knight. Miss Thea. Forgive me."

With that declaration, Mr. Osborne fled the scene of his heartbreak.

"I cannot! Do you not see!" Susan wailed so clearly through the house.

"Why would she say no?" Thea asked.

"Not now, dearest." Elizabeth turned to Sally. "Is there any reason she would refuse him?"

Sally curtsied. "I have heard her say she is not in his class, miss, and a man of his situation should be looking to someone more worthy."

Elizabeth sighed. "Thea, stay here. I shall go after him."

James opened the door for her, and she rushed outside without coat or bonnet or proper footwear. "Sir, wait! I beg you! Please stop."

Mr. Osborne continued to walk away.

"Mr. Osborne, sir! I request an audience." Elizabeth used her eldest sister voice. The one that announced she was displeased, and would not accept a refusal.

To his credit, Mr. Osborne only took two more steps before stopping. He turned and walked back to her where she stood in front of her aunt's house drawing the attention of neighbours' servants and delivery boys.

He bowed when he reached her. "I apologize, Miss Knight. That was rude of me."

"Sally tells me Susan has struggled with the differences of rank," Elizabeth said, unsure of how to navigate this situation. "I do not know how to explain it, to you or to her. But I feel that I should, at least, speak for my friend and the sorrow I know she must be feeling."

"Miss Knight, I did not delay…" He frowned. "My hesitation, Miss Knight, has never been due to the circumstances of her birth. But rather I wished to both give her the time to grieve the passing of her aunt, and to also warm to the truth, that I find in her the worthiest of women, and there are none that could replace her in my heart."

"Please, allow us to speak to Susan. Just for a moment."

"Forgive me for saying so, but she has refused me."

"My dear sir, she would not be the first woman to refuse an offer of marriage only to regret it once the shock has worn off." Elizabeth cleared her throat, realizing that she had used a rather harsh tone with him. "Allow her the opportunity to recover her senses. Then, in a few days, write her a very pretty letter. I am certain with a little sleep, and tea—"

The front door swung open, and a red-eyed Susan rushed down the stairs. "William! Please! I am so sorry!"

"My dear," he said.

"I do not know what came over me," she declared.

Mr. Osborne took off his hat. "I did not mean to offend you."

"You did not!" Susan cried out. "I only feel so unworthy..."

"There is no other woman in England as worthy as you. Or as kind. Or gentle. Or good. Or as beautiful. I want you to be my wife, but only if that is your desire."

Elizabeth did not know how to extract herself from this intimate moment, and decided the best way was to simply walk backward toward the house, never making eye contact. Then, she turned, when they were clasping hands in the street, and carefully escaped up the steps to the front door, which she pushed open.

"Well?" James asked, trying to look over her shoulder.

"I believe love is about to triumph," Elizabeth said.

"Thank the lord!" Alice cried out. "Finally, she can be wed and happy."

"For a woman who swears she will never marry," Elizabeth said, "I am surprised to see you in such support of matrimony."

"Susan deserves all that she desires, and that is Mr. Osborne. And, he adores her. And, more importantly, she adores him, since I would not abide her marrying for anything other than love. I would support her for the rest of her life than see her degrade herself like that."

"Thank you for that, Alice," Elizabeth said dryly.

"Well, it was what you were all thinking," Alice said, looking at Thea and the maids who'd gathered with relieved expressions on their faces. Then she smiled. "But none of that signifies anything since they are madly in love with each other, and she is about to be a wealthy woman. And good for her."

It was Aunt Cass who walked through the door first, and not the happy couple. Aunt Cass was beaming, and Susan was crying again, though in happiness.

"Look what I found on my step, making a spectacle for the neighbours," Aunt Cass said. "My permission has been asked for this marriage. I did not expect that as I approached my front door, I assure you."

Mr. Osborne cleared his throat. "Well, as Miss Markson has no living family, I turn to you, her friend and companion, and indeed to all of you members of the Ladies Occult Society, to ask your permission."

Elizabeth was certain Mr. Osborne had planned a speech, but it was pointless since he was drowned out by the exaltations of the others. Even Mrs. Cook came rushing from the kitchen, for fear someone else had died. When she was told the happy news, she wept in happiness, embraced Susan, and then declared she must be back to the kitchen lest her buns burn.

Elizabeth glanced toward the dining room. Well, there would be no occult work today. And a small, selfish voice worried that their little group would never be the same now that a man —a husband—was about to enter the picture. Soon, children. And then soon, too many responsibilities.

She watched Susan lead Mr. Osborne into the drawing room, where the others followed. She fell in, and kept her smile serene, for she did not wish a glum expression to sour the mood. For truly, Susan Markson was about to be safe and protected for the rest of her life by not just any man, but a man she adored. What more could a woman wish in life?

It was certainly more than she hoped for herself. So, she would be happy for another's good fortune.

Chapter 15

THE HOUSE WAS abuzz for the next two hours with wedding plans, as well as Aunt Cass suggesting every single town within a two-day ride of Bryden where they could purchase an estate. Then, plans for dinner parties to become better acquainted with the Osbornes. Then, plans for pearls, jewels, gowns, and bonnets. It took nearly two hours for the happy couple to extract themselves from Aunt Cass's giddiness, and only then by announcing poor Mrs. Osborne knew of her son's plans and must still be at home waiting and worrying of the outcome.

Susan grew more animated and flushed with each passing moment, and by the time she departed the house, looked the perfect image of a bride-to-be.

Miss Thorne decided to leave with Thea at that time, as well, for Cassie and Mr. Baldwin had not yet arrived to fetch Thea. Alice announced she planned to scold Cassie severely for abandoning her sister to strangers, and thought it would be an excellent joke.

"I am so happy for her." Aunt Cass dabbed at her eyes and said, "It is days like these I miss my George."

"Oh, Aunt," Elizabeth said. "Uncle Spencer would not want you to cry over him! If he were here, he would be teasing you for it."

"That horrible man," Aunt Cass said with great affection. "He was always pestering me like that. Why did I marry him again?"

"Well, if I recall the tale correctly, you were impressed by his income, and he maintained you were unable to resist his handsome, charming self." Elizabeth snickered. "I have come to suspect both hold a little truth."

They chatted on like that for the afternoon, along with the usual writing letters, answering invitations, and a few neighbours coming by for the news about the proposal outside. A letter arrived from Mr. Grant stating he would be returning soon, as he'd found several excellent prospects.

The two ladies were quietly writing their letters when they heard a carriage pull up and, a moment later, there was a knock at their door.

"Perhaps someone has come to propose marriage to you."

"Let us hope he is rich," Elizabeth said.

"Mrs. Henry Thorne," the footman called out as Maria was ushered in the room.

"Oh, good day, Mrs. Thorne!" Aunt Cass said.

Maria curtsied and said, "Forgive me for dropping in unannounced, Mrs. Spencer, but there is news from Bryden and I must speak with Elizabeth in private, if you do not mind," Maria said, interrupting all greetings.

"Is Papa…"

"Your father…does not improve, but there is another issue I wish to discuss, but please, Mrs. Spencer? May I be so incredibly rude?"

"Do not worry about me!" Aunt Cass said and stood up. "I should take a short rest in any case, with all of this walking about in the cold. It is good to see you, and I hope your news is not too grave. I shall see you are not disturbed."

With that, Aunt Cass left and closed the door behind her. In the distance, Aunt Cass could be heard giving orders to leave them alone.

"What is the matter? Is it G? Isabella?" Elizabeth burst forth, worry overtaking her.

"Henry wrote to me. I have come as quickly as I could," Maria said.

"You rushed to London? For that?" Elizabeth said. "Oh, was it because I had not written?"

"Yes, partially, I delayed for a day thinking your letter might have been slow arriving. However, G said she could endure two days back at home, and did not wish to come to town, so I hired a carriage and have come as quickly as possible. Do not be angry with Henry. Be angry with me, if you must."

Elizabeth put her hand on her chest and stumbled her way to a chair. "Maria, I honestly thought you were here to tell me my father was gone."

"Oh Elizabeth. I had not considered that. Oh, how foolish of me to worry you! I had only Henry's reputation in my mind and did not think. Oh, how stupid I am! I was selfishly thinking of only ourselves!"

"No," Elizabeth said, gasping for air. "There is no apology necessary. I. Forgive me. I cannot seem to catch my breath. The distance. You travelled all this distance. I had assumed…he was gone."

Elizabeth slapped her hand against her chest several time, just gulping down air. With the manner of Maria's arrival, she had been certain the end had happened. "Pray, ask the footman…ask for some wine, please. Just a glass."

Maria immediately opened the door and demanded someone fetch Miss Knight a glass of wine immediately. Within seconds, Maria arrived back at her side with a goblet mostly full of red wine. She sipped, slowly, for a light head would not be sensible.

"Oh Eliza! I had not even considered how my actions would appear." Maria collapsed on the sofa, nearest to Elizabeth. "Please forgive me for causing worry."

"You left G?"

"She insisted," Maria said. "She said if she went home, then she could distract your father until I return."

"But what excuse did you tell her?"

Maria's face was grave. "As much of the truth as I am permitted."

Elizabeth let out a breath and took another sip. Her heart was struggling to settle, and she turned her mind to setting her thoughts in order. The structured, sensible flow of ideas, questions, and information. That was how she would fix this.

"Henry said you did not take the news about poor Amelia well, and he feared he caused a rupture between us," Maria said into the silence.

"The circumstances of her birth are not her fault, and I would be distressed to discover Mr. Thorne thought I was harsh with the girl."

"Not her. Him."

Elizabeth stared at her wine as she realized how angry she was with Mr. Thorne. Recalling their encounter and how he had not come to visit, as was his usual course, she considered that perhaps her expression, if not her words, had been harsh.

"What is in your heart? Say what you are thinking."

Elizabeth wished to keep her anger close, to keep it secret and hers alone, but it appeared she had failed to keep her emotions in check. Maria was here as a wife, not as her friend. Elizabeth understood that much.

She took another sip of wine before saying, "I realize Mr. Thorne is not the first man to take advantage of a woman without family, of lesser rank. And I know Henry Thorne should have known better."

"You have never sounded more like your father than you do right now."

Elizabeth looked at her friend sharply, shocked that Maria would speak to her in such a manner. Her words were clipped, angry. "Forgive me for my bluntness, but I cannot lie to you. He should have known better."

"Yes, he should have. And she should have, too."

Maria pressed her lips together before speaking again. This time, her voice was calmer. Her emotions and defence of her husband pushed deep within to present facts. Elizabeth allowed her the silence and time to find her words.

"Henry was young when he met Amelia's mother. She was the daughter of a poor curate, as if any curates except our Mr. Sinclair are anything but. She was of age, well educated, and about to begin her life in service as a governess. Henry met her. You can suppose the rest."

"Yes, clearly I can," Elizabeth said.

"When her situation was clear to her, Henry removed her to the country with some trustworthy friends who concocted a dead husband to protect her reputation. No one knew her there, and a widowed distant relation of the large Thorne family? Very conceivable. But it was there, in the country, that she met the local blacksmith. Older, kind, and who did not care in the slightest about a baby that was not his. She married him, and did not tell Henry until after the ceremony."

"But why did Henry not marry her before the baby was even born? It is not uncommon in Bryden for the poor to delay marriage until the first born is about to come into the world. Henry could have." Elizabeth sucked in a breath. "I suppose his family would not allow it."

"You must think very little of Henry," Maria said, deep disappointment in her voice.

"I have had the highest regard for Mr. Thorne, and I have found my faith in him gravely shaken," Elizabeth confessed in the whisper. "To abandon her after using her…"

"Elizabeth! How could you think so poorly of him? I would not have married him if he were such a scoundrel. Surely, you must think better of my judgement than that! He offered, and *she* rejected."

"But why? In her situation?"

"Why destroy his future? What good is reputation if faced with poverty? He could be more use to her and to Amelia if he did not marry her. With her new husband, she was safe. No one cares about the local blacksmith marrying a young lady with an infant."

"I had not considered that," Elizabeth confessed.

"Henry insisted Amelia be sent to school, to a proper one in town. He visited her there, regularly, as a wealthy man supporting one of his poorer relations. God knows he wouldn't be the first doing that, nor the first man to use that excuse to cover up illegitimacy. And, in the end, being at school spared her from the illness that made her an orphan."

"I truly have found no fault in the girl! Nor her mother," Elizabeth said.

"Then what is your anxiety?"

"I had to hear about it from Henry in the street! Not from my friend. But on the street."

"I made a promise," Maria said.

"And I understand that, truly I do. Truly, I do." Elizabeth thought back to begging Mr. Thorne not to tell Maria about the book in her position. How she had not told her own sisters. But that was not what bothered her. And she had to confess it. "If I am to be honest, it hurt me to know that I, your oldest friend..."

"Was not privy to the things that a wife and husband might share?" Maria finished the thought for her. When Elizabeth nodded, Maria said, "Henry told me about Amelia when he proposed. In fact, he told me about her before he did. He told me about his gambling, about a widow of rank that took a fancy to him for a time, all of his sins. He laid them before me, then said he would come back the next day and ask me a question. If I could not accept his history, he said to instruct the servants to deny him entry."

"That is not the exact story you told me," Elizabeth said.

"Perhaps not, but the part where I told him I did not need to sleep on it, and that he could be a man and ask the question right then and there? That was true." Maria chuckled. "I was in love with him, and I did not care about some natural child in his past. I would do all I could to protect her, to befriend her, and to ensure her own reputation. If anything, knowing he did not toss them out of his memory improved him in my estimation. He did as a gentleman should."

This stung Elizabeth, far more than it should have. She understood the intimate nature of the relationship, in the descriptive manner Maria explained it to her. But then it had not occurred to Elizabeth that the very nature of that intimate act would bring on other forms of intimacy, of a trust that no two friends would share.

Because to share one's life, one's soul, one's body with another was very different than a friendship of daily tea and gossip.

"Have I offended you?"

For the first time, even including Mr. R, Elizabeth suddenly realized what she had been denied in life, and what she would never have. Not simply a husband. Not only protection. Not someone to bicker with amiably. But a companion to walk through the world, to know there would be no secrets.

"Not at all. I am merely surprised."

She would not allow this to destroy her faith in her friendship, nor her own trust in Mr. Thorne. It was a painful lesson to learn, but learn it she had.

Elizabeth smiled at her friend. "Please, however it is in your power, let Henry know that I do not hold him in a lower light, nor do I hold any actions of his against his dear Miss Amelia, who is blameless in all things. Assure him that I will call upon her when she arrives at Vane Park, and I will even embrace her as your own daughter, if that is your wish."

"It is," Maria said. "I shall never have my own, now you understand why I know that. It is me. It is my fault."

"It is not about fault!" Elizabeth declared.

Maria chuckled. "That is what Henry says."

"On that Mr. Thorne and I agree."

"He also says that it means we cannot have separate bedrooms anytime soon."

"Maria!"

"It is true!" Maria said laughing. "And for my part, I do not wish him that far down the hallway whenever my feet are cold."

"You are impossible!" Elizabeth said. "But, perhaps, you did choose well all the same."

"I believe I did," Maria said with a smile. "Now, let me tell you about Bryden. There is no real news to report, which is perhaps the best. Mrs. Knight is suffering a mild malady, she says to say, so she has not had the energy to be a regular correspondent."

She listened to Maria's small details from Bryden, with no new news, for which she was grateful. More worries about the old bridge, and how the country had been getting rain as opposed to town for once. Elizabeth steadied her heart, for Maria needed the comfort of knowing her friend did not judge her husband (however tempting it was). Her friend did not need to know what caused the ache in Elizabeth's soul, or even to know of the ache's existence.

No. That was for Elizabeth's quiet solitude. For if she were not to have a husband to share those thoughts, then she would not share with anyone else. And slowly, quietly, hardened her heart when Mr. Sinclair was finally mentioned.

Chapter 16

February 23, 1811
Saturday

MISS KEATS AND Alice spent the morning with Elizabeth —Susan was shopping with Mr. Osborne's mother—and they decided to work on the sisters' spellworking with disastrous results. Miss Keats and Alice offended Mrs. Egerton by not paying attention when she gave instructions on what was needed, and even Miss Gibbs, when summoned, found herself making glib comments about the giddiness of young ladies.

Elizabeth found herself unequal to the energy of Miss Keats and Alice, and felt rather excluded at times. She would not say so, of course, and assumed her feelings were simply of jealousy; Miss Keats had been the one to write to Elizabeth first, but Alice had taken over the friendship. Of course, as she chided herself inwardly, women were allowed to have more than one companion.

Having done nothing but offend several ghosts—the sisters refused to come forth after a while—Elizabeth decided it was best to call the visit to an end.

"Ladies, it appears this fine sunny day is affecting us. Shall we put away our books?"

The ladies protested that they would heed their lessons, and they apologized profusely for not turning their full attention to the occult.

"I do not take offence," Elizabeth said. "I find my own attention fading today. Might I suggest you both go off in search of Susan to spy on her purchases?"

Miss Keats' face beamed. "That is an excellent idea!"

"Oh, will you not come with us?" Alice asked.

Elizabeth made excuses, and it did not take many to convince the two ladies to hurry off after their friend. That left Elizabeth alone in a room with Miss Gibbs and Mrs. Egerton.

"In our time, Miss Thorne's parents would have married her off to someone on his deathbed," Mrs. Egerton said.

"And then Miss Keats could've been hired to be her lady's companion. All reputation-saving," Miss Gibbs added.

"To allow them to carry on in such a manner!" Mrs. Egerton said.

"Scandalous," Miss Gibbs said.

Elizabeth frowned at the door where her friends had just exited. "They are merely giddy young ladies. I do not see the harm."

A look between Mrs. Egerton and Miss Gibbs said they held a different opinion, but all held their tongues.

"I forgot how difficult the Wynn sisters were," Mrs. Egerton said, changing the subject.

"Indeed!" Miss Gibbs said. "I do not recall them being this impossible. If they were alive, I would give them a sore throat to force them to stop speaking!"

"Did I misunderstand the nature of healing magic, Miss Gibbs?" Elizabeth interrupted the ghostly discussion. "For I have been of the belief that it was not that focused."

Miss Gibbs gave a happy shrug. "Just keep healing sore throats until the right person is afflicted!"

"Please do not give our Miss Knight a bad impression of past occultists," Mrs. Egerton said sternly.

Elizabeth chuckled and said, "I do not believe our dear Miss Gibbs did anything of the kind."

"Oh, she did," Mrs. Egerton said with a sour expression. "*Once.*"

Miss Gibbs said nothing, but her wicked smile was confirmation enough.

"Miss Gibbs!" Elizabeth said. "How shocking!"

"Oh, no one died!" Miss Gibbs said.

"Our town was completely cut off for weeks for fear of plague!" Mrs. Egerton said. "Letters were not even allowed in!"

"Ah, but we had all of those officers roaming about, once the authorities determined it was merely a sore throat amongst the delicate young ladies," Miss Gibbs said. "My, what fun we had that summer."

Elizabeth put her hand over her mouth as she giggled. "Miss Gibbs! You are terrible!"

But the story of Miss Gibbs' mischief uplifted Elizabeth's spirits and soon she found herself fortified with cold ham and a jam tart, a little tea, and then, finally, she found herself restless. Her aunt had left on business, she'd said, and so Elizabeth decided she would accompany Sally part of the way to the shops for her own errands.

The conversation was light with the new housekeeper, who mostly was worried about doing the job well, despite reassurances that she had already been doing the role for some time. But "housekeeper" brought forth an image, it was true, and a young woman it was not. But Aunt Cass knew her own mind, and if she wanted Sally, then Sally she would have.

She caught the sight of a gentleman walking toward them. He did not recognize her as quickly as she did him, but his face brightened at the sight of her.

"Who is that gentleman, miss?" Sally asked.

"Mr. Sidney Sinclair," Elizabeth said. "My father's curate."

"Ah." Then, with a slight hesitation. "He is a very handsome young man, if I may be so bold, miss."

"Oh, I do not believe there is a single person in England who does disagrees, including himself," Elizabeth said. Then, when he came into speaking range, she said, "Mr. Sinclair! I thought you were still in the country."

He walked up and bowed deeply. "Alas, I had to break the news to my mother that I am richer than her. You can imagine the scene."

"I am certain she was delighted about your inheritance," Elizabeth said. "Sally? You do not have to wait for us. I know you have a great many errands today."

Sally curtsied, and said, "Yes, miss." Then when she was behind Mr. Sinclair, she looked over her shoulder at his very fine figure.

"That is my aunt's new housekeeper."

"She is very young!" He looked over his shoulder and caught her looking back. She smiled brazenly, before turning her attention back to her own tasks. He looked at Elizabeth, his own brazen smile upon his face. "Too young for me, I fear."

Elizabeth made a very unladylike sound, that approached one of Mrs. Egerton's groans. It made Sidney laugh.

"I have also been to the bank, and Mr. Grant already had everything arranged for me. So it is now official and my first purchase was Mr. Thorne's little cottage. My mother approves of my good sense, apparently. For once."

"Little! I believe it has three bedrooms upstairs, not counting the servants' rooms!"

"What are three bedrooms!" Mr. Sinclair said. "So, where are you off to today? Do you require company? I was walking in the direction of your aunt's house, in any case, to pay a visit, so we can return if you wish."

"Oh," Elizabeth said. "I'm flattered."

He gave her a curious expression. "I had worried you would be angry with me, for leaving your family."

Guilt hit her. She had been thinking of herself, of her own secret delights, when her family was nearly all in London because of Mr. Sinclair's hard work to care for their father's whims.

"Oh, Sidney," Elizabeth said. She cleared her throat. "I would never be angry with you. Of course you had to come to town! Your mother could not be informed by a letter, for such an important thing! Come, let us walk back to my aunt's and you can tell me all about Bryden, and then your poor mother's expression when she discovered the truth."

"Oh! She already knew. She has more spies than any general in history!"

"And she did not tell you?"

"No! My father wished to write, to say the subterfuge was no longer necessary but no! That woman decided to make me suffer. Mothers! You know how they can…Oh, Elizabeth. Miss Knight, how could I be so thoughtless!" He stopped walking and bowed deeply. "I am mortified."

"I took no offence," she said. "And I love hearing about your mother. That poor woman! So many terrible children who keep secrets from her."

"Have you been talking to my mother in secret, Elizabeth Knight, for those were her exact words!"

Elizabeth chuckled. "I have not yet made the acquaintance of your mother, I assure you. However, perhaps one day."

"As I have said before, that is my greatest fear in life," Sidney said. "Now, I must file my report. First, your sister has written you an impossibly thick letter that I have in my pocket. She says not to worry about her, that your father has been resting, and his moods have improved greatly with her arrival."

"Is that the truth?"

"He has been resting more than usual. I visited him before I left yesterday, and he was in his chair reading his newspapers and seemed very content."

"How is Isabella?"

"No great concern there. A slight malady, she says, but normal for one so far along in her condition, I suspect."

"Do you believe he's over the worst then?"

Sidney shrugged. They walked like that in silence, weaving around servants from Sir William's who all greeted her before hurrying off to their duties. Once alone again, he answered her: "There is always hope."

They walked along then, with not much more to say. He asked about the weather, and she about the state of the roads. She mentioned how dry it was in town, and he said it hadn't stopped raining in days. He came in a hired carriage, and she talked about her aunt's improved health. Boring. Safe. Dull.

"When will you move into Rose Cottage then?"

"It has been unoccupied for some time, so Mr. Perkins says I need to have the chimneys cleaned first, of course, and then we need to have some girls come in to scrub the walls and floors. Then, Mrs. Perkins will decide if it is ready for the carpets."

Elizabeth laughed. "Your situation is similar to my poor brother's! He is running into the same circumstances with his new abode, though my sister, Mary, is not making the task easier."

"Will Mrs. Fitzharding allow him to move in without tearing down the building to the ground and rebuilding in her image first?"

"I have been asked to intercede," Elizabeth whispered.

"Why are we whispering?" Sidney asked, also in a whisper.

"Mary has spies everywhere."

They shared a laugh and continued the walk to her aunt's house. After all, they were good friends, and good friends should be allowed to walk and laugh.

BY THE TIME they arrived at her aunt's door, Elizabeth found her worries had been unfounded. She enjoyed his company, and did not suffer any melancholy at seeing him, nor in the walk. Indeed, the continued news that her father improved, that G was settled, and that all was well boosted her spirits higher than they'd been since her arrival in London.

Indeed, she could carry on in this manner for some time.

She invited him to come sit for a quarter of an hour, of which he happily accepted and declared himself without any obligation for the remainer of the day.

"Surely your mother wishes you to dine with her tonight? Especially as you plan to leave for Bryden tomorrow!"

"Family dinner," Sidney said with great derision.

"For shame, sir!"

However, once inside, James said that Aunt Cass had not returned home, but that there was a gentleman waiting for her on a matter of business.

"A *young* gentleman," James emphasized. "I do not know him, however."

"Shall I leave?" Sidney asked. "I would not wish to interfere in your business."

"I cannot imagine who it would be, that the servants do not know. Perhaps it is one of the inquiries to a shop in town, about a special box. They were hoping to have it ready for me before I departed for Bryden."

"A box?" Sidney asked as James accepted his heavy coat, hat, and gloves.

She waved a hand. "Come, I am certain there is no business this young man has with me that you cannot hear."

"What if it is a proposal of marriage?" Sidney said with a laugh.

"Then I will be doubly shocked, as I have no time at present to turn my attention to a wedding."

"Oh Miss Knight!" Sidney said. "Your poor aunt must despair of you!"

"I am her favourite, and I can do no wrong," Elizabeth said in a haughty tone.

Elizabeth did not recognize the gentleman in the drawing room waiting for her, but Sidney clearly did.

"Arthur! What the devil are you doing here?"

This Arthur fellow jumped to his feet at their arrival, and accepted Sidney's outstretched hand. "This is Miss Knight, yes? We have not been introduced."

"Miss Knight? This is my brother-in-law's brother, Mr. Arthur Worsley. Arthur, this is Miss Knight. The butler told us you were here on business."

"Indeed. Um…"

"Well, what business do you have?" Sidney asked.

Sidney was not smiling. Oh, his face was serene, and pleasant, but it did not reach his eyes. Those were questioning, suspicious, and his tone matched. Elizabeth turned back to the man, all of them still standing as she had not taken a seat nor invited them to. Mr. Arthur Worsley was a very handsome man. The kind of man that made any woman under twenty-five catch her breath. Tall, but not too tall. Broad, but not in a displeasing manner. Wore his breeches very well indeed.

And had a rather guilty expression upon his face.

"I see I do not need to call for tea," she said, gesturing at the pot, cups, and a simple platter of food. She sat down and invited them to do so. The two gentlemen sat opposite of each other, with her forming the top of the triangle. She smiled. "So, how may I assist?"

"Well," Mr. Worsley said, clearing his throat. "I have come to inquire about a private book sale."

Sidney's reaction would have made her suspicious of this man regardless, but the mention of a private book sale? She guarded her expression. "Are you selling or purchasing, sir?"

Mr. Worsley glanced at Sidney, but found no support in that quarter. He pulled folded paper from a hidden pocket and passed it to her. "Purchasing, on behalf of the Royal Occult Society."

She took the folded sheet of paper, but did not unfold it. "I have not sold any books in some time now, sir, and to speak very frankly, my aunt has stated the Royal Occult Society is not welcome in her house after the scene on her front steps."

"Many of us are very…embarrassed by the scene that took place here during your book auction," Mr. Worsley gave her a wide smile. It faded at Sidney's unyielding stare. "We have been in search of a number of books, and it is no secret that you are amongst the preeminent collectors of occult manuscripts."

She opened the folded paper. Two columns of book titles, year of publication, and a sum of money next to each. She recognized several. Some she still owned. Some she sold.

And three were her autograph books.

Elizabeth possessed enough experience that the listed prices were reasonable in principle, but that did not signify anything, for not a million pounds would tempt her to sell the autograph books. To sell the books would be to sell Mrs. Egerton. To sell Miss Gibbs. To sell the Wynn sisters. To sell the countless lady occultists she had yet to meet.

None of that really signified anything, as she'd also told that odious Mr. Baxter of the Royal Occult Society that her autograph books had been destroyed.

Curiously, though, her expensive book was not on the list. So that was a small relief.

She refolded the paper. "I do not have a list of my library at present, as it is in Bryden. However, I would be very willing to write home and request they send it. I do not believe I have any of these, but I am happy to check."

"None of those?" He asked.

"As you know, I inherited a great number of books, and have sold many of them. I do not wish to promise something I cannot deliver." She stood abruptly. "However, my youngest sister is at home at present, and I shall send for my list. If I find any particular book you desire and I wish to negotiate the sale, I shall have Mr. Grant approach you. I believe you know him."

Mr. Grant had once been an attorney for the Royal Occult Society, who had been dismissed because he defended her honour in the manner of a proper gentleman. Oh, they knew him.

"Yes," Mr. Worsley cleared his throat. "Yes, of course. But pray, *none* of the titles seem familiar? Perhaps you might wish to take a second look."

She did not do as he suggested. "One of the botany titles is familiar, but I believe I already sold that one to Mr. Osborne. Have you checked with him?"

"No, oh no. I thought...I thought I should speak directly with you as an excuse to make your acquaintance." He glanced at Sidney. "Forgive my forwardness, of course."

"If I find there is anything I wish to sell, should Mr. Grant address the letter to you at the Royal Occult Society? Will you receive such a letter with those directions?"

"Yes...yes, of course."

"Then, I am very happy to have made your acquaintance today, and I will not take up more of your time."

It took Mr. Worsley longer than it should have to recognize the dismissal. In fact, it took Sidney bidding him good day before Mr. Worsley took the hint. She did not move from her position until she heard the front door close behind him. It was then she let out a breath. She tossed the letter upon the nearest chair and began to pace.

How dare that man show up in her aunt's house in such a manner? And the gall of the man to act like he was doing her a favour, when it was the Royal Occult Society who had attempted to turn her father and her own brother against her!

And to dare show his face in this house, after the trouble they had caused for her! She should have demanded the footmen drag him from the house for all of the neighbours to see!

Sidney remained silent as she paced, though he moved to the window. From there, he made no secret that he was gawking out on to the street to watch Mr. Worsley walk away.

"Elizabeth, forgive my forwardness, but I believe you just told a falsehood to Arthur."

She stopped her pacing to stare at Sidney. "And why would you say that, sir?"

He removed his finger from the curtains and allowed them to fall back into place. "Because I know you."

Several unkind words warred within her mind, before she could bring herself to speak with the neutrality expected of her. "Forgive my forwardness, sir, but your Mr. Worsley came to trick me."

When Mr. Sinclair did not say anything, she said, "The Royal Occult Society has thus far attempted bribery, intimidation, threats, and trickery. All have failed, so I suppose they have debased themselves with an attempted flirtation to gain access to my book collection. Will they attempt a seduction next? I will not tolerate such treatment."

Sidney walked to the open door of the drawing room, and closed it. He leaned against it and asked, "What do you possess that makes them threaten a young lady?"

Every fiber of Elizabeth's self-survival told her not to whisper a word to a rich man. Every piece of skin and bone that made a person real screamed in her mind to lie to him. If her trust was misplaced, if she had allowed her affections to deceive her, he could do more than ruin her: he would *destroy* her.

And yet.

Her heart, betrayer that it was, said she should trust this man she called a friend. If she could not trust him, right now, in this moment, then who could be trusted? Certainly not herself.

And, after all of the discussions of late about husbands and wives, and the intimacy of their bond, the loneliness and isolation of Elizabeth's heart ached more than ever. She had never felt so alone as she had this trip to London, and she knew she could never go back to how it once was. Her childish notions of life and friendship had been shattered. She would never know love, not in the way of lovers.

"I apologize, I did not wish to force a confidence," he said. "I asked only in concern for your safety and wellbeing."

"I have, in my possession, a book worth three thousand pounds that my family is not aware of its existence, and I have three books that hold the ethereal existence of centuries of ghosts, of which two speak to me upon command."

She blurted it all in one breath. Terror filled her, the horror of knowing she had just exposed the most vulnerable part of her soul.

Sidney stared at her, his face going through several expressions before he bowed. Deeply. "I am honoured that you would entrust me with such information."

"Please do not tell anyone," she whispered. "It could ruin me."

He put his hand on his chest, over his heart. "I will protect your secret with my very life. I swear it to you, to God himself who will condemn my eternal soul if I betray that oath."

Elizabeth's jaw trembled. "Truly?"

"My dear Miss Knight! Elizabeth, my friend. My dearest friend," he said with such urgency it startled Elizabeth. He cleared his throat, realizing the forcefulness of his own tone. In a more reserved manner, he asked, "Is the book for your protection when you father is called to heaven?"

She nodded.

"And these other books, will they be for sale?"

She shook her head. "No. Very few people know of these four books. The Society had an awareness and some knowledge of my uncle's collection, and have been taking extraordinary measures to obtain some, or all, from me. At one point, they attempted to trick my own brother into hiring highwaymen into stealing it from me."

"My God!"

"Sending a handsome young man to my aunt's house is not overly offensive, in that light."

"Would we consider him handsome?" Sidney asked.

Elizabeth laughed. "Well, some young ladies must for the Society to think he would have me dissolving like sugar."

"They clearly do not know you," Sidney said with a chuckle, one in which she shared. "Elizabeth? Did you mean what you said, that you have ghosts that you can speak with?"

"Indeed," she said cautiously.

"How extraordinary," he said. "I have many acquaintances in the occult world, though none I would call a friend outside of yourself, of course. I have heard this was a skill in the past, and that there are records of it, but that the talent was lost."

"Not lost, sir. Just hidden. I would never have allowed those awful men to have my autograph books—that is what they are called—for they were left to me by my uncle. He left me many others with the clear intention for me to sell them. Then my cousin, David Leigh, gave me the entire occult library from my uncle's house, also with the expectation that I would sell some of it." She sighed. "But none of that matters now. I have two—nay! Four now!—of the ghostly occultists resting within the book's pages. No, I would never betray them in such a manner as trading them for a little coin. No, sir. To me, that would be the same as trading away one of my friends. I could not do that. As for the other books in my collection? Well, those will be for Mr. Grant's attention I suspect, when the time comes."

"And do these occultist ghosts appear at your whim? Might I be introduced, for example?"

Elizabeth continued to be amazed at how easily the world accepted she talked with ghosts when not even the Royal Occult Society could at present. "Mrs. Egerton, one of the ghosts, does not like men, and, unfortunately, I do not know how to summon other ghosts without her assistance."

He smiled. "No men? Not even charming ones with a substantial inheritance?"

"She would find you less repulsive in that light. Perhaps." The curtains about the room all moved at once. "I believe that is my warning to stop, sir, lest I offend Mrs. Egerton."

"Well, I do not wish the wrath of an occultist ghost, I assure you," Mr. Sinclair said, laughing. He was interrupted by the door and the sound of Aunt Cass' voice. "Ah, let us act natural, to avoid raising suspicions."

"Suspicions of what?"

"I am not certain myself!"

They were both laughing when Aunt Cass walked into the room to greet her company.

SUSAN RETURNED ONLY to beg everyone's permission to stay at Mrs. Osborne's, who wished to get to know her future daughter-in-law better. Aunt Cass reminded Susan she was not her mother nor her mistress, but laughed anyway as she gave her permission. Elizabeth, too, said she was not remotely offended. Besides, Alice was with her parents for the next two evenings due to family obligations, and even Miss Keats was being kept busy by her sister-in-law. Cassie and Thea were, of course, enjoying the Baldwin's hospitality.

"Go!" Aunt Cass had said.

Which left Elizabeth alone, writing in her room by candlelight. She felt no animosity toward the others. She had been relying on the occult and the busyness of town, all of the rushing here and there, and the constant flow of visitors to keep her mind off of her father.

But with only her fireplace and a thick candle in a glass lantern in a mostly silent house, she was left alone with her fears and feelings. There, she began to tread too close to being low, of the melancholy of isolation and loneliness.

Therefore, the only choice left was for her to write a letter to G, asking her sister about the state of the roads, about the pantaloon adventures, about what they had for dinner that evening. Nothing. Meaningless nothings.

She left the letter unfinished and took out her occult journal, where she had made extensive notes concerning Miss Gibbs' locket, the sisters, and the nature of summoning. Aunt Cass coughed, but only occasionally, having once again exhausted herself out visiting and enjoying the freedom afforded improved health. She always recovered, but Elizabeth feared her lungs could not keep taking the damage of breathing in such filthy, diseased air as in town. She hoped Mr. Grant found an agreeable situation for her soon, and selfishly hoped that solution would be within an easy distance of Bryden.

Elizabeth worked until she needed to stir her fire, adding another log. She could have called for a footman to do it, but she knew how to stir a dwindling fire. She should make the attempt now, for there was no knowing how her days would go. Her father, even if he was recovering, or even recovered fully, would not live forever. One day, he would be called to leave this world. On that day, she would be called to leave her own earthly comforts.

Stirring a fire would be the least of her worries on that day.

Tired of her own thoughts, Elizabeth summoned Mrs. Egerton to help her with possible reasons Miss Gibbs' half of the locket did not work. Elizabeth made a list on a sheet of paper, scratching and adjusting as necessary. When happy with the resulting possibilities, Elizabeth carefully wrote them out into her occult journal. When the ladies were together, she would summon Miss Gibbs and they would investigate each idea in a sensible, methodical manner.

"Perhaps we should abandon the notion of any useful summoning on the Wynn sisters at present," Elizabeth said, utterly defeated. "I fear if we cannot join poor Miss Gibbs to a locket to allow her to see the world, then how are we to work with two sisters who despise one another and yet seem determined to be bound together in that dislike for all eternity."

"Do not say that within hearing of either," Mrs. Egerton chided, "or we will never get any peace from those two."

Elizabeth chuckled and continued writing. She read aloud and then wrote down Mrs. Egerton's comments. It was companionable silence off and on, nothing awkward.

Until Mrs. Egerton decided to ask a question. *The* question.

"Are you in love with Mr. Sinclair?"

Ink splattered. Quickly attempting to clean up her mess, Elizabeth laughed and said, "Whyever would you ask that?"

"In my time, we never allowed such familiarity before the marriage was arranged. Such matters as a life partner can not be trusted to the young." Mrs. Egerton watched Elizabeth clean and blot and settle herself. "Your Mr. Sinclair dresses in such a ridiculous manner."

"I admit Mr. Sinclair does wear his collars higher than what is necessary for the country, I will grant you that, but he is very well dressed for the age in which I now live," Elizabeth said with a chuckle. Then, she winced a little at Mrs. Egerton's piercing gaze.

When it was clear Mrs. Egerton wanted more than that, she said, "I find myself…I find. I shall regret when he leaves Bryden."

"He has purchased property. I cannot understand why you would think he has a scheme to eventually leave. And you, my dear, have not answered my question."

"Would you be angry with me if I was in love with any man?"

"Any man? I would be gravely disappointed. You deserve more than *any* man."

"That is very kind," Elizabeth said meekly. "And him?"

"I find myself growing fond of him, despite his inability to dress himself like a sensible man, though I do prefer that blue coat of his. It is a very manly colour."

"He does wear that coat well," Elizabeth whispered.

"Is that your only word on the subject?"

Elizabeth swallowed hard past a lump in her throat. "If he were a poor curate, or the son of a clergyman? Perhaps I would have deluded myself by now that his polite smiles were more than friendship. But I do not have that luxury with such a gentleman, no matter how I feel every time he calls me Elizabeth. I ask that you do not pry further into my heart. For I have only just discovered its secrets, and now that I know what is there? I have begun to harden myself."

"Oh my dear Miss Knight," Mrs. Egerton said. "Then I pity you."

"Do not." Elizabeth smiled at the ghost. "I have no expectations. Now, let us turn back to the occult, shall we? I find it very diverting."

Chapter 17

February 25, 1811
Monday

ELIZABETH WAS FACED with a sea of cloth samples. All blue. And all to Elizabeth's eye, the *same* blue. She even turned the display to catch the sunlight pouring in from the window in hope of finding subtle differences. They still appeared to be the same blue.

"Well?" Susan asked nervously.

"They all seem very elegant," Elizabeth said. "Which do you prefer?"

"I do not know!" Susan said. "They are all so expensive."

"My dear Susan!" Aunt Cass said. "We have discussed this at length. I shall be purchasing your wedding gown. All that is required of you is to choose a fabric, and then my seamstress will make you whatever gown you so desire."

"But it so expensive!" Susan said.

"What about this one?" Elizabeth asked, pointing at one of the blue swatches of silk. "That would make a very pretty gown, and then you would have something to wear to dinner parties."

"Dinner parties!" Susan exclaimed.

Aunt Cass glared at Elizabeth. "My dear girl. The entire purpose of marrying a rich man is so that you do not have to worry about money. Isn't that right, Elizabeth?"

"Indeed it is! Susan, my dear, you must listen to my aunt. If she says she will purchase your silk, you must allow her. Otherwise, she will purchase all the silk in London and then we will have to go into trade to rid ourselves of it. Think of the scandal!"

"Thank you, Elizabeth," Aunt Cass said dryly.

One of the footmen entered the drawing room with a silver platter. He presented to Elizabeth. She recognized Mary's handwriting and opened it immediately.

> *My dear sister, I find myself alone and in need of light company and conversation with someone who will not aggravate my head. Do not assume this is a summons if you are busy with other tasks. Only if you wish to escape the tedium.*

She offered a smile and said, "There is no alarm. Mary wishes some sisterly companionship today if I am available."

"Mary?" Aunt Cass asked. "Why, yes, you should go!"

"Indeed you should!" Susan insisted. "Mrs. Spencer and I can fight about silk and lace without your assistance, I assure you."

"I do not wish to break up our little party!" Elizabeth said. "This feels very rude! And Mary said it was not a summons. She is only lonely, I believe."

"Elizabeth," Aunt Cass said, "if Mary wishes to heal the breach, you must accept the offering when it is made."

"If I am to be honest," Susan said, "I am exhausted from decisions. I have barely been engaged and I already wish to elope."

"Truly, you will not be offended? Mary so rarely asks in such a manner that I feel I must attend her, for no other reason than to calm my own worries."

They assured her they would not, so she left soon after. The weather was decent enough to make the short walk to Mary's, and Elizabeth found she enjoyed the brisk walk in the February air. Once arrived, she assumed she would be ushered to Mary's closet, as they all called the small, north-facing room. Her sister had said it had once actually been a closet that servants rearranged for when her head pains were upon her. It was windowless, but had bright paper on the walls, and the furniture was all comfortable, with plenty of blankets and pillows for Mary's comfort.

However, Mary was seated near a window with sewing in her hands when Elizabeth arrived. They greeted each other, and tea was ordered. Her husband was gone for the day, visiting his family. She had declined, due to having awakened with head pains. However, it faded after a good breakfast and some time alone. So she found herself quite alone and at peace, but perhaps light on company.

"Why did you not invite the girls?" Elizabeth asked as the maid brought in the tea things, and a platter of delights. "I'm certain at least one of them would have been happy to visit, as well."

"I considered it, as I have barely seen them since their arrival in London. But I must confess I do not believe my nerves can handle how loud they can be, especially Thea. Is that very unsisterly of me?"

"Between ourselves and these walls? I frequently understand why our father loses his temper, for there are days I also wish to rant and throw pillows at the three of them."

That made Mary chuckle. Elizabeth went through the charity basket on the floor and found some children's clothes in need of finishing, so spent a few moments setting up needlework and mending alongside her sister. While doing that, she told Mary about Susan's engagement and the discussion about silk.

"I did not mean for you to come if you had company! I am certain I was very clear in my letter."

"Oh, do not distress yourself over it." Elizabeth threaded her needle and said, "I find myself in rather good spirits to sit quietly, sewing clothes for the poor, and having tea with my sister. Is there any word from Bryden?"

"I received a letter from G this morning. She has returned to Vane Park. She says Isabella is unwell, and felt unequal to keeping G company. Of course, you know what Georgiana is like in her letters. Three paragraphs could not contain how there was no cause to dismiss her, for she could have been assistance, she assured me. However, Isabella wished the solitude."

"I hope it is nothing serious," Elizabeth said. "I have not received a letter from Isabella in several days now."

"Neither have I," Mary said. "My last report was from Mr. Thorne, when he visited before leaving for Bryden."

"Mr. Sinclair visited us on Saturday, and returned to Bryden yesterday. He reported my father quiet, reading mostly, but no immediate problems," Elizabeth said.

"Perhaps we are finally past the point of worry," Mary said. Then she sighed and said, "Now, we can turn our attention to worrying about Aunt Cass and Isabella."

"Well, Aunt Cass continues to improve, and when Mr. Grant returns from the country, he may be able to persuade her to leave town."

Mary held up her sewing for a moment to inspect her work before returning to her seam. "Would it be too much to hope for her to move near Ashbrook?"

"I would not object to her being nearby, I confess," Elizabeth said.

Half an hour passed in such a manner, and Elizabeth found herself rather enjoying Mary's company. Her sister had been trying, had taken words to heart, and Elizabeth found forgiveness stirring within her. More then forgiveness. *Understanding.*

"I met Mr. John Baldwin last Friday," Mary said casually.

"And what is your opinion?"

"Cassie seems to think highly of him," Mary said.

"And what is *your* opinion?" Elizabeth repeated.

"I could find no fault in him. He seems an excellent young man. A bit flighty, perhaps, but that might be due his age more than any fault in his nature. What are your thoughts?"

Elizabeth gave a little shrug. "I met him at G's coming out ball. I think I would have liked him, even if I did not know he had a thousand a year."

"Eliza! Be sensible."

"I am! But since it seems no man in England wishes to marry me, I must worry about my sisters securing their futures."

Elizabeth had meant the words in jest; in fact, she'd laughed when she said them. Mary did not laugh. She stared at Elizabeth, clearly working up her courage for something.

"Mary, what is it? I was only teasing myself."

"Is there something between you and Mr. Sinclair?"

It did not surprise Elizabeth that Mary had asked, given Thea's slip at dinner about the entire Sidney/Elizabeth situation. Silly of them to have thought the others would never hear; in Bryden, even the trees gossiped.

But she smiled, priding herself that she was hardening to it all. "Mere friendship, and only that, I assure you."

Once again, Mary hesitated, mulling over her words. "Would you be inclined to feel more?"

Elizabeth looked about the room, but there were no servants about. "Mary…"

Mary held up a hand, hoping to silence the protests. Elizabeth allowed her sister to speak on the topic she wished most to avoid. "You do not even call Henry Thorne by his Christian name, a man we have known for a very long time. You struggle to call my husband by his name. Yet, *Sidney* seems to easily roll off your tongue."

"Of what do you accuse me?" Elizabeth demanded, heat rising in her heart.

"Of nothing," Mary said. "Please. I do not know how to speak to you about… Eliza, we used to be closer than any two people alive. Mr. Rutherford is the only other man I know of that you have referred to in the intimate. And now, Sidney Sinclair. What am I to think? So simply answer my question. Would you be inclined to feel more?"

"Mr. Sinclair—Sidney, if you wish—is an excellent man. There is a kindness within him, and he will one day make an excellent, kind husband, and father. But." She held up a hand to silence her sister. "*But.* Even if we set aside my poverty, my lack of beauty, my age, and the complete and utter disrespect I have shown him on a regular basis, my younger sister is in love with him. I would be a terrible example to other sisters if I were to disregard her feelings in this matter."

"If you do not wish to answer the question…"

Mary was pushing, far too deep for her liking. Elizabeth did not wish to lie, not now. Not as they were finally attempting to repair the bridge between them. And yet, Mary had bumped against a very sore bruise, and Elizabeth could only use humor to deflect. "I assure you, I thought I was answering the question. On what point do I offend you?"

"I know I have made many mistakes, and they are the reason we are no longer friends."

"Mary…"

"Do not deny it. I have allowed hurt and bitterness, and well. It does not matter the reasons, for I still did make those mistakes." Mary put down her sewing to give Elizabeth her full attention. Her eyes were full of tears. "I know you never approved of my marriage to James."

"Those were not my words," Elizabeth protested. She glanced about her to ensure he was not about the room. "He is an excellent man."

Mary pulled out a handkerchief and dabbed at her eyes. "May we, for today, attempt to put aside all of …all of it."

"That is all I have ever wanted." Elizabeth's words caught in her throat. "I have missed having a sister that was my friend, and not someone I have to parent."

"Then I shall be very blunt with you. I do not just love my husband, Elizabeth. I am in love with him. The starry-eyed way that Thea looks at Sidney Sinclair is the way I look at my James when no one can see me."

Elizabeth's mouth dropped opened, and it moved several times before she managed to say, "Then I am happy you took your own path."

"I need you to know that I did not love him when I married him. I was terrified, in fact. Terrified of what…well, the things that a wife is expected to do and that I would be called upon. But we worked that one out in our own time." Mary snorted, lost in her own memories. She smiled, though. Smiled in a way she had not in front of Elizabeth for a very long time. "The first few months of our marriage were complex, as we discovered each other."

"And what did you discover?" Elizabeth asked, almost frightened to know the answer, but also desperate to understand the quiet trust and comfort between a man and a wife. She did not see that at home, and longed to know it existed in places other than novels.

"I discovered I loved him. That I had fallen *in* love with him. That I was not only happy with him. Safe. Protected. But that I could not imagine my life without him in it, and that I would not trade him for all of the men in England nor for all of the gold in this country."

Elizabeth had never heard Mary speak about a man with such conviction, and she knew she was hearing the truth of it. So her next words were filled with all of the joy in her heart. "Then I am so relieved, and so truly happy for you."

But then, Elizabeth's curiosity would not allow it to rest. For she asked, "But why tell me this?"

Mary drew in a deep breath and slowly let it out. "I want the same for you."

"As do I!" Elizabeth chuckled. Mary's fervour was worrying her. No, that was not right. Mary was worried.

About Elizabeth.

"Mary, I am happy."

"Do not lie to me."

It shocked Elizabeth to be spoken to in such a manner, and perhaps more so by Mary.

"Do not give me that shocked proper young lady expression, Elizabeth Knight. I know you too well. You are not happy. You have not been happy in ages. And the older the girls get, the more unhappy you become. The reason I keep inviting you to Ashbrook …" Mary sighed. "I thought you enjoyed being with the children, and so I pushed that, thinking it was what you wished. I had never meant to turn you into our governess. It was never my intention. I was only attempting to rescue you. And instead, I made the wedge between us worse!" Mary gasped out a sob and covered her mouth with her hand. "Forgive me."

Elizabeth had a choice then. She could lie. She could misdirect her sister.

Instead, she decided to be brave.

Elizabeth put down her sewing and stood up from the chair. She crossed the gulf to sit next to her sister on the sofa. She did not look at Mary, not at first. Then, she inhaled, decided it was time to forgive, to accept, and walk across the bridge.

"Was it James' idea to invite me today?"

She laughed between her tears. "It has been his idea to invite you for six months. I have not had the nerve, but after the dinner party…Even I knew I needed to muster my courage. And, I must point out that you have still not answered my question."

"No, I have not."

Mary sniffled and wiped her nose. "Will you?"

"I do not find it easy to speak of what is in my heart."

"And I find it difficult to admit when I am wrong, Elizabeth."

"Despite Mr. Sinclair's professed love of the countryside, I believe the time will come when he will leave us behind. And I have begun to feel the weight of that," Elizabeth's voice trembled. "And I have begun to harden myself against that eventuality. For my own sake."

Mary gripped her hands in hers. "I did not know. I wish you had told me! I would have done everything in my power to encourage…Even now, just speak the word and I shall, with your permission, do all that I can to promote your happiness."

"No, please Mary. I beg you, you must not tell anyone. Not even your husband!"

"I do not keep secrets from him! Or, we have agreed to not keep secrets from one another, and I cannot go back on that. It is…" Mary seemed to struggle for words. "It is how we…"

"I do not wish to pry into your marriage! But surely you are not required to announce the details of my heart unasked!" Elizabeth declared. "I do not want Mr. Sinclair to find out! It would destroy what little joy I have. What I want—nay, what I need—is for Sidney to always think of me as a friend. I wish him to always greet me fondly, to call on me with the future Mrs. Sinclair, to write Isabella sporadically, always leaving a line or two of some foolishness about his collars or his boots to tease me."

"But why only that when you want more?"

"I am nobody, a near penniless spinster. That is all I can hope for!"

"Oh, stop your nonsense!" Mary raised her voice at Elizabeth, shockingly. "Setting aside that I am your sister, and that my husband's name carries weight, you are also friends with Maria Thorne, of all people, and your aunt is Mrs. George Spencer. Do not think of yourself as a nobody, first and foremost, Miss Elizabeth Knight. If you have been thinking you will be living above a butcher's shop when our father is gone…oh indeed, you have been, haven't you?"

Elizabeth did not answer, for indeed, she had considered that.

"As if we would allow it!"

"I cannot ask…"

"Ask? There is no asking!" Mary insisted. "Enough with this, Elizabeth! You do not have to shoulder our entire family's problems upon yourself."

"All of the money must go to Charles! If Miss Talbot is as poor as everyone says…"

"We are planning to give Charles a thousand pounds of our own money so that he can marry his Miss Talbot! That, his income, her dowry, and his curacy? Provided they don't have a child every ten months they might survive without starving to death."

Elizabeth's mind wanted her to say ten different things, but all that blurted forth was, "Are he and Miss Talbot that serious?"

"He has said nothing to me, but I have heard it from James and Mr. Thorne that apparently he is absolutely in love with the girl and is only waiting to establish himself to ask for her hand."

"I had no idea," Elizabeth said in all astonishment. "No one tells me anything."

"I did not know myself until Charles arrived in town, chasing Miss Talbot, I might add."

"I do like her," Elizabeth said.

"As do I," Mary said.

Elizabeth smiled. "Look at us. Agreeing."

"What shall this world come to?" Mary said.

They laughed, a short bark at first, followed by loud unladylike laughter.

And Elizabeth, with the skill of an elder sister, distracted Mary into discussing Miss Talbot and Charles' potential marriage, as opposed to her own heart.

Elizabeth had not left the sight of Mary's doorstep when a carriage stopped and offered her a seat. It was Mr. Grant, returned from his house hunting, and she happily accepted. They arrived at Aunt Cass' slower than it would've taken her to walk, in all truth, but she enjoyed Mr. Grant's company and found it was the perfect opportunity to discuss something in private.

"Mr. Grant, might I take this opportunity to ask you a question of business."

"Well, of course Miss Knight! If it is in my ability, I shall be happy to comply."

"I wish to hire your services in the future, if I might be so bold."

"Indeed Miss Knight? What do you need?"

"There is a very expensive book in my possession that…I fear…I shall need to sell one day soon. Might I, when the time comes, write to you with the particulars for the auction?"

"Yes, of course, but why not simply engage Mr. Osborne?"

"The book is estimated to be worth three thousand pounds."

Mr. Grant gasped. "Oh. Oh, yes, I see the issue. You will need to sell this at Sotheby's. Yes, that is the best place for a book auction. Yes, yes. You will need a representative there, for you, of course. Would you prefer to be anonymous? I would act as your agent."

"Yes, please. That is exactly what I wish. You understand my situation, surely."

"Of course, of course! May I therefore write to you with the particulars, with fees, costs, all of those things, so that you are aware of how to price your book when going into auction. I shall consult Mr. Osborne, with your permission. That way, when the unhappy event occurs, you will not need to worry about details during a grievous time. Would that be acceptable?"

"Oh yes, Mr. Grant. Thank you so much. That is exactly what I would wish."

"I cannot promise that I can keep this from your aunt—the woman has supernatural talents at sniffing out gossip—but I shall try. To please you."

They talked business until, finally, the carriage pulled up to the house. She thanked you profusely, letting him know this greatly reduced her worries.

"Excellent. Now, let us go break the news to your aunt that I have found tolerable lodgings *deep* in the country."

Elizabeth laughed. "How deep?"

"They make Bryden look like London's rival," he said as he offered a hand for her to leave the carriage.

After the usual greetings, tea, and formalities, Mr. Grant got down to business. He unrolled three sheets of paper with tracings he'd made. "Apologies for the hurried nature. I am no artist, sadly, but I have attempted to capture the building plans as best as I could. Now, this first one is excellently situated. I have not seen it, I confess, but if you are interested, I shall ride out tomorrow. The rent is fair, and the grounds excellent, but it is located about an hour north of Coventry."

"I do not believe I know a single soul there," Aunt Cass said with a frown.

"That is why I did not make the journey, I confess. Now, there is a second option, about twenty minutes by carriage from Mrs. Fitzharding's house. A bit large for your needs, if I were to offer my opinion, but the rent is less than you would make letting out this place."

Aunt Cass sighed and said, "I would have to get a carriage just to visit Mary every day."

"Aunt!" Elizabeth exclaimed.

"Well! I only speak the truth."

"That brings us to the third. In Wollerton, near Vane Park, in fact. Now, I walked from the house straight to Bryden Rectory to accurately record the distance and time. I called on your father, Miss Knight. He was asleep, but your stepmother says to pass along that she continues to feel a little under the weather, just a slight tiredness, nothing to cause alarm, but that Mrs. Thorne and Mr. Sinclair have both been sending their housekeepers and they are all well cared for at present."

"Oh, thank you for doing that, sir! That was most generous," Elizabeth said. "My sister and I have been worried, as neither of us have heard from Isabella."

"Well, she says not to be alarmed, so I feel we must honour her wishes and not worry ourselves." Mr. Grant laughed. "Now, where was I? Ah, yes, I timed the walk at forty-two minutes, cutting across only an apple orchard, since I did not know the state of lady's footwear in the country. So provided Miss Knight is allowed to walk that distance without a chaperone, daily visitation will be easy enough. However, it is a little small for my tastes, and I fear one chimney smokes. On the good side, however, it is available for outright purchase."

"What about the cottage on Mr. Thorne's land?" Aunt Cass asked. "I am certain he was attempting to sell that."

"That is no longer available! For I did call there, as well," Mr. Grant said. He leaned forward and said in a loud whisper, "Apparently, a young man of means has spoken to Mr. Thorne about purchasing the property outright, but I know no other details. They said you would know, Miss Knight."

All eyes turned to her. "I believe I am still sworn to secrecy."

"You are impossible, Elizabeth Knight!" Aunt Cass declared.

"As silent as the grave, that one," Mr. Grant said in agreement.

Aunt Cass asked Elizabeth and Mr. Grant to stay as she gathered the servants. Elizabeth was still recovering from the visit with Mary, and was feeling her world closing in on her. But she sat, and answered the questions of the servants, until Aunt Cass nodded.

"Then it is settled. I shall be moving to *deep* in the country. May God have mercy upon my soul," Aunt Cass said gravely.

Elizabeth laughed. "Aunt! It is not that bad!"

Chapter 18

February 26, 1811
Tuesday
The Middle of the Night

HARD POUNDING UPON a door startled Elizabeth from her sleep. At first, she thought it was a dream, but then she heard voices, shouting, and heavy footsteps rushing up the stairs. She managed to bolt from bed and have her dressing gown in her hand when the frantic knock came at her door, as opposed to Aunt Cass'.

"Miss Knight? Miss Knight!" That was Sally.

At nearly the same time, she heard, "Mrs. Spencer!" in a man's voice; James the butler.

"I am awake!" Elizabeth called out as she struggled with her gown in the darkness.

The door opened to candles, servants, and chaos. In just her nightshirt, Sally curtsied and said, "Mr. Sinclair is downstairs with a carriage. He is here to fetch you immediately."

"Oh God," she whispered.

She was half down the stairs before realizing she was still struggling with her dressing gown. She stopped only long enough for Sally to catch the troublesome sleeve and Elizabeth wrapped herself before appearing before Mr. Sinclair barely dressed. As it was, she was barefoot, with a braid slung over a shoulder, with her sleeping cap on to protect her curls.

Her own self-consciousness vanished at the sight of Sidney's exhausted, drawn face, highlighted more and more as the footmen rushed to light candles.

"What has happened?"

She heard Aunt Cass coming down the stairs, and Sidney turned to give her a short bow before turning back to Elizabeth.

"Forgive me, Eliz—Miss Knight. Mrs. Spencer. Forgive my arrival."

"What has happened?" Elizabeth repeated, and with less patience this time.

"There is no easy way to say this, but you are needed in Bryden." He removed his hat, then wiped at his red eyes. "I apologize. We have been riding through the night. Miss Knight, there is no easy way to tell you. Your father was taken with a fit yesterday. No, Sunday. I do not remember what day this is, I apologize. He has slipped into a dream state of which we cannot rouse him from. He has taken to his room. He mostly sleeps, but wakes screaming at times. Or yelling at imaginary people. He mistook me for his father. When I attempted to correct him, I sent him into a rage." Mr. Sinclair ran his hand through his disheveled hair. "He had been screaming out for you for hours before Mrs. Knight begged I come.

"His father?" Elizabeth whispered. "But he has been dead for years now."

"So Mrs. Knight informs me. She begs you come home, miss. All of the servants but Julia have been dismissed, for he has attacked several of them. He often mistakes Julia for you, so she has been pretending to be so. God forgive us, but it is the only way to calm the man."

"Can Mr. Collins not do something?" Elizabeth interrupted.

"Mr. Collins cannot be seen by your father, for he believes he is his brother, apparently the one..."

Elizabeth raised a hand. "Yes, I know which brother. Oh good God. I shall leave as soon as the horses are rested."

"No need," Mr. Sinclair said. "I took post horses, and these are fresh."

"My sisters! We must…we need to get them."

"Begging your pardon, Elizabeth, Miss Knight, forgive my forwardness, I have not slept since your father's fit. Mrs. Knight and Julia both beg that the girls not come, not even Mrs. Fitzharding." He drew in a breath. "I have already stopped at the Fitzharding's, as they were along the path. I have informed her, and she will go to your sisters to explain."

"But they…" Elizabeth said. "Where is G?"

"Vane Park, she could not abide… Elizabeth, it is very dire. You must come."

"Miss Knight?" James bowed. "Write a note for your sisters and I will have two of the men deliver it for you, before you leave. I promise."

"Your father is in such a state that Mrs. Knight, Mrs. Thorne, my housekeeper, and Mrs. Thorne's housekeeper…everyone agrees. The girls should not be exposed to this, no matter the heartbreak of not saying their goodbyes." Mr. Sinclair gulped hard and his voice trembled. "Indeed, he is not my own father and yet I have found it very difficult in my own heart."

One of the footmen came around the corner from the direction of the kitchens. He was still in only a nightshirt and a dressing gown still open. "Mrs. Spencer? Mrs. Cook has the fires started, and there is cold food in the kitchen for your guest, as well as the coachmen. She has called over to Sir William's, as well, to inform them, and they are sending over hot water, as they were already awake with the laundry."

Elizabeth had not moved. She knew she must move; she must write her letter. She must do *something*. But to deprive her sisters of the opportunity to see their father one last time? Of course, dignity was to be maintained, and perhaps the others knew best. That the wailing of two young girls losing yet another parent would be too much for the dying. Even G abandoned home. Perhaps that would be the balm to soothe the injustice of it all.

"I can never repay your kindness, sir. For coming all this way in such haste," she whispered.

"I would never accept repayment," he said quietly.

They stared at each other, for far too long she knew. Bryden was not a leisurely walk, and any night journey such as this would be dangerous for a multitude of reasons, including something as simple as an unseen hole or a fallen tree. But he'd been with her father, been with Isabella and G, and despite not having slept while tending the dying, he came to her.

"Mr. Sinclair, you must be exhausted," Aunt Cass said, interrupting their confused silence. "Come into the drawing room and have some tea and something to eat while we ready the carriage."

"Miss Knight?" Sally said beside her. "Come, write your letter as I pack your things."

Elizabeth wrote disjointed messages of encouragement and apologies. She also wrote notes for Alice, Susan, and Miss Keats, for they were to meet again the following day. She asked Sally for the time; it was just after two in the morning. That day. They were to meet that day.

The letters were dispatched with two footmen who could run the distance and back safely. Sally stopped packing to assist Elizabeth with dressing and pinning her hair up so that her braid was not out.

Elizabeth's trunks were being carried down the stairs when the footmen returned from the Baldwin's residence with a letter for Elizabeth. Sally held up a lantern. The letter was in Mary's hand.

> *Mrs. Baldwin has superior experience with such an ailment as what our father suffers and has spoken with the girls, explaining the circumstances of her own mother's death. Cassie and Thea do not feel equal to witnessing such a scene, and I shall remain here with them, under Mrs. Baldwin's invitation.*
>
> *Charles will abide by Mr. Sinclair's instructions, but he and James will return to Bryden as soon as the carriage is ready. They will call upon Vane Park and beg rooms so that they will be nearby to support you.*
>
> *If you need me, Eliza, please write by express and I shall come as quickly as possible. All of my love, and we will pray for your safety tonight.*

From that point until the first station post to change horses, Elizabeth found everything a blur. She knew she'd successfully done all necessary tasks to now be inside the carriage, with the first touches of dawn fighting to break the horizon's darkness. But there were gaps in her jumble of memories, and she could not put them in order, not for a thousand pounds.

They were outside of town now, beginning the long journey back to Bryden. She was in the forward-facing seat, Sidney across from her. Both had heavy blankets over their legs, and Elizabeth had another wrapped about her shoulders. Conversation had been frantic to now, a jumble of questions repeated thrice, no doubt, with Sidney answering each time with patience. The various interventions, the deceptions of servants and professionals to offer aid, and her father's increasingly erratic, terrifying last hours before Sidney's departure to London.

Later she would have time to reflect if they had made the correct choices. She left her siblings scattered to the wind, while she rode now toward her duty. Sidney's eyes were dark, and the skin puffy from lack of sleep.

He'd fallen asleep for several minutes before gasping awake, looking about him in confusion. His gaze landed upon her, and she could see it took him a moment for him to ground himself in this world and not the one of dreams.

"My apologies." He shook his head and then smiled at her. "It has been a long day. More than a day now. I believe I have lost track of all time and place."

"I would not begrudge you your sleep, sir," she said.

"I would feel guilty knowing I left you alone," he said.

"As long as you are here, I am not alone," she whispered.

The look he gave her was one she'd never seen before directed at her, and she regretted leaving her sisters, or even Charles, in London. For the exterior lanterns cast shadows inside the carriage, along with the first streaks of the gold and red across the sky in the east. The dancing light, as the carriage moved with the irregularities of even the most well-kept road, gave his face a sympathetic and gentle appearance.

"I would do anything for you. For your family. Anything your family required of me, I would be happy to grant if it were in my power to do so."

His words were full of sincerity, even if his voice had a hoarseness that came with fatigue and travel. He was not teasing her. She regretted the intimacy of being here, alone. Oh, that Bryden was only an hour away!

Oh, that Bryden was a week away, sang her heart, even as her sense warred with how selfish that thought had been.

"I shall find a way to pay back this kindness," she said.

A curiously sad expression came across his face. "Friends do not tally debt."

"Nevertheless," Elizabeth whispered. Embarrassment flooded her that she'd allowed her voice to dip so low that he probably would not even hear her over the sound of the horses and carriage. She mustered her courage. "Nevertheless. I do not wish you to think ill of me, to think that now you have your inheritance, that I would take advantage, that I would…"

Words failed her, for none existed that could express what was in her heart. All she could do was fiddle with the blanket covering her legs.

Yet, he seemed to understand her for he said, "Of all the people in this world, you are the least likely to misuse me. In fact, if I had my own way, I would ... I would...my dear Miss Knight." His voice grew colder, sterner, as he spoke her name. As if he had to muster his own courage. She recognized it, for she had to fight it was well.

And she had a duty to protect this man, in this moment where sense was being removed by exhaustion, by worry, and the intimacy of dawn. She would not have him utter even so much as a hint of something he would regret by noon's bright light.

So she smiled, for women such as herself, who were poor, and about to become poorer still, needed friends more than they needed flattery. "I am your friend, sir, and will never forget your kindness. And know in your heart, always, that it was not your wealth that I befriended, but rather because I know you to be a respectable gentleman, and one that I find myself honoured to call a friend. Now, and forever."

"Friend. Yes," Sidney said. Then he laughed, a nervous, inappropriately loud sound. "I believe I understand now why society frowns upon young men and young women sitting alone in moonlight. It tricks them of all sense."

Elizabeth laughed, very similar to his. "I believe worry and fatigue makes our feelings so much more passionate than they actually are, and that is why a great many mistakes have been made in moonlight." She glanced out the window at the eastern sky. "Thankfully, we are chasing the evil moon away. Sense is now rising once more."

Sidney yawned, an unguarded gesture of a man beyond caring about propriety. He appeared too tired to even cover his mouth as he did so. His head lulled a little, and she worried he would fall asleep mid-yawn. But he gave her a small smile. "Mrs. Knight will be relieved to have you home, I think. She is very distressed."

Guilt flooded Elizabeth, for she had turned her attention away from the troubles at hand. This was not the time to indulge. It was not the time to be selfish, to consider only her feelings. No. She must ... she must.

She looked out of the carriage window. The sun was almost over the horizon now. It would warm the carriage, as well, though they had heavy blankets about them to chase away as much chill as possible. She felt for the coachmen and horses, who rode all night exposed to the cold air.

When she turned back, Sidney's head was leaning forward, bouncing with the carriage's movements. He continued to force himself to stay awake for her comfort, despite his own fatigue. The kindest thing she could do was lean against the side of the carriage and attempt sleep. She nestled one of the pillows Sally had provided into a comfortable position and leaned against it, though she had no inclination toward sleep.

If nothing else, he would awaken to see her resting and it might give him permission to do the same.

Though, before she closed her eyes, she looked at his sleeping figure, part of her relieved they did not speak words that he would soon regret.

And yet.

She closed her eyes and felt a small disappointment that she did not say more. Just for once in her life, to care about only herself. But that was not her destiny nor her duty, and she would not debase herself for a fantasy that could never be.

Chapter 19

THEY ARRIVED AT the rectory late morning, having made excellent time at all of the post stations. Once Mr. Sinclair had fallen asleep, and stayed asleep for some time, Elizabeth found him to be more moderate in his words, for which she was grateful. For, she did not sleep well, and her nerves were raw when he stepped out of the carriage first to assist her down the step.

No one waited for her at the door. No one came rushing out of the house to greet her, as was the norm for the rectory. Just silence.

Mr. Sinclair reached back into the carriage to take possession of her writing desk, the one item she would not allow out of her sight, not even in such dire circumstances as this. The coachmen stepped down to begin unloading the trunks, and Elizabeth thanked both for their excellent driving through the night. She invited them to go around back to the kitchen for something to eat. They declined, saying they would unload the trunks and then have a good meal and a rest at the inn when they returned the horses.

The front door flung open as Julia—looking even more exhausted than Sidney—gasped, "Oh Miss Knight! I am so happy to see you."

"Julia!" Elizabeth gasped. "Look at the state of you."

Tears welled up in the poor girl's eyes. She curtsied to Mr. Sinclair and said, "Sir. Thank you for fetching her. Mrs. Perkins says to tell you to hurry home, if you please, as all of our servants are at your house at present."

"But why?" Elizabeth asked.

Julia curtsied. "So that whenever Mr. Knight falls asleep, I can sneak them back in to assist me, miss."

"Excuse us, miss," the older of the coachman said, "where should we place these?"

"Inside the door for now," Julia ordered as she moved to hold the door open for the men to bring in the trunks.

"Has he worsened?" Sidney asked.

Julia curtsied. "He got out of bed yesterday, not long after you left, to shout at Mr. Collins and he fell down the stairs! He attacked…Mr. Collins, sir. It was such a struggle to get him back into bed, and finally, forgive me Miss Knight, I pretended to be you and that was how it has been."

"Oh Julia!" Elizabeth said.

"Mrs. Green has been allowed to visit Mrs. Knight still, though Mr. Knight doesn't know her. He also does not remember Mrs. Augusta Knight. Only your mother, miss."

Elizabeth blew out a breath. This was not a conversation to have with the coachmen present, good men she was sure they were all the same, but what was to be done unless she, Julia, and Sidney hauled in the trunks. And she doubted anyone would allow that.

"Sir?" The elder coachman interrupted. "Begging your pardon, but we'll take your trunk to the residence now. Would you like to come with us?"

"Miss Knight?"

"Please, go rest. Thank you for all that you have done." She curtsied deeply.

He gave her a sharp bow and said to Julia, "Come immediately if we can assist, no matter how small."

Julia curtsied. "At once, sir."

They waited for the carriage to pull away. Elizabeth moved her writing desk between hands, as it was growing heavy. Then, she asked, "Before I go inside, tell me the truth about what I face."

"Mr. Collins is waiting at Mr. Sinclair's, and he said to delay you if possible. However, if I might be bold to offer my own opinion miss? Your father is in grave danger, as is Mrs. Knight."

"Isabella?" Elizabeth whispered. "What is the matter?"

"Mrs. Green is upstairs now, miss. I overheard Mrs. Knight say that she has not felt the baby in some time. Forgive me for gossiping, miss, but it is most likely she will bring a stillborn."

Elizabeth placed her free hand on her chest in hopes of calming her heart. It did not.

"When you visit Mr. Knight, miss, it is important you do not touch him," she said. "He might recognize you, but if he does not, you do not wish him to bite you. Or worse, miss. And I know Mr. Knight would never wish to do you that kind of harm, so please for his sake. He does not know what he is about."

"I understand." Elizabeth drew in a long, deep breath and then let it out. "Where is Georgiana?"

"Vane Park still, miss," Julia said.

She took a hard look at Julia and asked, "When was the last time you ate, girl?"

"I...I do not remember. Yesterday, I think? I had a cup of tea this morning, I remember that."

"I do not want you to do a stitch of work, not a stitch, do you hear me? Not until you have eaten a full plate of food. I do not care if it is merely bread and jam, but you must eat a full plate of it. I shall go upstairs and deal with my father and Isabella. Go. To the kitchen with you."

"Yes, miss. Thank you, miss."

Elizabeth walked inside after Julia, and waited for the girl to disappear before putting her writing desk down. She took off her bonnet, dropping it on top of her desk. Then, one more deep breath. She began the climb up the stairs, acutely aware of how loud the steps were, how they creaked, and how one in particular groaned with the slightest pressure.

She did not visit her father, for she heard harsh, ragged snores coming from his room. Instead, she went to her own bedchamber, surprised to hear muted voices within. She delicately knocked at the door and opened it cautiously.

Isabella was propped up on Elizabeth's bed and immediately burst into tears at the sight of her. She held out her hands and Mrs. Green shushed them to keep their voices down.

"Oh my dear girl, thank you for coming home," Isabella said between tears. The women embraced and Elizabeth looked at Mrs. Green for a report. "What should I know?"

Mrs. Green patted Isabella's hand and said, "You rest. I shall inform Miss Knight, both on your care and her father's. You must keep up your strength now, remember. I shall order more broth from Mrs. Perkins."

Mr. Knight called out, demanding to know who was walking about. Mrs. Green put a finger to her lips and said, "It is Mrs. Green come to fetch Miss Knight to consult on a matter of ladies."

Elizabeth could not hear her father's reply, but Mrs. Green motioned for her to quietly descend the stairs. Once at the far end of the house, Mrs. Green seemed to relax. "My dear Miss Knight, thank you so much for coming home. Your poor sister, Miss Georgiana, could take no more and I sent her away before she was forever altered. I hope, in time, she shall forgive me and Mr. Collins."

"I am certain she shall," Elizabeth said. "Please, tell me all that I must know."

"Where is Julia?" Mrs. Green asked, looking about her.

"I have sent her to eat something. She could not remember the last time she had a meal, so I said she was not to work until she'd eaten a plate of something, I did not care what."

"You are such a kind young lady. Mrs. Thorne has written to Ashbrook, to the housekeeper in your sister's absence, informing her of the situation. She dispatched a kitchenmaid, and a chambermaid, both whom are currently at Mr. Sinclair's house, as he is the closest of everyone. Both those women, the housekeeper assures us, are excellent, steady women who will not be affected by Mr. Knight's tempers. Some of your more tender servants have been sent to Vane Park. Others are now at Mr. Sinclair's to assist."

"But how can they help if they are across the field? Forgive the question, I am very tired and I cannot think straight."

"Indeed, miss, there is no offence. They are washing the laundry there, as well as preparing all of the meals, and then carrying everything back over." Mrs. Green licked her lips. "Miss, I wish to be as delicate as I can, but you must understand that your father, dearly respected man that he was, is little different than a small child right now. The laundry alone…"

Elizabeth gasped out a breath but nodded. "Yes, of course. Foolish me, say no more. I would not wish to embarrass my father by us discussing any further detail. Julia told me about the fall. Can Mr. Collins not do anything?"

Mrs. Green shook her head. "The fear is that laudanum will kill him at this stage, for Mr. Collins and I have both seen this malady before. There is not much time."

"How little?"

"I have seen hours, days, and once even a month."

"Good God, a month of this? The poor man."

"Your stepmother is not in her right mind to make any decision, in her condition. Your brother is not here."

"He will be in Bryden later today. I believe that is the plan."

"But he is not here, right now. And the only person who can give permission to ease your father's suffering is his wife. So my dear? I ask you to consider intercession."

"But you said it will kill him."

"My dear, I have never seen a single living person come back from this," Mrs. Green said. "Why let him suffer?"

Elizabeth said she would have to make that decision on her own, after seeing her father. Mrs. Green said she understood, and begged Elizabeth's forgiveness for putting Isabella in her bed. "For her own safety," was Mrs. Green's reasoning.

So with Mrs. Green departed, Elizabeth walked back upstairs. Her father heard her footsteps, calling out angrily to whoever was on the stairs.

"Elizabeth, Papa. I'm home from London."

"London is it? Well, come in, my girl, come in." His voice was hoarse, slurred, but she obeyed him. He was in bed, with no interest in getting up. "My dear, I've not seen you all day. Look how much you've grown. I swear you're taller every time I see you."

The sight of him took Elizabeth's breath away. As much as she attempted to prepare herself, nothing could have. Only experience would have given her the necessary strength, and she thanked God that she has never had that experience before now.

For this would haunt her for the remainder of her days.

"Of course I am taller. You always said I would be taller than you one day."

"One day, my dear. You will be as tall as me, I am certain."

She never quite made her father's height, and it had been a joke amongst the two of them, back when Augusta was still alive, and there was still laughter in this house. Her jaw trembled and she sucked in a breath. "Sorry, I nearly sneezed."

"Did you catch cold in London?"

"No, sir. My hair was tickling my face."

"Have you seen Charles walking? I have not yet."

She did not know how to reply. Should she correct him? Sidney had said he had made that attempt, and it had sent her father into a rage. But, would playing along with this dream be a lie? What was even truth in this moment?

So, she said, "I am certain you shall catch him walking."

"They do not feed me," her father said, in a tone completely different than just a moment before. He stared directly into her eyes and said, "Anytime I speak back to him, he locks me in the closet. Well, I will fight back one of these days."

He gripped her hands tightly, and she flinched from the pain. But she held on and said, "I will help you fight back."

"Good," he whispered. "Good."

And then, confusion washed over his face. "Elizabeth? What are you doing here?"

"Returned from London, Papa."

He grunted, and closed his eyes. He was snoring a moment later.

Elizabeth could not say how long she stood there before she managed to gather herself, but she finally stirred. Quietly, carefully, as to not wake her father, she gathered dishes into a basket. She tidied the room, and removed soiled linens that were in a corner. Her father's mattress was ruined, even with fresh hay she did not think the smell would come out of the fabric now. But, that was for another day.

Today, she reminded herself. *Concentrate on today.*

SHE CAREFULLY WALKED down the stairs, first with the linens and placed them in their appropriate basket for the laundrymaids. Then, she retrieved the basket of dishes. She found Julia asleep on the floor, held up by a sack of flour. Mrs. Perkins was in the kitchen, and she put a finger to her mouth. Another two maids she recognized from Vane Park both curtsied before they turned back to scrubbing.

Mrs. Perkins motioned for Elizabeth. She poured hot broth into a mug with torn bread. In the faintest whisper, "For your father, so he will not choke."

Elizabeth carried on like that, running the errands for the servants who could not risk being seen above stairs. Julia soon stirred to assist, but Elizabeth wanted to ease the girl's load, so she attempted to tidy her father's room as best as possible, bringing up fresh water, linens, clothes.

He opened his eyes sometime close to dusk and said, "Lucy, what are you doing here?"

Elizabeth could handle the shouting, the hitting, the biting, the screaming agony of her father's imagined horrors. She could handle him seeing her as a child still. However, it was then she realized being confused with her long-dead mother was a cross too heavy to bear alone.

Tears ran down Elizabeth's face and she clenched her jaw so tightly her head flashed with pain.

"I have missed you so, my dear love," he muttered.

She dropped the rag in her hand, unable to control the shaking in her hands. She could not cry out, and risk a change in his nature. She could not risk upsetting Isabella.

"God shall join us together soon," he said. And then he was mercifully asleep once more.

Elizabeth walked out of his room, leaving the rag on the floor, leaving her work all behind. She had to escape, to quell the anger inside her. She had never felt so enraged at God in her life. No matter his sins, no matter his transgressions, no person should ever endure what her father's mind now suffered.

She sucked in a breath and walked into Cassie's room. With the door safely closed behind her, Elizabeth called Mrs. Egerton and Miss Gibbs. Miss Gibbs wore a modern gown, in all black, with black ribbons in her hair. Mrs. Egerton wore the mourning gown of her time, with a severe black hat perched on the side of her heavily curled wig. Both presented imposing, somber figures.

"Thank you, ladies, for appearing," she whispered.

"Miss Knight, I wish to both offer my sincerest regrets on your father's present situation, and to offer whatever comfort or assistance I can."

Elizabeth inclined her head. "Thank you, Mrs. Egerton. I find myself ill-prepared."

"My dear girl, no one is ever," Mrs. Egerton said with a kindness the ghost so rarely used. "I do not believe God created us to be prepared."

"Miss Knight?" Miss Gibbs said. "I offer my wisdom, if that is what you wish."

Temptation flashed in Elizabeth's mind. Her life would suffer without her father in it. From a practical, financial sense. They would have to leave this house, as it belonged to the Church and was not their own. Another rector would move in, and they would be abandoned to the world. Even their strawberries would belong to another.

Mr. Collins would arrive soon. She expected him. She was to convince Isabella to ease her father's final days. That was her duty, as the eldest. To bring sense and order and dignity.

"My father never recovered from the coughing sickness," she said. There was no question. Just the truth spoken aloud. Mr. Collins will be here soon. I must make a decision."

The ghosts silently waited, allowing Elizabeth the opportunity to discover her own mind.

"My heart says I should use the occult, to risk everything to save my father tonight." Elizabeth said the words aloud, the words that had been quietly stirring within her. "It says I should risk another who is stronger: myself. I have had the sickness before, and it was barely more than an annoying cold. In fact, my largest complaint was that I had to live in my room alone without any company for fear I was contagious."

Miss Gibb's expression was grave. "Are you asking me to teach you how to take your father's suffering?"

"Miss Knight, I must caution—"

Elizabeth held up a hand. "Ladies, I love my father. Despite his flaws, his mistreatments, and his utter carelessness. I love him. I have so many memories of sharing secret moments with him, that I will carry to my own grave one day. I will wrap them in my heart and keep them safe."

Tears formed in her eyes. "But I do not wish to die myself, and I fear…I fear. As much as it pains me to be so unbearably selfish in this moment, selfish I must be. I pray it does not change your good opinion of me, but if it does, then I am sorry for it, but I shall not swerve on the path I have chosen. Only forward now, and may God's will be done."

"His will appears to be the death of your father," Miss Gibb's said.

Elizabeth allowed the tears to drip down her cheeks. In a whisper that took the strength of her entire soul, she said, "Then, the Lord's will be done."

Both ghosts curtsied, deeply, before disappearing. Left completely alone in the world, Elizabeth took a moment to find calm. She had condemned her father to death and she would, one day, have to face God and her own father to explain herself.

May God have mercy upon my soul.

Chapter 20

ELIZABETH GAINED CONTROL over herself in time for the apothecary's arrival. She quietly escorted him to Isabella, with an exhausted Julia dragging an overflowing basket of clothes up stairs. Mr. Collin's weight caused one of the stairs to squeak. Elizabeth winced. But no noise came from her father's room. She escorted him into see Isabella, who had to be roused from her own slumber.

"Miss Knight, it is very good to see you," Mr. Collins whispered as she closed the bedroom door. "Mrs. Knight. You are looking well."

"Since Elizabeth has returned, all of my strength is gone."

"That is only natural," Mr. Collins said. "Miss Knight, though, might I suggest we send Julia home tonight? The poor thing is tripping over her own feet. When this sad affair is over, we must all strive to do something special for the girl. Perhaps a new bonnet? Nothing too flashy, she isn't of that class, and she's not that sort in any case, but we must do something."

"I know exactly how to ensure Julia is compensated," Elizabeth said. When in doubt, those of a working class of society preferred coin and plenty of it. She would ensure additional payment for Julia.

"How is the wound, sir?" Isabella asked.

"Oh, healing apace, thank you ma'am. Thankfully, the bite wounds did not fester," Mr. Collins said. At Elizabeth's confused inquiry, he said, "One of the more unfortunate parts of this occupation is that the patient sometimes attacks those most able to assist."

"Oh, Mr. Collins, I am so sorry," Elizabeth said.

"Speak nothing of it," he said. "The apothecary's life is not all giggling babies and quiet, stoic death. Many of us are attached to this world, and grasp it with both hands, even as God calls us home. Those stubborn in life are often stubborn in death. I take a lot of comfort in that, actually."

"I thought you said Charles would be here by now," Isabella said weakly.

"I understood he and Mr. Fitzharding were leaving this morning. They should be here by now, I would think. Or have at least sent word," Elizabeth said.

"I heard the bridge near Eastmore finally gave way, no surprise with how much rain we've gotten this winter," Mr. Collins said. "You were lucky to have passed it when you did, for it collapsed sometime this afternoon. If they left this morning, they will have to go around. They might head toward Ashbrook and then make the rest of the journey here in the morning." Mr. Collins took a deep breath. "Therefore, I recommend we discuss Mr. Knight's suffering without your brother."

"Oh Elizabeth, I do not know what to do," Isabella said.

"Mr. Collins, please speak plainly to me. Will my father recover?"

He shook his head. "I consulted Mrs. Green, as well, and I assure you I am not the kind of apothecary to dismiss the knowledge of a midwife. We both feel very strongly that your father has little time now. It is most likely his heart. Perhaps an infectious malady as well? It is difficult to say. There is no medicine created that can stop this. Only a miracle can."

"Is a miracle then possible?" Isabella asked.

Elizabeth felt a prick of guilt, for she could be that miracle. But she had made her secret choice.

"I would never say that I know more than God, nor claim to know when He will heal the sick, but in my experience, your husband's condition is not one that attracts miracles."

Isabella put her hand over her mouth and wept silently. Elizabeth went to her, taking her free hand into hers. "Mr. Collins? If my father could tell us his wishes, what do you think he would want?"

"He would want you to ease his suffering," Mr. Collins said.

"Elizabeth, what will Charles say if we make this choice without him? The son and heir!"

"My dear, you are his wife," Mr. Collins said. "We are not planning to kill the poor man. No, indeed, I would not allow that. However, as his wife, you can say it is time to administer comfort to a dying man, to ease his remaining time. That is all I recommend."

Elizabeth squeezed Isabella's hand and nodded her consent.

With tears in her eyes, Isabella said, in a rather strong voice, "Please ease his suffering."

Long past tears, Elizabeth said in a quiet voice, "May the Lord's will be done."

Chapter 21

WITH MR. COLLINS departed, Elizabeth made the decision to send Julia home. Mrs. Perkins had left and returned sometime during the evening—Elizabeth was losing track of the goings on of the house —but she approached Mr. Sinclair's housekeeper and asked to speak privately with her in the study. Mrs. Perkins followed her and asked how she could be of service.

"Mrs. Perkins, forgive what I am about to ask. My father is asleep, finally, and Mrs. Knight is also able to rest. I am exhausted beyond all words, and I have only just arrived. Poor Julia lost her own mother only months ago, and she should not be here in this house when…when the unhappy event takes place. Be it tonight or a month from now."

"I understand your fears, miss."

"I know my father relies on her, for any number of reasons related to his illness, or perhaps it is merely that a maid about the house is a constant and trustworthy face, I do not know. What I do know is that, in my soul, I know she should not be here."

"Miss Knight, you only needed to ask," Mrs. Perkins said. "I shall take her away, right this moment with your permission."

"Please do not dismiss her," Elizabeth said. "I also rely on Julia. Forgive me, Mrs. Perkins, I cannot think straight."

"With your permission, miss, I shall take her back with me and feed that girl until she falls asleep in her plate, if that will give you peace tonight."

Elizabeth's jaw trembled, but she managed to push down the emotions. Hard. "It would be of great peace to my mind."

"Do you wish me to send over a footman or a maid to sleep here tonight?"

Elizabeth shook her head. "The house is just across the field, and I believe we will finally have a good night's rest. It appears my brother is delayed by the bridge washing out, so we will see him either sometime very late tonight, or perhaps in the morning. The fires are all lit, and I believe we should all rest while the opportunity is here."

Mrs. Perkins emptied the house of servants with both speed and silence. Julia did not even come to protest, too exhausted from her own suffering. Then, in the quiet of a near-empty house, Elizabeth and her candle walked back into her father's study. Such a strange place for her to find comfort, but she was compelled to stand there now.

She did not dig through his papers or belongings. That would be Isabella and Charles' duty. Instead, she closed the door, to stare fondly at the forgotten plank nailed to the doorframe. She ran her hand along it. Six Knight children, their heights carefully recorded year over year, by their father. With the heights of her mother, father, and Augusta all measured as well. If Isabella were to provide a seventh Knight, her height and that of her little one would eventually have graced the record. That would not happen now.

So many memories were on this simple piece of lumber. She had been the tallest of the children, for a very long time, until Charles finally overtook her and, then, his own father. There were good memories that day, as they laughed over Christmas wine that Charles was finally the tallest of the Knight clan.

In all of the despair, darkness, and fits of temper, there were the good memories, too. Some would dwell on the bad. She knew Thea did, and would. She would repeat the bad memories in her mind, torturing herself until exhausted. She would speak to her sister about it, when Thea returned home. Or, maybe she would write a letter in the morning. Not tonight, though.

Tonight, Elizabeth wished to be selfish. To hear the sounds of the only house that was her own. She knew this house the way she knew her own hand. She would miss this place, the only place that felt like home.

The curtains moved, and Elizabeth invited the ghost to come forth. However, she was surprised that it was not Mrs. Egerton; it was Miss Gibbs, and only Miss Gibbs. The ghost was dressed in the modern style, but still in all black. She wore a black bonnet on her head, and was not her usual cheerful self. She curtsied and said, "I have noticed you have not requested my assistance for your stepmother."

Elizabeth ran her hand along the height plank once before pulling away. "Isabella's challenges are not in the realm of my assistance, and I cannot inflict her situation on another. I have enough sins on my conscience this night as it is."

"My purpose, my *true* purpose, is to be useful. I wish to be certain you have not changed your mind in regards to your father."

"You are very kind, but Mr. Collins had given my father a small draft, only enough to hopefully allow for a peaceful rest." Elizabeth said. Then, in a moment of honesty, she added, "I understand what you are asking me, and why. I wish you to know that."

Miss Gibbs did not say anything. She did not grin. She did not laugh. She stood solemn in the study, with only one candle in a glass lantern to light the room.

"I am a woman of duty. That is why God put me on this Earth, and I have endeavoured to always act in a manner that will not have me…" She sighed, struggling for the words.

"Miss Knight, you are not required to answer to me. I am not God."

"No, but one day I shall face him with my choices this day," Elizabeth said.

Miss Gibbs said nothing. She offered no comfort, no contradiction, no support. Elizabeth knew then that this choice must be hers and hers alone, and the ghost could not interfere. Would not. Should not. Elizabeth found she had no animosity toward Miss Gibbs in that moment, for the ghost did not wish to be the blame of another's choice. No, indeed, it was Elizabeth's decision and hers alone.

She held the power to bring her father back from the brink of death, and her selfishness, her own attachment to life, her worries about her sisters, her fears and loves, all pounded against her soul and she lacked the courage to give her life for his.

Elizabeth tried, oh how she tried, to convince herself that her father would not wish the loss of a child to save his life. She did not believe herself. Not that she believed her father was that evil of a man, but rather she could not convince herself she made the choice in consideration of her father's feelings.

She made the choice in consideration of her own.

She must trust God's will. That was the only thing that allowed her to hold her resolve.

Miss Gibbs did not disappear. She stood with Elizabeth, in silence. In a house never so silent before. No soft-footed maids dashing about. No young boys running in and out with deliveries and messages and parcels. No John the Bailiff with his heavy footfalls walking through the kitchen path to the study. No girls shrieking at each other, in excitement, anger, or anticipation.

Just the silence of sickness. Of worry. Of waiting for the end of all things.

Merciful silence, for Elizabeth did not know if she could endure being called her dead mother's name again. Or hear the hints into her father's past that made him afraid of being locked in a closet. Though, she knew enough. One could not live with a person for all of their life without history slipping through unguarded moments. The rift with his brother. How his own father's name was a curse.

And yet. *Yet.* The death of Mr. Knight would destroy their little family. They would be forced to leave the rectory. The Church would offer his widow no pension, no annuity, no support. They would bury him and find the cheapest accommodation possible. Hopefully, kindness and humanity would allow it to be in that order, for there were plenty of tales to the contrary.

But how would her death solve anything? Even if she did not die, her health would be irrevocably injured by such a desperate action. There would be no guarantee her father would still not succumb to the merest illness going about the village next winter. She could take the sickness, but she could not repair the damage. It could all be in vain.

"Miss Gibbs, I say this as a dutiful daughter, but also a dutiful sister. Saving my father at the risk of my own life—I know that is always a choice—would still be failing my duty to my sisters. I must allow God, and God alone, to guide our lives."

Miss Gibbs inclined her head. "God's will be done."

"God's will be done," Elizabeth whispered.

The ghost disappeared, leaving Elizabeth alone once more. She walked about the house, with her lantern casting shadows on the walls, exaggerating the sizes and shapes of the furniture. She loved this house. She had never really formed that thought in her mind before now, but knowing she would soon need to abandon it —that it was real now, surely it was real—she found herself mourning.

Mourning the loss of her father, of course. Mourning the loss of another sibling, most likely. But it was mourning the loss of this life she led, with her kitchen garden, her potatoes, her roses, her new strawberries they'd planted. There was even the new pear tree that she would never taste its fruit. It would not be hers.

Several letters had arrived during the day that Elizabeth had not read, so she sat down to the dining table and opened her letters. Most were simple notes, offering assistance, soup, joints of meat, and various cakes and sweet biscuits. Those she would answer in the morning.

No.

No, she should answer them now. These good people deserved her attention. Her grief was not her duty. Her duty was to bring order to the chaos of life.

So she gathered paper and pen and ink, and wrote. All began the same. *On behalf of my father and Mrs. Knight, I thank you for your thoughtfulness in this trying time for our family.* Some offers she could easily direct to Mrs. Perkins or Vane Park, as she was not aware of the current system that supported the house with a sick man who dismissed all the servants.

Some of the offers, though, were easy to accept or reject. Oh, they had plenty of tea stores, but thank you so much for such an extravagant offer. Actually, their jam supplies were running low, and a jar of gooseberry jam would be very happily received, as tarts could be made for Isabella once her situation improved. Other offers she kindly rejected, or asked for a delay until they knew more if the patient would recover. She emphasized in those letters her profound gratitude, and expressed that her refusal was only to avoid overwhelming her exhausted servants.

Elizabeth discovered a letter from G in the pile, one that must have gotten lost in all of the chaos of the household. She opened it, preparing herself for the passions of a youngest sister about to lose yet another parent.

> *Please do not write if you are the least busy. I understand very well how difficult it is in the house, as the servants are all bringing news to us as fast as possible. I am so sorry I could not stay home any longer, and please ask Isabella to forgive me for abandoning her. I told Mrs. Green and she put me in the kitchen so that no one could hear me crying. I feel so very embarrassed that I was unable to be as you would have behaved. I know you are not crying and disrupting the ill. I know how I am to behave, and I want you to know I tried very hard to be good, indeed I did. But it was so difficult! And Papa! He did not know me, not even a little, and I thought I could be brave but I could not.*
>
> *I have been crying at Vane Park, and Maria is very kind. I told her she should come to support you, but she said you would write if we were needed, so we sit here mourning my father before he is even gone. My heart is broken.*

Elizabeth dabbed away the tears in her eyes and wrote her sister a letter for the morning, before even finishing reading the letter. She needed to write with the feeling immediately in her heart, as if G was in front of her speaking. A very kind, supportive letter about how bravery comes in many forms. And that how, yes, society expected everyone—but women in particular—to keep their emotions in check, to never display violent raptures. Never wailing sobs of unabashed mourning. Calm. Always calm.

But.

But, Elizabeth reminded her sister, they were only human. And people could not always control themselves, so it was important to remove oneself from a situation as to not cause extra distress. Elizabeth praised her sister's sense, for her knowing at such a young age that she was not equal to the task before her. By speaking up, by being honest and forthright, G could be removed from the house in a quiet and dignified manner so that the ill and suffering ones upstairs would not have to witness G's grief.

> *You did very well, G. Never forget that, no matter what comes in the hours or days ahead. I am so very proud of my little sister, who is not so little anymore I fear. Who is turning into an excellent, dutiful, and kind young lady. One I am proud to call sister.*

Then, Elizabeth continued to read the letter, and that is when her own heart failed her.

> *But when it was clear that we needed you, Mr. Sinclair came to ask my permission. Indeed, he did! He was so brave riding out to Vane Park, was he not? And getting the carriage and the horses, and doing it all by post. And so late in the day, after having been up with Papa for two straight days! Did you know that? I wager he did not tell you, because when I tried to tell him how brave he was, he said he was only doing his duty as a curate!*
>
> *Imagine! No other curate in England would do such a thing for only fifty pounds a year, and especially not one with so much money as him! I know of the cottage and the inheritance, but I am sworn to secrecy so please do not tell anyone, for I am not to say.*
>
> *And then I could barely sleep for I worried so much about the bridge near Eastmore because everyone said the*

> *rains would make the old thing collapse and I worried that Mr. Sinclair would die, and then I worried you would die, but he got you here as fast as any horses could bring you! I will always think him the very best of men.*

The letter struck Elizabeth's heart, and a sob escaped her. She clamped her hand over her mouth, lest she wake or distress Isabella. In all of the haste to return home, it took Georgiana to articulate what she could not: Mr. Sinclair did far more than the regular duty expected of a man in his position. He did the duty of family. He saw the Knight household as an extension of himself, and acted in a manner that the actions of all other men would be compared to him.

Elizabeth summoned Mrs. Egerton, for companionship in the dwindling hours of the evening. She read G's letter to the ghost, who nodded and said, "I believe your Miss Georgiana is finally ready to outgrow her foolishness. She made a very proper choice in removing herself. Many have struggled to do the same, and have brought nothing but distress and worry to those they confess they wish to help. But this nonsense about Mr. Sinclair! The man hired some horses. Let us not pretend he invaded France for your family."

"Oh Mrs. Egerton! Where is your sense of adventure!" Elizabeth said with a chuckle. "Surely, young ladies fell in love in your time, with the wide-eyed expression of does."

Mrs. Egerton laughed. An improper laugh, as Augusta Knight would've said. "Oh, we loved in my time. We longed, we desired, we wept over young men who rejected us. But we were sensible."

"It is a sin to tell lies. Young ladies are silly about men no matter the age in which they were born, and I believe the young men were no better."

Mrs. Egerton smiled and said, "Well, some of us were stupid to be sure, but not all of us."

Elizabeth thought about Sidney's face as she rushed down Aunt Cass' stairs. The pain. The fatigue. The knowledge of what he had to escort her to face. And how he did it without complaint, without asking a farthing, or a favour. How they whispered to each other in the carriage. How the worry and the intimacy of the night made them dance so close to the cliff's edge, where duty would have bound him to honour his words, if they had not managed to stop themselves.

"Tell me, Mrs. Egerton. Were you ever in love?"

Mrs. Egerton's long exhalation moved the opened letters on the table. "Oh, I once looked at a young man the way you look at your Sidney."

"He is not my Sidney, madam, and I do not believe I ever said I was in love with him."

"My dear girl, it is not a crime to fall for the charms of a young man, especially one who is not dependent upon his family for anything in life. There are far worse mistakes a woman could make." Mrs. Egerton sighed. "And, your sister was correct about one thing."

"Only one?"

"He was very brave to make that journey at night, and then to escort you back with such gentlemanly comportment." She lifted her chin. "I believe my opinion of him is higher than any man I have seen thus far, excepting perhaps your excellent departed uncle."

"Uncle Edward was very special," Elizabeth said with a smile.

"And I believe Mr. Sinclair is a very singular man."

"Sidney will no doubt make a woman very happy one day." Elizabeth cursed her voice for shaking.

Mrs. Egerton had a curious look upon her face when she said, "Oh, I believe he will make a very deserving woman happy, if I am any judge."

"I hope she is deserving of him," Elizabeth whispered.

"Good night, Miss Knight. You should sleep."

"Good night, Mrs. Egerton. I shall try."

Elizabeth only stayed up another half of an hour, just long enough to finish her letter to her sister and seal the others. She thought on her words with Mrs. Egerton and decided she would bury her feelings deeper. She did not want anyone to know the secrets of her heart, for them to whisper about her. To expose her to the world.

She would be very poor soon.

She would have to sell her book to support her sisters.

She would let him go.

"Just let him go, Elizabeth," she whispered to herself as she climbed the stairs. "Let him go."

Chapter 22

THE RAIN HAD started just after she'd gone to bed in Cassie's room. Thankfully, she had changed into her brown morning gown earlier in the day and did not bother to undress for bed. Without anyone to assist in the house, she wished to be decent if called upon. She had made the decision to remove her stays after the second boom of thunder, however, as she could not get comfortable.

By the fourth time the thunder woke her, Elizabeth decided sleep was futile. She wrapped a shawl about her and walked out to the upper drawing room. There were still embers in the fireplace, so she stirred the fire to life, and slowly built it back until, finally, she could put a log upon the blaze. Her father did not approve of ladies touching the fireplace, but she felt an odd sense of pride that she could do this simple task.

She found her mind wandering as she lit the candles in the room. Thankfully, Aunt Cass would take a house nearby. The walk there and back was safe and rather pretty. Doable every day, except in heavy rain or snow.

Mary could take in a couple of the girls in rotation. She could even take in Isabella and the baby, if that is where God's miracle decided to reach.

Charles was soon to move into his own curate's residence, and that would be large enough to take a girl or two on occasion.

If she could marry off Cassie to her Mr. John Baldwin…

Elizabeth shook her head, angry at herself for treating Cassie as a burden, the way so many talked about her. Her own father. Augusta. Mary. Charles. Even Aunt Cass, on occasion, slipped a comment about her refusal to marry. As if she planned her life to be a spinster! To sink further and further into poverty the older she grew. No one of precarious income would dare admit to such stupidity. It was fine for the Miss Alice Thornes, with a dowry of ten or twenty thousand, whatever it was. The Alice Thornes of the world did not need protection; the Bank of England did that for them.

The Susan Marksons of the world, however? They did not have the pounds, shillings, and pence to protect them. They needed to attract the Mr. Osbornes of the world. And, there were far more Susan Marksons than Mr. Osbornes.

No, she would encourage Cassie to marry her Mr. Baldwin only if that is what she wished. She would not push. Nor, though, would she discourage. Mary's words about her marriage echoed in her mind. Mary was happy. She knew Mary was safe, but happy? In love? How could she be so wrong about such a basic thing?

But they argued all of the time! *Husband*, Mary called him.

But then again, Maria always complained about Henry Thorne, too. And, when the news of Amelia reached Elizabeth's ears, what did Maria do? Defend the love of her life.

Then, a thought, as random and as rapid as her thoughts had been all evening. *I hope he is dead.* Elizabeth regretted the thought, the angry, bitter, resentful thought that was not even based in anything but the rapid succession of emotion in a too-tired mind.

She did not want her father to die. She had never been close to him, for she could never be what he wanted her to be, no matter how hard she tried. Too many memories were of anger, frustration, and sadness.

There were memories of laughter, too. And, if God willed it, her father would recover and there might be more good memories to form later in life. Elizabeth had come to realize that her attachment to her father was the hope of better memories, of better times, of better days. They rarely laughed at the same thing, but when they did, there was a joy upon both of their faces finding that common ground.

Of course, those moments made Elizabeth more acutely aware of the gulf between them: daughter and father. Of people who knew one another and yet were strangers. The curse of family.

She thought of her father's suffering, of the terror and confusion he also must have been experiencing, and she blew out a breath as she stared at the fire she'd made with her own hands. Perhaps it was not cruel to wish him to die, for no other reason than to end his suffering. No man should suffer in this manner. No one should.

She heard a moan of agony, and went to her father's room, taking one of the candles with her. She stepped in as quietly as the floorboards allowed her, but her father did not stir at the light. She noticed his eyes were open.

Elizabeth feel the gulf all the more, for they told her how much distance had to be crossed.

"Papa?"

Nothing.

His mouth was open as well, as if he were frozen in mid-gasp.

Elizabeth gulped and moved the candle in front of her father's face. She held her breath. The flame did not flicker. Neither did her father.

She let out a breath, turning away when she did so as to not put out the light. She did not cry out, nor did she weep. The exhaustion was too great now, and yet, she knew in her heart she was bound for hell. For what she felt in that one moment, standing there, was relief. For surely no man would want to live through the hell he had endured.

And while the uncharitable would say hell would be worse than anything she could imagine; she had already lived through hell. And knew, more was to come now that the head of the household was gone. Oh, there would be far more to come. The living hell would begin, with the slow degradation of her life, of her reputation, of her existence. Until, finally, death would be a release for her, as well.

But, right now, she was still Miss Elizabeth Knight, and she would do her duty.

She put the candle down and pulled the blanket over her father. Over his body. She did so, even as she fought the gasp of grief that wished to escape her. She breathed through clenched jaw, the air hissing and sucking against her teeth. Under control, she walked out to Isabella, to wake her, to tell her the news.

"I am awake," gasped Isabella.

Elizabeth opened the door at once, and saw her stepmother standing in the corner, hand gripping the chair. The moan she'd heard had not been her father. It had been Isabella.

"Did I wake you?" Isabella asked.

She had not even heard Elizabeth up, lighting the fire, walking to her father…

Isabella needed to know, but silence was all she could manage. Her nerves gave out. She still did not weep. She just…could not go on.

Isabella hissed as she gripped the chair harder. "Is he gone?"

Elizabeth nodded.

Isabella closed her eyes, just for a moment. "I am sorry for you, my dearest."

Then Isabella's voice hitched in her throat. She sucked in a breath, trying to hide the harsh, pained sound that escaped clenched teeth.

"Isabella...how long has this been going on?"

"Since this morning," Isabella said. "I did not wish to make your burden worse."

Elizabeth stared at her, the words just a jumble in her brain. Until she suddenly felt the urgency. Her father, God rest his soul, did not need help any longer. Isabella, however, did.

"I shall fetch help," Elizabeth sputtered. "Sidney!"

"Who?" Isabella asked, buckled over now.

"Mr. Sinclair!" Elizabeth blurted.

"I may need you to hurry," Isabella wailed.

She should dress, put her stays on, get her hair pinned into place. Isabella cried out. No, there was no time. Speed over propriety.

She rushed downstairs to the door where her father's greatcoat hung on a hook. She sucked in a breath, then grabbed it and shoved her arms into the heavy garment that would protect her from the rain. Likewise she put on his heavy boots, the ones he wore outside when in the fields. Too large, too wide, but she had to get through the field between her and Sidney.

She ran through the rain, through the mud, through the weeds. She tripped and fell into a mud puddle, but she did not care. She wiped her face as best as possible and continued to run. She had sent Julia away because she … it did not matter why now. She had done so, and now there was no one to help Isabella but her.

It took forever to reach his house, despite seeing it across the field. There were no candles in the windows, no rooms alit. She did not care. She pounded upon his front door, pounded, and called out his name. Begging for help.

Dogs howled and barked the warning of intruders.

Thuds inside.

A light in an upstairs room.

Another light growing closer.

She was calling out, pounding the door, just unable to stop herself. Desperation had overtaken her senses.

She nearly fell into the house when the door swung wide. Still in his nightshirt and nothing else, Mr. Perkins held a fire poker in one hand, and the door in the other.

"Miss Knight! You look like you've seen the devil!"

"My father is dead, sir, but Isabella! Isabella requires a midwife this very moment, and I cannot leave her to fetch Mrs. Green myself. Please, I beg of you, to send…"

"Elizabeth!"

Elizabeth looked past Mr. Perkins to see Sidney rushing down the stairs, attempting to stuff his shirt into his trousers. "Oh sir! I beg of you, I need assistance!

She did not get to say much more, for Mrs. Perkins was shouting orders for everyone to get to the rectory, to Vane Park, to send riders to Ashbrook, to get Mrs. Green, to fetch Mr. Collins. Most of the servants were still in nightshirts, many with bare feet, as they rushed to their duties.

Mrs. Perkins shouted, "Ready the carriage!"

Mr. Perkins left the door to Mr. Sinclair, as he began shouting his own orders for the footmen. "Get Julia! Her mistress needs her!"

"Will you come in to wait?" Sidney asked as he held open the door with his foot, struggling to get his suspenders over his shoulders.

"I cannot be away from Isabella. She is all alone!" Elizabeth said.

"Sir! Your boots!" Mrs. Perkins said, rushing to his side.

A footman joined her, thrusting his master's greatcoat at him.

"Go! I shall be along as soon as the carriage is ready," Mrs. Perkin's shouted. "Go!"

Sidney shoved his bare feet into the ugly boots he wore in the fields, and pulled the coat over his half-dressed state. He motioned at Elizabeth, and they hurried across the muddy field, her heart pounding in her chest that she did not lose a stepmother tonight as well as a father.

Chapter 23

ISABELLA WAILED AND screamed, as Elizabeth and Sidney paced the drawing room floor. Over the course of the night, people from all over the village poured into the house, bringing food, clean linens, offering assistance, sending their maids, whatever needed to be done. With Mrs. Green's arrival, Mrs. Perkins removed herself from aiding Isabella and instead took charge of the household. Mr. Collins paced in and out of the room, providing updates to Elizabeth, issuing orders to the servants for various items needed. On through the night.

Sidney offered her a generous glass of brandy, which she at first refused, but then accepted when Mr. Collins urged her. Occasionally, she would glance in the direction of her father's bedchamber during her pacing, thinking she should go to him, sit by him, do a duty. Only she could not find it within her. Her courage was spent.

Somewhere in it all, Elizabeth slumped against the wall in the hallway, just sliding down to the floor. Head lulling. The brandy could not chase away the chill in her bones now, the weary exhaustion of too little sleep and too much worry. She knew she should fix her gown. Fetch a blanket. Not sleep on the floor. Her body no longer knew how to stand. Falling. Falling.

Slipping on ice.

Heart pounding in distress.

Isabella's screams.

Head lulling.

"Elizabeth?" came a small voice.

"G?"

"Easy now," a man's voice.

"Sidney?"

"Easy now," he whispered.

He gently pulled her toward his chest. She fell forward, resting her head against his body, not caring about propriety, or rules, or society. She was simply too tired to care. A weight pressed against her shoulders. Her back. Delicate women's fingers expertly pulled the ends across her chest.

He began to push her back, away from him, and she muttered protestations. She did not wish to move. She wished…she wished…

Then, the sensation of falling. Her eyes jolted open, but all she saw was Sidney. Lowering her to the floor. Gentle, confident hands guiding her down. Her head landed on softness.

"Elizabeth, rest," he whispered.

A weight wrapped about her feet. Then, another on top of her. A soft voice whispering she was covered and very decent.

G. Sweet, sweet G.

"News?" she whispered.

"Nothing yet," Sidney whispered.

"They sent riders to Ashbrook, in case Charles and James are there." G came into view and touched her sister's face. "I'm here now."

"I'm sorry about Papa," Elizabeth whispered. Her jaw trembled. Tears trickled out of her eyes. She was so tired.

"I'll watch for when Charles comes," G whispered. "You need to sleep."

"I am on the floor," Elizabeth protested.

"Just sleep," G said. "Mr. Sinclair, make her sleep."

"Elizabeth," Sidney whispered. "You must sleep now."

"Promise to wake me," Elizabeth whispered.

"I promise," G said.

"Promise."

"I promise," Sidney said.

Dreams followed. Voices that faded near and far, whispers, screams, weeping. Elizabeth was certain she was awake, and then startled into waking only to drift back to dreams. In the dream, Sidney was with her, both resting in grass. He whispered, words she could not hear, and yet they made her smile. Then, he was next to her in her bed, still smiling, still whispering, only now telling her to wake.

"Why are you in my bed?" she whispered.

"Elizabeth, wake up," Sidney said. A hand touched her shoulder.

Elizabeth jolted from sleep, disorientation filling her with fear and dread. How was he in her bedchamber! Had that all been real? What had happened! But then, reason took a hold of her a heartbeat later, and she let out a long breath, calming herself. She had fallen asleep on the floor.

"There is news," he said. He was crouched beside her.

"Is she…?" Elizabeth could not finish the question.

"Mrs. Knight is weak, but alive for now."

She accepted Sidney's hand as he helped her to her feet. He bent over and picked up a blanket, which she used to wrap herself. Her hip and shoulder ached from being on the cold floor, and she stretched her neck to attempt to ease the cramping.

It was then she had a good look at Sidney. He wore a different shirt than previously, and wore a vest and a clumsily-tied cravat. There was a jam stain down the front of his vest. He also had his good boots on now. His eyes were puffy, with dark shadows.

"Did you sleep, sir?"

"There are gaps in my memory," he said with a kind smile. Then, he said, "I am so sorry to tell you this, but there is more news."

"Stillborn?" Elizabeth guessed.

"Stillborn son. I am so sorry to give you the news. Your brother wished to tell you, but I shall say you guessed."

"Charles is here?"

"Downstairs. He only arrived in the last hour, but he did not want to wake you."

"Isabella is alive, though?"

Mr. Sinclair nodded. "Mr. Collins informs me that we must do all we can to avoid her developing a fever. The next two days will be the worrisome period. He and Mrs. Green agree."

"After that?"

Mr. Sinclair smiled gently. "Then, she most likely will have the time to mourn her husband."

"I must go to her," Elizabeth said, gathering up the ends of her blanket.

"No, they gave her laudanum. Mrs. Green and Mrs. Perkins are both asleep in her room. Mr. Thorne and Mr. Fitzharding are downstairs with the carriages. They await your permission to go fetch your sisters in town."

"Why me? Charles is here."

"Charles—he does not wish to be called Mr. Knight at present, so forgive any familiarity the servants have tonight—and Miss Georgiana wished to wait for your opinion, but neither wished to wake you." He offered her a tired smile. "And, we all needed to know Mrs. Knight's situation, in any case."

"Where are they?"

"The dining room, I believe," Sidney said.

Elizabeth nodded and said, "Thank you. For your kindness. Throughout all of this. I do not know how I could have managed it without the assistance of your household."

He reached out, as if he wished to take her hand. But he caught himself, pulling back before he allowed the fatigue to overtake his sense. He bowed. "It was truly my pleasure. To be of assistance, I meant to say. To assist your family."

She took in a long breath and gave him a smile. Then, she walked down the stairs to face her responsibilities. The supportive one. The sensible one.

The one who let her father die.

£50 in the desk.

£16 remaining from her biannual payment.

£24 savings from the sale of her books.

£8 in pin money or thereabouts.

Nearly one hundred total in ready money in her possession. Now.

"Oh, Elizabeth!" Charles said as he rushed to embrace her.

He wept, as hard as he did when his own mother had died. She reached out an arm to invite G into the embrace, and the youngest sobbed as she was enveloped by her older siblings.

"The bridge was out, and several carriages were stuck in the mud, including ours. We had to keep stopping to help. So, we ended up having to go the long way around, so we thought we had time to stay at Ashbrook." Charles wept. "I am sorry I was not here."

She gripped him tighter. "None of that, Charles. None of that."

He wept on her shoulder, and she stood on her toes so he would not have to bend over as far. "None of that."

Mary would take in some of the girls. She had enough money to find an establishment for herself and Isabella.

"Don't worry, Charles. Don't worry. I was here."

Three thousand pounds. She would write to Mr. Grant immediately.

Historian's Note: The Spoilers

A LOT HAPPENS in this book that assumes the reader will just go along with it, even if they don't know the specific history. There's a couple of spoiler things, however, that I wanted to explain. One is rather small (the brothel joke) and one is rather large (Mr. Knight's death).

"I should inevitably fall a Sacrifice to the arts of some fat Woman who would make me drunk with small beer." – Jane Austen, in a letter to her sister, Cassandra

I wanted Elizabeth to make this comment, to reference the risks for poor, unprotected women in the city, and recognize she would never suffer this fate. However, there was too much to explain, from "fat woman" to explaining what a "bully" was and, eventually, "sacrifice." So while I modernized the words a little to not require as much explaining, but I wanted to talk about it.

In my book, *Hustlers, Harlots, and Heroes*, I define a "fat woman" as:

slang for a bawd, or a brothel owner. They'd prey upon young, innocent girls arriving in London, often from the country. They'd use various methods to coerce (and sometimes, force) the girls back to the brothel, where they'd be held against their will or would be too afraid to leave.

A woman such as Jane Austen, and indeed our own Elizabeth Knight, would never be prey to such a character. These women had both friends and family of consequence and means. For the estimated one in five London women who engaged in sex work (directly, indirectly, or in adjacent industries that supported it), many did not have such friends.

With that said, of course, not all were victims, and many were there by choice. When faced with a life of being a maid-of-all-work, a teenage girl might decide sex work would preserve her health and sanity longer than that of a £5 per annum job of long hours and hard work.

Mr. Knight's death was difficult to write, as I will explain in my author's note below, but it was also difficult in a social rules sense. This is a world where there are rules for everything, and dying and death are just amongst those.

For readers who know my experiences when my own father died, it might come as a surprise that I wrote a story where the Knight children did not get to say good-bye—only Elizabeth. However, there is a stoicism that was expected at all times, even in death. Women often did not attend funerals. They weren't barred, but rather they had to maintain that quiet dignity. As you can see in the final chapters, women would have been exhausted. They were up at all hours with people in and out of their house. The body would remain in the house to be dressed and prepared for burial. While a midwife could be called to assist, a wife might also have to do the task, or even servants.

Throughout all of this, with the worry and lack of sleep, and finally the grief, women would be expected to be in control of their emotions, and not displaying their feelings publicly. Stoicism in all things.

Calm dignity.

Head held high.

Never let them see your heart.

Elizabeth could do that when her sisters could not.

Author's Note

I COULD NOT have predicted how both my personal corner of the world and the entire planet would change when I sketched out the series outline for *Ladies Occult Society* back in 2018. Elizabeth was always going to lose her uncle in *A Magical Inheritance*. She was also always going to lose her father in this book. The trouble turned out to be the path to get us here.

Originally, this series was supposed to be an epidemic story. No, not a covid book. Rather, in 2018, I felt too many people didn't really understand epidemics and outbreaks of illnesses that wiped out people. I would be on social media explaining basic things about sickness before the age of antibiotics or the wide acceptance of germ theory.

If you go back, you'll see that there are series hints about Charles having experienced an illness that set him back years. Later, the rectory's own cook becomes sick. And finally, in this book, we were to start at the beginning of the outbreak, with Mr. Knight catching it, most of the girls becoming ill, leaving Charles, Elizabeth, and Isabella to care for them.

However, by Christmas 2020, it was obvious to me I could not write a pandemic book. However, I still had a father to kill off, a brother to rehabilitate, and a sisterly relationship to mend. Charles was the easy part, as I could simply have the characters bring his recovery into the forefront, as opposed to the hints in the background that probably slipped the minds of readers. Also, by now (late 2023, when I'm writing this note) nearly everyone understands the long-term effects of serious illness, both on the body and the mind.

Also in 2020 or early 2021, I decided Mr. Knight would die in the way he does in this book. I based it on my own mother's health and behaviour just after my father died (Christmas, 2018). Two months later, she landed in the ICU with heart problems. So, I felt it would work well with Mr. Knight's overall character.

Unfortunately, due to Newfoundland being closed for travel (to control the virus), I did not see my mother again until August 2021. Due to the trauma of breaking a femur, surgery, gangrene, another infection, and the ongoing issues with her heart, she did not know me. Not in any real way. I shall spare you the most horrific details, as those are the moments to use in writing horror and not a slice-of-life fantasy, but my mother was stuck reliving one of the most terrifying moments of her life. And I had to sit there, and experience it, over and over, through her eyes. Occasionally, I still have nightmares.

But, Mom lingered until February 2022, and I was faced with another difficult decision regarding this book: re-write the last half of this book *again*, or muster the courage to face editing a story that was very close to my own mother's death with all of the pain that encompassed. You have read my choice, though thankfully, Ladies Occult Society is my world, and so I gave Mr. Knight a significantly kinder death than my own mother's.

I know readers will celebrate the end of Mr. Knight. It was never my intention to make him this hated, for I always saw him as a victim as much as the women. For me, the villain of this tale has always been society and not Mr. Knight. For his story is not done yet, and there is more to be revealed.

And, well, I think we all know what these characters want to happen in the next book. Speaking of which…

Coming Soon

The finale to the beloved Ladies Occult Society series.

Miss Elizabeth Knight dedicated her life to her duty as a woman, a daughter, and as an elder sister, and the reward for that sacrifice was poverty and heartbreak. Except, there was another path now. And it will take her sisters, her friends, and some very determined ghosts to break Elizabeth's old habits. For happiness is around the corner, if she can just be brave enough.

About the Author

KRISTA D. BALL is apparently an award-winning author, something that shocked her mother who went to her grave believing it was a lie. After all, Krista writes lies for a living. Born and raised in Newfoundland, Canada, the quickest way to get on Krista's nerves is to pronounce it New-Found-Lund. After obtaining a degree in British History, Krista needed to justify her student loans. Twenty-five books later, including three non-fiction, the loans are finally paid off, but now she's not qualified to do anything else but write books. Expect more in the future. That wasn't meant to sound like a threat.

Also by Krista D. Ball

Ladies Occult Society
A Magical Inheritance
A Ghostly Reqest
In the Society of Women
A Lady's Choice (*forthcoming*)

Collaborator
Traitor
Fugitive
Rebel
Regrets Past

Tales of Tranquility Series
Blaze
Grief
Interlude (short story collection)
Fury
Schemes
Liberate
Ambush

The Dark Abyss of Our Sins
The Demons We See
The Nightmare We Know
The Sins We Seek

Spirit Caller Series
Spirits Rising
Dark Whispers
Knight Shift
Mystery Night
Dead Living
Blood Family
Dead of Knight (*forthcoming*)

Nonfiction

What Kings Ate and Wizards Drank

Hustlers, Harlots, and Heroes

Appropriately Aggressive

As Dinah Lewis

First Impressions

Love in the Spotlight

www.ingramcontent.com/pod-product-compliance
Lightning Source LLC
Chambersburg PA
CBHW020755250626
47155CB00003B/1088
* 9 7 8 1 7 3 8 0 7 4 6 6 2 *